TITANS

ALSO BY KATE O'HEARN

TITANS

- BOOK 1 -

KATE O'HEARN

Aladdin

NEW YORK LONDON TORONTO SYDNEY NEW DELHI

ALADDIN

An imprint of Simon & Schuster Children's Publishing Division
1230 Avenue of the Americas, New York, New York 10020
First Aladdin hardcover edition July 2019
Text copyright © 2019 by Kate O'Hearn
Jacket illustration copyright © 2019 by Even Amundsen
For information about special discounts for bulk purchases, please contact
Simon & Schuster Special Sales at 1-866-506-1949 or business@simonandschuster.com.
The Simon & Schuster Speakers Bureau can bring authors to your live event.
For more information or to book an event contact the Simon & Schuster Speakers Bureau
at 1-866-248-3049 or visit our website at www.simonspeakers.com.
Jacket designed by Karin Paprocki
Interior designed by Mike Rosamilia
The text of this book was set in Adobe Garamond.
Manufactured in the United States of America 0619 FFG
2 4 6 8 10 9 7 5 3 1
Library of Congress Cataloging-in-Publication Data
Names: O'Hearn, Kate, author.
Title: Titans / by Kate O'Hearn.
Description: First Aladdin hardcover edition. | New York : Aladdin, 2019. |
Summary: "When Titans Astraea and Zephyr find a human boy on their world,
they must figure out how he got there and why. What they uncover is a plot
to take over Titus and ultimately the universe"— Provided by publisher.
Identifiers: LCCN 2018035204 (print) | LCCN 2018041330 (eBook) |
ISBN 9781534417069 (eBook) | ISBN 9781534417045 (hc)
Subjects: | CYAC: Titans (Mythology)—Fiction. |
Animals, Mythical—Fiction. | Mythology, Greek—Fiction. | Fantasy.
Classification: LCC PZ7.O4137 (eBook) | LCC PZ7.O4137 Ti 2019 (print) |
DDC [Fic]—dc23
LC record available at https://lccn.loc.gov/2018035204

For my family.
And for the misfits and dreamers—
keep reaching for the stars!
I love you all.

TITANS

1

"I KNOW WHAT I SAW, AURORA. THERE WAS a human on Titus!"

The sound of her parents' distraught voices woke Astraea from a deep sleep. They had never sounded like that before, but it was the fear in their tone that really caught her attention. Climbing from her bed, she crept to the door and opened it a fraction to listen to what they were saying.

"My father said you are mistaken. There are no humans here."

"Hyperion is lying!" her father insisted. "No matter what he claims, there was a human woman here."

"But it is impossible. Humans are banned, and

access to the Solar Stream is forbidden without permission. There must be some other explanation."

"If there is, please tell me, because I cannot think of one," her father said.

"I do not know," her mother replied. "But if a human was found on Titus, it would mean disaster for us all. I am sure my father would have told me."

"Your father is not telling anyone, and that is why I am so worried. The woman was terrified and crying as he took her away. He was taking her toward the new wing of the prison. But we haven't finished building it yet. Why would he take her there?"

"I—I just do not know. Perhaps I should ask him again."

"If he denied it once, I am sure he would do it again. But something strange is going on. At work we have found these thick puddles of gray matter. We have no idea what they are or where they are coming from. I told him about those as well, and he said nothing."

"This is madness. My father enforces the law; he does not break it," Aurora said. "He would not associate with humans, especially now. Perhaps she just looked like a human but was a Titan or Olympian."

"I *know* the difference. She was definitely human."

"What are we going to do?"

"I do not know. But I was thinking perhaps we should . . ."

Their voices trailed off as they moved deeper into the house, but Astraea had heard enough. Her father had seen a human taken away by her grandfather. But how was that possible? Everyone knew that contact between Titus and Earth was forbidden. Anyone caught going there, or bringing a human here, would be severely punished.

Astraea closed her door and wandered over to the window. It was late and the stars twinkled brightly overhead. Taking a seat on the sill, she watched a group of young night dwellers playing a game of kickball. The sound of their soft laughter drifted toward her, even though they kept their voices low. She had met a few night dwellers before, but they were a mysterious bunch who kept to themselves and only ventured from their homes after dark, since the sunlight was deadly for them.

Watching them play, she knew she should go to bed. The following day was going to be very busy, and she needed her rest. But the brief exchange left her unable to sleep. What was a human doing on Titus? How did she get here? And why was her grandfather keeping it a secret?

Astraea's kitten, Hiddles, leaped up onto her lap and meowed softly. The rainbow tabby fluttered his tiny wings several times and settled down. Astraea petted his fluffy, warm fur and smiled at his soft purring. She leaned down to his head and whispered, "I don't want to go tomorrow. Do you think Mom would believe me if I told her I was sick?"

Hiddles looked up at her and licked Astraea's chin, then lay his head down again.

Astraea sighed. "You're right, she wouldn't believe me."

It was just before dawn when Astraea finally grew sleepy and climbed into her bed. It felt like she'd only just closed her eyes when a voice outside her window started calling her name.

"Astraea, are you up yet?"

Astraea moaned and rolled over. "No. Leave me alone."

"Come on, we're going to be late for the opening day!"

Astraea pulled the covers over her head. It couldn't be time yet. She had only just gone to bed. "Go away, I'm sleeping."

There was movement beside her bed, and suddenly her covers were wrenched away.

"Hey!" Astraea started pulling them back, but they were locked firmly in the teeth of her best friend, Zephyr. "Let go!"

"Get up!" Zephyr said through clenched teeth. Her gleaming white head and neck were stretched through the window to reach Astraea's bed. As soon as she started to back up, Zephyr knocked all the marble ornaments off Astraea's bedside table.

"Zephyr, stop! You're wrecking the place!" Astraea clung to the covers, was dragged from her bed, and hit the floor with a loud thud. She got up, secured her grip on the bedcovers, and started to pull them back in with all her strength. "I said let go!"

"No, you let go!" Zephyr whinnied.

The tug-of-war continued as the two strong Titans pulled the covers. Zephyr was by far the stronger but was only using her teeth. Astraea had both arms wrapped around the fabric and had planted her feet firmly on the floor. She flapped her small wings to add to her pulling strength.

"Give up now," Zephyr called through her teeth.

"Never!" Astraea cried. "You give up!"

Inch by inch, Astraea was slowly dragged closer to the window. She put a foot up on the sill to give herself more leverage, and then her second foot, until she was standing on the sill, leaning back and straining against Zephyr's strength.

The sound of a tear started. "Uh-oh," Astraea called. "Zephyr, stop, it's going to . . ."

The downy cover ripped in half, throwing both Astraea and Zephyr backward in different directions and filling the bedroom with a shower of soft white feathers.

Astraea landed hard on her backside. Outside the window, Zephyr nickered and coughed. After getting to her feet, Astraea peered out and burst into laughter. Zephyr lay sprawled on the ground in the middle of a cloud of down. Her wings were askew and her equine body was smeared with mud. She sat up and spit out the remnants of the duvet.

"Look what you've done!" Zephyr rolled over and climbed back to her four legs. She held up a golden hoof. "I spent all morning getting ready, and now I'm filthy. My hooves need polishing again!"

"You started it," Astraea chuckled.

Zephyr snorted, "Oh that's special, blame me. *You* should've been up already and you know it. Today everything changes."

Astraea groaned. "Don't remind me." She leaned out the window and lowered her voice. "I have to tell you something, but you can't say a word to anyone."

"Ooh, a secret. I love secrets." Zephyr trotted closer.

Astraea checked to make sure no one was listening and kept her voice soft. "Last night I heard Mother and Father talking. They said a human woman was found on Titus. My grandfather took her away."

"A what?" Zephyr cried, and looked around fearfully. "A human is here?"

"Quiet!" Astraea hushed. "I don't think anyone is supposed to know about it. But my parents were really upset."

"No kidding! If a you-know-what was really here, they could cause an epidemic. They're filled with all kinds of terrible diseases. You could go blind if one touches you."

"What?" Astraea cried. "No, that's just a myth."

"No it's not. You-know-whats are filthy, disgusting creatures." Zephyr looked around again and raised her front hooves as though she expected a human to jump out at her.

"What about Emily Jacobs? She's from Earth and she's not disgusting."

"She's not human," Zephyr said. "She's Xan."

"But she used to be. And her father and Joel are still human and they're not infectious."

"That's because they lived on Olympus long enough to be cured. But if there are new ones here, there's no telling what could happen. How did she get here?"

Astraea frowned and mused aloud. "I really don't know. But if it's true, why is my grandfather hiding her?"

"Maybe to stop a panic."

"Could be," Astraea agreed. "I think we should miss the opening ceremonies and start our own investigation."

Zephyr started to laugh. "Nice try, Astraea, but nothing is going to stop us from going to the opening of Arcadia. We're doomed, and there's nothing we can do to save ourselves—even if a hundred you-know-whats appeared here."

"But this is more important!"

"Maybe, but we can't do anything about it. We have to go. Your mother will kill us if we don't."

Astraea sighed and shook her head. "I've been dreading this for ages. School—who ever imagined Titans would have to go to school? And why do we have to go when our parents didn't?"

Astraea didn't hear her bedroom door open or her mother enter. She jumped when her mother said, "We did not have to go because we were too busy trying to survive being locked away in that prison, Tartarus. This is a great day, the joining of the Titans and Olympians in education. It has been a difficult adjustment for all of us living together here. Perhaps now we will be unified."

As her beautiful mother came closer, she frowned at the mess in the bedroom. Downy feathers covered every surface, and half the torn duvet lay on the floor. She picked a small feather from Astraea's hair. "Do I want to know what happened here?"

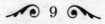

Astraea and Zephyr looked at each other. They both said, "She did it," at the same time.

Astraea's mother sighed. "Why did I even ask? I do not care who started it. It ends now. And I want this mess cleaned up when you come home."

"We will clean it up," Astraea promised. She noticed small worry lines around her mother's eyes. "Is everything all right? You look tired."

Her mother smiled, but the expression didn't reach her eyes. "I did not sleep well last night, that is all." She looked out the window. "Zephyr, please come in. Breakfast is ready and waiting for you on the table."

Zephyr's head bobbed up and down. "Thank you, Aurora. I will be right in."

Astraea and her mother watched Zephyr trot away and disappear around the side of their home. Zephyr was right. She had spent some time getting ready. The feathers on her wings were neatly preened and her coat glistened with health and care—except where it was now smudged with dirt and dotted with down feathers from the duvet. From behind, she was the spitting image of her father, Tornado

Warning, a clone from Pegasus who had come from Earth. From the front, a large black blaze on her chest revealed that her mother had been a midnight-black winged mare from Titus.

"She is looking lovely this morning," Aurora commented.

Astraea grinned and touched the neatly folded wings on her mother's back. "You've been busy too. Your feathers are glistening and you've perfumed them."

Aurora sighed. "Astraea, please, how many times must I ask you to speak properly? We do not say 'you've' but 'you have,' and we say 'do not' rather than 'don't.' You know I do not like this abbreviated language you and Zephyr have picked up."

"But it's how everyone talks. Besides, Emily Jacobs speaks like this, and she's a Xan. She's really important."

"Emily Jacobs is a human from Earth who became a Xan. Granted, the ancient Xan were an admirable race that once protected the universe. And yes, they gave us the Solar Stream that we use to travel from world to world. But they are gone except for Riza and now Emily—who still has the heart and mind of a

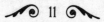

human. Her involvement with the Olympians was a fortunate accident and nothing more."

"But she's done so much for us. She saved us all from those monsters that destroyed Olympus."

"Yes, she did, but with the help of Riza and your cousins Jupiter, Neptune, and Pluto. She did not do it alone. It took teamwork."

"Well, I still like her."

"And so you should," her mother admitted. "She has done many admirable things. But that does not make her the best role model for you. She is impetuous and was never taught to speak properly. You and your friends are not human. You should not strive to be like her or speak like her."

"But I like speaking like Emily. It's cool."

"Cool?"

"It's an expression I heard Emily's friend Joel say. It means it's good."

Aurora sighed again. "You are not going to change, are you?"

Astraea grinned. "Not if I can help it."

"All right, I surrender," Aurora said. "If I cannot get you to change how you speak, you will at least try to look nice for the opening ceremonies. Now, what about your wings? Would you like some fragrant oil to get your feathers shining?"

"For these?" Astraea opened her small, immature wings. The feathers were the soft downy gray of youth. It would be some time before they molted out and were replaced with white flight feathers large enough for her to fly. At this point, they were more of a nuisance than a blessing. "I'm just going to tuck them in and cover them up."

"Cover them? Why? Your wings are beautiful. Everyone knows they will grow. Why are you so ashamed of them?"

"Mother, look at me!" She opened her wings again and spread her arms. "They barely reach my wrists. I look like a cherub. Until they grow large like yours or Grandmother's, I'm just going to keep them hidden."

Her mother smiled gently and combed back the hair from Astraea's face. "A cherub's wings are much smaller than yours and you know it. Believe me, what you have now is nothing to be ashamed of. I was exactly the same when I was your age. All Titans with wings are. You just need time."

"Yes, and until then, I'm going to cover them up."

"Suit yourself," Aurora said. "But whatever you decide, do it quickly. The opening ceremonies will start soon, and your grandfather expects us to be at the front of the gathering."

Astraea groaned.

"That is enough of that," Aurora chastised. "Zephyr is waiting for you. So finish getting ready and come down for breakfast. Then we can head over to Arcadia. Your father has already left."

"I'll be right down."

While she dressed, Astraea's mind kept going back to the previous night. It was obvious that her mother was trying to act as though nothing was wrong, but the news of the human woman appearing on Titus was something they should all worry about. As soon as the opening ceremonies were finished, Astraea was going to look into it to see if she could learn more.

After a quick meal, Astraea, her mother, and Zephyr left the house and joined the legions of Titans walking toward the newly completed school.

"Wow, there are more here than I expected!"

Zephyr commented as she looked all around. "I didn't think there were this many Titans."

Aurora nodded. "Tartarus was a large prison with many, many levels."

Zephyr snorted angrily. "And after all that, we're expected to be friends with Olympians, when they were the ones who imprisoned us?"

Aurora stopped and faced Astraea and Zephyr. "Listen to me, you two. What happened in the past is just that, *the past*. You were both born after Tartarus. And yes, these are trying times as we all adjust to living together on the one world after the destruction of Olympus. But we must try to find a way to get along. This new school might be the only way for true unification."

"Or war," Astraea said doubtfully.

"Do not even think that!" Aurora said. "Believe me, none of us want to go back to the dark days of fighting and strife. Peace is the only way. We just have to find a way to get along with the Olympians. The alternative is unimaginable."

"But what if the Olympians don't want to get along with us?" Astraea asked.

"They will," Aurora said. "We have no choice. This is the only world we have left. We *must* find a way to live together."

Zephyr snorted, "Why does it have to be us kids who are forced to get along? We're the ones being made to go to school with them."

Aurora smiled gently at her daughter and Zephyr. "That is because you are the hope of the future. Both of you are part of the first generation born outside the walls of Tartarus. You are the ones to ensure peace." She paused again. "Tell me, have you even considered how the Olympians might be feeling this morning, knowing they are leaving their region, Olympia, to come into our region to go to school?"

Astraea looked at Zephyr and could see that they were both thinking the exact same thing. They didn't care how the Olympians felt. To them, Olympians were refugees at best, invaders at worst.

"It will not be as bad as you expect, you will see," Aurora said lightly. "I am sure in a few days' time you will have made a whole new set of friends, and some may even be Olympian." She walked on and looked back. "Now come along. They are expecting us."

Astraea looked over at her best friend and raised her eyebrows. "Olympian friends? I'd rather hug a Hundred-hander—and they smell horrible!"

"I'd rather have a human friend," Zephyr said. "And you know how I feel about *them*."

2

JAKE REYNOLDS PUT ON A CLEAN T-SHIRT and then ran a comb through his long blond hair. He pulled on his baseball cap and stood back, checking himself in the full-length mirror. Then he nodded. "Lookin' good, dude. . . ."

On the way out of his bedroom, he picked up his backpack and skateboard. He called out to his mother in the living room "I'm going now, Mom—catch you later."

"Jake, wait." His mother appeared. "I want you to take Molly with you."

"But, Mom—"

"No, Jake. If you want to go out, you are going to

take Molly with you. Just to the pier; she's going to meet your father there for their day out. Then you can go off with your friends."

"Why doesn't Dad come here to get her? Or maybe Richard can take her."

"You know your dad and stepfather don't get along. It'll turn into a fight and I really don't need that today." She rubbed her swollen belly. "The baby has been kicking up a storm and I'm really feeling the heat."

"This sucks," Jake complained.

"Please, Jake, just this once, would you do something I ask without turning it into a drama? You know I'm going to need your help when the baby comes. It's only a couple of weeks now. With Richard working away so much, I'm counting on your support."

Jake looked at his mother and sighed. "Fine, Mom, but you owe me for this."

"I know, I know." She smiled. "You can put it on my bill."

"Don't think I won't." Jake leaned down to kiss his mother on the top of her head. He had only recently turned thirteen, but he was already much taller than

her. His father was a retired basketball player, and by all accounts, Jake was going to be as tall if not taller than him. "Where is the Mole?"

"She's just getting ready. Molly! Come on. Your brother is waiting!"

Moments later Molly arrived. His sister's light brown hair was uncombed and hanging long and unkempt down her back. She was wearing stained denim shorts and a ripped top.

"Aren't you gonna get changed?"

Molly looked down at herself. "I did."

"Yeah, right. I don't want to be seen with you if you're going out like that."

Molly harrumphed and put her hand on her hip. "Just coz I don't spend hours in front of the mirror like you do doesn't mean I don't look nice."

"You look like a slob. Ever heard of something called a brush?" Jake looked at his mother. "Mom, tell her."

"Molly, your brother's right. Go comb your hair and change into something nice for your dad."

"Mom!"

"Do it!"

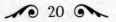

"I don't even want to go out with Dad!" Molly grumbled as she stormed off and slammed her bedroom door.

"And brush your teeth!" their mother called after her daughter. She turned back to Jake. "You know it's been rough on her with the baby and all. Just give her a few minutes."

"But the guys are waiting for me."

"Let them wait. Please just get your sister to the pier and wait for your dad. Then the rest of the day is yours."

He grinned mischievously. "If I do, can we order pizza tonight?"

"You're negotiating with me?"

Jake nodded and crossed his arms over his chest. "If you want peace, you gotta sweeten the pot a little."

His mother smiled. "You want terms? Okay, pizza tonight if you promise not to fight with your sister on the way."

Jake hesitated. "Wait, I was just supposed to take her to the pier. You didn't say anything about not fighting with her. For that, I think we need extra toppings. . . ."

"Jake!"

He grinned again. "Okay, deal. I take the Mole to the pier with no fighting and we have pizza tonight—with two toppings."

She sighed in exasperation. "Yes, fine, pizza with two toppings. Now just wait for your sister. I'm going to go lie down for a while. This California weather is getting to me—I'll never understand why we left Detroit."

"Because you didn't like the cold," Jake said.

"Well, it's better than this heat," his mother said. "Be back around seven and we can order in." She rose on her toes and kissed him on the cheek. "You've got your phone and helmet?"

Jake turned around to show his backpack. "Yep, in here."

"And you'll wear your helmet?"

"Duh, Mom. 'Course I will."

"Just checking," she said.

Molly returned wearing clean shorts and a T-shirt. Her long hair was pulled back in a ponytail.

"That's better," his mother said. "Now both of you be good and have fun."

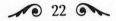

It wasn't a long walk to the Santa Monica Pier as they made their way from their apartment building on Olympic Boulevard down to Ocean Avenue and toward the water. But as they neared the beach, the Saturday crowds and tourists were out and filling the streets around it. Traffic was heavy as people fought over parking places. Jake changed routes and took a quieter street.

"I hate Saturdays here," he said, trying to start a conversation with his moody sister. "It's like, 'Hey, dude, I'm a tourist, can I take your picture?' like I'm some kind of freak or something."

"You *are* a freak," Molly said glumly.

"You're the freak," Jake said. "You're always like life has squished your kitten or something. Would it kill you to smile?"

Molly stopped and put her hands on her hips. "As a matter of fact, it would. So just shut up and take me to the pier."

"*So just shut up and take me to the pier . . . ,*" Jake mimicked his sister's whiny voice.

"Grow up, Jake."

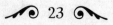

"You grow up," he said back. Jake might have promised not to fight with her, but Molly was making it almost impossible. To avoid the situation getting worse, he put his skateboard down, climbed on, and glided down the sidewalk.

"Oh yeah, that's adult," Molly called. "Just walk away."

"I'm boarding away, and it's better than talking to you. . . ."

Jake had gone only a few feet when he heard Molly scream. He looked back, his eyes widening at the sight of someone—or something—grabbing his sister.

"Hey, you, let her go!" Jake was still on his skateboard, and it cut sharply to the left. He tried to correct himself, but the angles were wrong. He lost his balance, flipped off the board, and crashed down to the ground, smashing his head on the curb.

The last thing he heard was his sister's terrified screams.

3

ASTRAEA WALKED BESIDE ZEPHYR AS THEY made their way through the thickening crowds. The whole new city was called Arcadium, but at its heart stood Arcadia, the massive school that would educate all the Titan and Olympian children together.

"Well, it is bigger than I thought," Zephyr commented. Her white head was raised higher than most of the Titans.

Astraea stood on her toes to see what Zephyr was talking about. "I can't see anything with all these people in my way."

Zephyr laughed. "That's because you're too short.

I can see everything. There are several large buildings. I thought there was only going to be one."

"There are too many students for there to be only one building," Aurora explained. "There will be a lower school for youngsters, a middle school for students your age, an upper school, and then a university for further education. From what I understand, each building has a number. Arcadia One is the largest and that is where they are holding the opening ceremonies. I have also heard talk of another building for adults who wish to take courses."

"Why would adults want to go to school?" Astraea asked.

"Just because we are older than you does not mean we want to stop learning. There is so much we can do now. We can study the arts, literature, and science, as well as many other subjects. I myself am considering taking some courses. I hear that some of the Muses are giving dancing and singing lessons, and Urania is going to give lectures on the heavens and stars."

Astraea stared at her mother in complete disbelief. She had never imagined that Aurora would

want to learn new things. "You going to school—
this I need to see!"

Her mother laughed as they continued. The
crowds were getting denser, and they were being
shoved on all sides as they filtered through the narrow streets of Arcadium to reach the area of the
opening ceremonies. Shops selling school equipment, books, and supplies lined the street, while
vendors tried to sell fruit and ambrosia cakes off
carts, but with the swelling crowds unable to stop,
business wasn't good.

"Wow, look at it, it's so beautiful," Zephyr teased.
She looked at Astraea and winked a large, dark eye.
"What an amazing place. You should see it. . . ."

Astraea shot a dirty look at her best friend. "I don't
care anyway. It's just a dumb school."

"Jealous," Zephyr nickered.

"Am not."

"Are too."

"Girls, please," Aurora said. "That is no way to
behave. We must set an example."

"An example for who?" Astraea asked.

"For everyone. Your grandfather is a very important

man. We must all behave in a way that does not bring disgrace to him."

Astraea wanted to say more, especially about her grandfather and the human woman, but she kept silent. Her grandfather was Hyperion—brother to Saturn, onetime leader of the Titans. He was also the uncle to Jupiter, Neptune, and Pluto, the Big Three who now governed both the Titans and Olympians. Hyperion served on the high council and was the head of security—which meant Astraea was part of the most influential family on Titus.

It was because of Hyperion's position that Astraea was expected to behave differently from other kids her age. It also explained why she didn't have any friends except for Zephyr. Everyone else was too frightened of her grandfather to speak to her.

They kept moving with the crowd until the large gathering slowed to a stop before the entrance steps to the Arcadia grounds. Astraea finally got her first good look at the school and gasped. Arcadia One was five stories high, with tall windows lining the sides, and it stretched farther than any building she'd seen before. There were tall white marble pil-

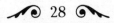

lars in front that reminded her of Jupiter's palace. The neighboring school buildings were almost as tall, but equally long.

"It's huge!" Astraea said. "Why do we need a school this big?"

"It is not only going to be used as a school," Aurora said. "There will be meeting halls and places for other gatherings. The design was based on Earth buildings that serve many purposes."

Zephyr tilted her head back. "Wait. Why did they use Earth designs when it's a quarantined world?"

"It is true that we can no longer visit Earth, but that does not mean they do not have some excellent ideas. This school is a good example. It will become a community center for everyone." Aurora led them forward. "Now come along. They are waiting for us."

Up ahead loomed a large stage with multiple chairs set up across it. There was also a series of chairs set up in front of the stage for the invited guests, while the rest of the huge gathering stood.

As they made their way to the front, Astraea noticed that most of the chairs were occupied except

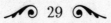

for a few along the first row. These were reserved for dignitaries and their families.

"There they are," Aurora called as they moved to the front row. Astraea's father and four older brothers were already there, dressed in their best Titan robes.

Astraea was grateful to her father for saving the aisle seat for her. She and Zephyr could stay together as she sat and Zephyr stood in the aisle beside her. Just as they settled, horns started to blare and the crowd began cheering the arrival of the Big Three.

Everyone turned and watched Jupiter waving to the crowd as he walked confidently toward the stage. He was tall, powerful, and commanding. Astraea noted how much he looked like Saturn, with his gray beard and neatly styled long hair. Jupiter was the oldest Olympian, but the blazing blue of his eyes still held a twinkle of youth. He was followed by his two brothers, Neptune and Pluto. Neptune, like Jupiter, also waved to the crowd and had a broad, beaming smile and eyes the color of the ocean, whereas Pluto in his dark robes did not smile, but nodded to the people who greeted him.

The Big Three were followed by Saturn, Hyperion,

and the Titan and Olympian high council. But everyone else who followed was quickly forgotten as Astraea inhaled at the sight of Emily Jacobs astride Pegasus. The winged stallion glowed in the light and held his head high and proud. The tall Xan, Riza, walked closely beside them, looking calm and stunning in her long robes. Then came Joel DeSilva, their Olympian friend, Paelen, and Pegasus's brother, the winged boar, Chrysaor—these were the Heroes of Olympus. They were followed by Emily's father, Steve, and Jupiter's daughter, Diana.

Astraea felt Zephyr react to the presence of Pegasus. A muscle in her friend's shoulder twitched in irritation as her whole body tensed. Her wings fluttered lightly. "What's *he* doing here?"

"I don't know," Astraea said. "Father didn't tell me that Pegasus and Emily were coming. I thought it was just the Big Three and the high council."

"Look at her, riding Pegasus like he's some kind of horse. It's disgusting, and he shouldn't let her do it. Well, if he's here, I'm leaving." Zephyr started to move, but Astraea reached out and caught hold of her mane.

"Zephyr, no, you can't go. We've been specially invited."

"I don't care. Being here with Pegasus is humiliating. The teasing is going to start all over again."

Zephyr had spent her whole life trying to prove that she was her own person and not just the offspring of Pegasus's clone, Tornado Warning. She never considered herself a relation to the Great Stallion of Olympus, though he always referred to her as his niece. Pegasus's presence at the opening of Arcadia would bring it all back to her. People would once again see how alike they were and call her his daughter.

Astraea leaned closer to her friend. "Zeph, stand tall and proud. You have every right to be here—more than he does, because you live here and he doesn't. He lives on Xanadu with Emily and her family. You mustn't let anyone see that he's bothering you."

"But he *is* bothering me," Zephyr whispered.

"Girls," Astraea's father warned.

All Astraea could do was rest her hand on her friend's neck and be there for her. She could only imagine how difficult it must be. Except for the black blaze on her chest, Zephyr was identical to Pegasus in every way, right down to the golden hooves.

"Just remember I'm always here for you," Astraea whispered softly.

The twitch in Zephyr's neck increased with each step Pegasus took. Finally the stallion was passing directly beside her.

Emily spotted them and waved. "Hi, Zephyr and Astraea. It's great to see you!"

"Hello, Emily!" Astraea waved back, flattered that Emily remembered her name. But for all her excitement, she was also concerned about her friend—especially when Pegasus looked directly at Zephyr and bowed his head. "Zephyr, it pleases me to see you here. I hope you are well. . . ."

"Pegasus," Zephyr responded, keeping her voice neutral.

Then they were gone, climbing the stairs to join the Big Three and the high council

Astraea looked at everyone on the stage and noticed something that most people wouldn't. The Big Three looked pleased to be there, as did most of the others. But when her eyes landed on her grandfather, she saw

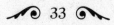

the intense expression on his face. He wasn't smiling like the others—in fact, his brows were knit together in a deep frown, while his eyes never stopped panning the crowd.

"Look at Hyperion," Astraea whispered to Zephyr. "It's like he's looking for someone."

"He's looking for a way off the stage," Zephyr responded. "I don't blame him. I want to go too."

"No," Astraea said. "It's not that. He's looking for more you-know-whats."

"You've got you-know-whats on the brain," Zephyr said. "You don't seriously think there would be any here, do you? Look around. Most of the Titans and Olympians are here. A you-know-what would have to be insane to come."

"Maybe, but look over there. That's Tibed." Astraea pointed to a heavyset, humorless man in the crowd. His dark eyes were intense, and he was motioning to Hyperion. "He works for my grandfather. Look how he's trying to get his attention. I bet you a bowl of nectar there's been another sighting."

Zephyr leaned closer to Astraea and whispered, "You're obsessed. But it's just to avoid today. If I can put up with *him* being here"—she indicated Pegasus on the stage—"you can put up with this ceremony. Let's just get through this and hope it doesn't get any worse."

Astraea looked from Zephyr to Pegasus and back to her best friend again. "You know, things might be easier for you if you get try to get along with him. He's a legend, and like it or not, you *are* related to him. You can't avoid him forever."

Zephyr gave Astraea a withering look. "Wanna bet?"

"Fine, I give up. Go on hating Pegasus for the rest of your life and see how far that gets you. But I like him. He's always nice to me, and I really like Emily."

Astraea's father nudged her and warned, "Girls, that is enough. Pay attention." The expression on his face showed he meant business.

Facing forward, Astraea kept her eyes on her grandfather until he seemed to sense her watching him and looked at her. Knowing she'd been caught, Astraea smiled at him. Though he didn't smile, the corners of his mouth did turn up a bit, but the intensity in his eyes remained. If she had any doubts about what she'd heard the previous night, her grandfather's expression removed them. Hyperion was worried about something, and it showed on his face to anyone who was really looking.

When everyone was settled, Jupiter came forward. He nodded his head to the crowd.

"Welcome one and all to this very special occasion. I know it has been an enormous adjustment, having all of us living together here on Titus since the destruction of Olympus. And at times it has proved to be very difficult. That is why I am delighted that we can begin to bring everyone together in this exceptional place of education—Arcadia."

The crowd roared and applauded until Jupiter had to raise his hands to calm them down.

"It also gives me great pleasure to introduce the one whose suggestion it was to build Arcadia. I give you Emily Jacobs."

Emily slipped off Pegasus's back, and the two of them came forward.

"Hello," Emily started. "It's wonderful to see so many Olympians and Titans standing together to celebrate the opening of Arcadia. Some of you may be wondering why you have to go to school. Well, as you may know, I come from Earth and grew up in New York City. When I was there, I liked going to school. It was where all my friends were, and where I could make more friends." She smiled as she looked over at Joel DeSilva. "I met Joel there. And at first we really didn't get along." Her smile broadened. "Did we, Joel?"

Joel shuffled his feet but smiled back at Emily. "Well, we were very different. . . ."

Paelen gave Joel a light slap on the silver arm that Vulcan had made for him when he lost his real one. "What are you talking about? You told me you two hated each other, remember?"

Emily grinned at her friends and then turned back to the crowd. "That's why school is so important. It's where you learn to get along with new people, people you think you might never like. For us, it was just people from different places, but here, the differences are amazing." Her eyes landed on Zephyr

"Why's she looking at me?" Zephyr asked Astraea softly.

Astraea chuckled. "Because you're so different!"

On the stage, Emily continued. "I know there's

still a lot of mistrust between the Olympians and the Titans, but maybe through this school, you'll discover that you have more in common than you thought, and maybe, very soon, you'll even find you have a lot more friends than you imagined."

Once again the crowd cheered and waved as Emily continued her speech. But on the stage beside her, Hyperion rose carefully to his feet and slipped silently away.

Astraea watched her grandfather jump down from the stage. He was joined by his security guard, Tibed, and a woman. Their expressions were serious. After a brief exchange, Hyperion looked back to the stage, bowed to his brother Saturn and the Big Three, and then started to walk away.

Something was up, Astraea could feel it. She rose and looked at her father. "Dad, I'm really sorry, but all this excitement is getting to me. I have to go to the bathroom."

"Can it wait?" he asked. "The ceremony has just started."

Astraea shook her head. "I know and I'm sorry, but it's getting urgent."

Finally he nodded. "All right, but hurry back. You don't want to be late on your first day."

"I'll be as fast as I can."

She nodded back to Zephyr. "I'll be right back." She apologized as she walked past her mother and brothers.

When she was free of the row, she ran down the aisle and made her way through the dense crowd gathered at the rear. Running along the back of the gathering, she tried to follow the path her grandfather had taken. But all traces of him and his people had gone.

Just as she was about to go back to her seat, she caught sight of her great-uncle Crius. He was Hyperion's younger brother and also part of the security aspect of the high council. He was leaving the gathering and walking with purpose. Every instinct inside her said this had something to do with Hyperion and the humans.

Keeping farther back, she started to follow Crius through the crowd and away from Arcadia. Once they left the school grounds, it was difficult to stay behind him without being seen. Wherever he was going, he needed to be there fast.

After a moment, Crius stopped. He turned and looked back in her direction. Astraea ducked down behind a flowering bush. Had he seen her? She crouched and waited. Crius looked around, as though he sensed someone there. Then he started to walk in her direction.

"Crius!" a voice called.

Astraea had never been so happy to see Tibed before. He ran up to her great-uncle and pointed in the opposite direction. "He is running toward the palace. Hyperion told me to go around this way to cut him off."

Crius nodded. His eyes trailed over to Astraea's hiding place a final time, and then he allowed Tibed to lead him forward.

Astraea's heart was pounding. She was sure her uncle knew she was there. But thanks to Tibed, he was now focused on other things.

Astraea left her hiding spot and followed but was careful to stay farther behind. Before long, they headed into the part of town that held the palace and was the center of power for Titus. After several minutes of dipping and dodging behind buildings, she heard shouting and then screaming. It was coming from Saturn Square, the open public square that celebrated the union between the Titans and the Olympians.

Surrounding the outside of the paved square were carved marble statues of the heroes from the final battle for Olympus. At the very center of the square was a large fountain. The marble statues at the top of it were a life-size Pegasus rearing high, wings wide and kicking out his front hooves. Emily Jacobs was on his back with her arms raised. Real fire shot from her hands and sizzled through the fountain's water flow.

At the base of the fountain, Astraea saw a man being held down by Hyperion and two others. He was large, strong, and young, and his clothing was completely different from what the Titans wore. Judging by the way Hyperion and the others treated him, he must be human. Though she was across the square, Astraea could clearly see that the man was terrified. He tried to fight his way free, but one quick blow from her grandfather knocked him out.

The unconscious man was dragged away. Astraea rose to follow, but before she could take her first step, a hand slammed down on her shoulder.

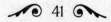 41

She jumped and turned to see the furious face of Tibed standing above her. "What are you doing here?" he demanded harshly. "You should be at the opening of Arcadia, not sneaking around in the middle of a security operation."

There was no excuse Astraea could think of to explain her presence. "Well, I, um . . ."

"Yes, spit it out," Tibed said. "Or have you nothing to say because you have been caught doing something that you know you should not be doing?"

Astraea stood at her full height, which made her taller than her grandfather's portly guard. "I heard there were humans in Titus. I wanted to see one for myself and maybe understand why they are here."

"Who told you there were humans in Titus?"

"I don't remember," Astraea said quickly.

"Well, whoever it was is wrong. There are no humans here."

"What about that man my grandfather just hit? He was human." The moment Astraea said it, she regretted it.

Tibed's round face went red with rage, and he moved in close enough to make her nervous. "You did not see anything here. Do you understand me? No humans, nothing."

"B-but—"

"But what?" he spat. "There are no buts. You saw nothing. Or do you want me to tell Hyperion you were spying on him?"

Astraea panicked. "No, please don't tell him. I promise I won't say anything about what I just saw. I'll go back to Arcadia and forget everything. Please don't tell my grandfather."

Tibed said nothing for several heartbeats as his hard eyes bored into her. He was only a hand's width from her face. Up close, there wasn't a trace of compassion or understanding in him. "What will you pay for my silence?"

"Wh-what?" Astraea choked. "I—I don't understand. I don't have anything."

"I do not want anything now," he said, leaning even closer. "But there may come a time when I need something—perhaps a favor, or something else. Then I will tell you what my silence today will cost you. You either agree now, or I will call Hyperion over. The choice is yours."

There was nothing about this man that Astraea liked. There was a genuine threat in his eyes that frightened her like she'd never been frightened before. She nodded her head slowly. "I—I understand. Thank you for not telling him."

Tibed didn't smile or react at all. But thankfully, he backed away. "Go on now, little girl. Go back to school and leave the adults to their work." He roughly released her and shoved her away. "Go on now, run, run away. . . ."

Astraea started to run. The horrible little man had treated her like a child, but she was not a child. She was growing up and becoming more and more aware of a terrible problem.

There were humans coming to Titus.

4

BY THE TIME ASTRAEA MADE IT BACK TO Arcadia, the opening ceremonies were finished and the speakers and guests were gone—including her parents. She was going to be in a lot of trouble when she got home. But at least she'd have time to think of a good excuse.

Astraea walked between the chairs that were being taken down by a group of satyrs, while the stage behind her was being dismantled by two giants. Farther ahead, closer to Arcadia One, Astraea saw long lines of students still waiting to be assigned their classes.

After a quick search, she found Zephyr hovering

at the end of one of the longest lines. Her friend raised her head and whinnied loudly when she caught sight of Astraea. "Where have you been? Your parents were furious!"

Out of breath, Astraea ran up to her friend. "You wouldn't believe it. . . ." She gulped air. "It's true, there are humans in Titus."

"No way!" Zephyr cried.

"Yes, I saw one for myself. There was a human man in Saturn Square. He was so frightened. Then my grandfather hit him."

"Why?"

"I think to quiet him down. He was screaming."

Zephyr laughed. "I would scream too if I came face-to-face with Hyperion!"

"That's not funny, Zeph. Don't you realize what this means?"

"Yes, it means that man is having a really bad day."

In the line next to them, a chestnut-colored centaur was staring intently at them. He was frowning and scratching his head. Finally he stepped away from the group of centaurs he was with and clopped up to them. His eyes settled on Zephyr. "You're Pegasus's daughter."

Zephyr immediately tensed, and her shoulder muscles twitched. She turned on him and scowled. "Excuse me? Do I look like Pegasus is my father?"

"Yes, you do," he said.

Zephyr's wings fluttered, and her eyes went wild with anger. "You take that back right now, centaur, or I'll make you take it back!"

"Zephyr, stop!" Astraea put her hand on one of Zephyr's fluttering wings to calm her. "Don't let him bother you. We have more important things to worry about."

"That's easy for you to say. He didn't just call you Pegasus's daughter."

"I know," Astraea said. "But I'm sure he didn't mean it as an insult."

"Yes, I did," the centaur said. "Her father is Olympian, but she pretends to be Titan by spending all her time with you—as if spending time with a stubby-winged child could help. She should be with her own kind in Olympia and not here at Arcadia with real Titans."

Astraea's eyebrows almost disappeared into her hairline. "*Stubby-winged?* Is that what you just called me?"

He nodded his dark head. "You are stubby-winged."

"Oh, you really shouldn't have said that," Astraea warned. "If you had half a brain, you'd get outta here now while you still can."

"Why? What are you going to do? Beat me with those baby wings of yours?"

Astraea started to chuckle and stepped back. Tibed had frightened her just a short while ago, and there was nothing she could do about it. She wasn't about to let this centaur do the same. She looked at Zephyr, bowed, and waved her on. "He's all yours."

Zephyr reared on her hind legs and kicked out her front hooves at the centaur, knocking him backward. "Astraea's wings aren't stubby and my father is from Earth, not Olympus—his name is Tornado Warning, not Pegasus!"

The centaur crashed to the ground and looked up at them in complete shock. "You kicked me!"

"Yeah, and I'll do it again if you don't apologize to Astraea right now."

The stunned centaur climbed to his feet. "How dare you kick me! Don't you know who I am?"

"Don't know and don't care," Zephyr said. "If you don't apologize to Astraea right now, I'll knock you down again!"

"Hey," another Titan said, stepping forward. "Leave Cylus alone, you filthy Olympian."

That comment caused a satyr to push forward and turn on the Titan. "Are you blind? She's a Titan, not an Olympian. And we are not filthy!"

"You are all filthy," the Titan said. "So shut up before I make you shut up."

A roar filled the air as a sphinx strode up to them. She was about Astraea's age, with blue-black hair and emerald-green eyes. The feathers on her wings were in shades of brown and black, while her lion's body was golden. "All of you stop it right now."

"Stay out of this, Seneka," one of the other centaurs said. "This is between us and the Olympians."

Seneka shook her head. "We all have to live here now. You can't keep fighting like this."

"We can do whatever we want," another Titan called. "And you can't stop us."

More Titans in the line started to mutter and call out to the Olympians, who also responded angrily.

"You all shut up," Cylus said. "This is between me and Pegasus's brat!"

Zephyr launched herself at the centaur again. Swinging her neck, she knocked him over and stood above him. "Pegasus—is—not—my—father!"

The students around them backed up and started to cheer and encourage the fight as Zephyr pounded Cylus with her front hooves. When Cylus rose again, he reared and kicked out his sharpened hooves at Zephyr, giving her a deep cut on her black blaze.

"Zeph, that's enough," Astraea cried, trying to pull her friend back. "You're bleeding!"

"Not till he apologizes!" Zephyr shrieked.

"Never!" Cylus shouted.

The ground beneath them shook as a giant almost as tall as Arcadia One and wearing a uniform charged into the fight. On the front of his pale blue lapel was the insignia for Arcadia—a blazing circle of stars surrounding a gold *A* on a midnight-blue background.

"What is going on here?" he demanded.

He separated Zephyr and Cylus with a massive hand. "Stop it, both of you." He looked around and shouted loudly enough to rattle windows. "You will stop fighting right now!"

Fear of the giant silenced everyone.

Astraea recognized the giant because he worked for her grandfather. Pushing forward, she called up to him. "Brutus, it was that centaur's fault. He insulted Zephyr and me."

Brutus looked down on her. "Astraea, what would your grandfather say if he knew you had been brawling on the first day of school?"

"It wasn't her, it was me. I was brawling," Zephyr said. "And Cylus deserved it. He called me Pegasus's daughter and said Astraea had stubby wings like a baby."

The giant bent down and faced the centaur. "Cylus, did you say that?"

Cylus wouldn't look up at him. One of his front hooves dug into the ground and he folded his arms across his chest. "I might have."

"Words wound," Brutus said. "You should know better." Then he looked at Zephyr. "Your father, *Tornado Warning*"—he glanced back at Cylus to make it clear who her father was—"may be wild,

unpredictable, and dangerous, but you know better than that. Violence is never the answer."

"It works for my father and it works for me," Zephyr said defensively.

"Well, let us see how well it works when I take you in to see Arcadia's new principal." Brutus looked at the gathered crowd. "All of you, get your class assignments and then move on. If I hear of any more trouble, you will answer to me."

The students around them returned to their lines with their heads held low. No one said a single word.

"Cylus, Zephyr, and Astraea," Brutus said. "You will follow me—now."

Astraea looked back at the sphinx and shrugged. "Thanks for trying, Seneka."

The three followed Brutus through the long line of students, past the faculty at the end who were doling out assignments, and finally up the steps to Arcadia One.

"Honestly, fighting on the first day?" Brutus stopped before the doors. His immense size meant he couldn't enter the school. "You should be ashamed of yourselves."

Astraea looked over to Zephyr. Her friend wasn't the least bit ashamed. The nerve in her shoulder was still twitching with irritation, and it wouldn't take much to get her fiery temper flared again.

"Wait right here," Brutus said. "I am going around to the principal's window to let her know why you are coming to her office. While I am gone, there will be no more fighting. Do you understand?"

"Yes, Brutus," Astraea said.

Zephyr's head was down. "Yes, Brutus," she said glumly.

When Cylus said nothing, Brutus bent down. "I asked if you understand. There will be no more fighting!"

"I don't see why I should be in trouble when Zephyr started it," Cylus insisted.

"You did!" Zephyr whinnied.

"Enough!" Brutus roared. The pressure of his voice caused the open school doors to slam shut. "This stops now! If I hear of any more fighting, your parents will be told." The giant stood up and stormed along the front of Arcadia One and around the side.

"This is your fault," Cylus said angrily.

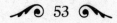 53

"Us?" Astraea cried. "You started it!"

"Yes, well, what are you going to do about it?" Cylus threw out his chest. "We're already in trouble."

"Not as much as you're going to be unless you shut up," Zephyr warned.

Astraea could see her friend was getting ready to fight again. She put her hand on Zephyr's neck. "Zeph, stop. Dad's already going to kill me for missing the opening ceremonies. I don't want to make it worse."

Zephyr's eyes were bright and her nostrils flared as she turned to Astraea. "But you know how I feel about being compared to—you-know-who."

"Yes, I do. But now's not the time to fight over it."

"Oh, so poor little Zephie doesn't like being called Pegasus's daughter," Cylus teased. "Well, too bad, because that is exactly what you are. Tornado Warning is just a dumb copy of Pegasus that can't even talk. If he is your father, then by definition, so is Pegasus."

Astraea gave Zephyr a calming pat. "Stay here." She walked over to the centaur. Up close he was much taller than her, as he defiantly stared her down. "I wonder what happened to make you so mean. Did someone take away your toys when you were a baby? Or are you just stupid, and being mean is your way to hide it?"

Cylus's eyes narrowed and his posture changed. "I am not stupid."

Nerve struck. "Yes, you are stupid if you keep causing trouble with Zephyr. You must know how strong Pegasus is. Trust me, Zephyr's just as strong. But she doesn't have his self-control. So if you want to keep all those pretty white teeth of yours, you'd better be quiet."

"I'm not stupid and I'm not scared of her," Cylus said, though he backed away two steps.

The ground started to shake as Brutus returned. He bent down to them. "The principal is waiting for you. You go in through these doors and straight down to the end of the hall. Her doors are right there. Sit down on the benches outside her office and wait to be called in."

"I should not be here," Cylus argued. "My mother is on the high council and is an adviser to Jupiter. She will be furious when I tell her how you have treated me."

"I would be happy to tell her myself," Brutus offered. "In fact, shall I go over to the palace right now and bring her here? Then you can tell her yourself why you were fighting."

Cylus stood defiantly before the giant, but when Brutus started to go, he called, "Never mind. There is no need to disturb her right now."

Brutus sighed and pointed to the doors. "Get inside."

The look on the giant's face left no room for discussion. They entered the school together and saw the madness inside as other students filled the main hall. They had already been given their assignments and were struggling to find their classrooms. Hall monitors of every shape and kind were helping to direct them.

The three said nothing as they continued forward until they reached a T junction where the corridor continued in opposite directions. Ahead of them were two large double doors with long benches set up on either side. A sign on the door indicated this was the principal's office.

One of the benches already had an occupant. A boy was sitting alone and looking very lost.

Astraea had never seen anyone like him before. His head was down and he was gazing into his folded hands. He appeared to be neither Titan nor Olympian. His skin was radiant silver, and he had a head of shocking black hair with lavender and blue highlights.

He had a sharp nose and full lips. When he looked up at her, Astraea almost gasped. His eyes were amazing—dark blue with silver flecks.

"All of you come in!" called a voice from behind the office doors.

Astraea patted Zephyr's shoulder and walked forward. Out of the corner of her eye, she saw the strange silver boy rise to follow. He was graceful and walked with a soft, soundless tread. He wouldn't look at anyone.

Cylus stopped and stared at him. He snorted, "What—are—you?"

"Cylus!" the voice called. "That is enough. Inside, now!"

"But have you seen him?" Cylus cried.

"Inside!" the voice repeated as the office doors flew open.

Astraea looked inside and couldn't see who opened them or how. She put her arm on Zephyr's back and slowly walked forward.

They passed through a spacious outer office, which held only a single marble desk filled with scrolls and parchments, then went farther ahead into the inner office. Inside, they saw a stern-faced woman dressed in flowing white robes and sitting on a three-legged stool. Her graying hair was piled high on her head, and she had golden sandals on her feet. There was no other furniture in the room, though there was an immense window overlooking all the other buildings of Arcadia.

Brutus was standing outside the window peering in.

"Thank you, Brutus," the woman called. "I will take it from here."

She turned back to the students, and her hard blue eyes bored into each of them, as though looking deep inside. "If you do not know my name, I am Themis, the new principal of Arcadia." Her gaze finally settled on Astraea. "Fighting on the first day? Really, Astraea, is that the example you wish to set for the younger students?"

Astraea dropped her head. "I'm sorry."

"So you should be. You have brought shame down on your family. I will, of course, have to inform your parents."

Cylus snickered and smiled smugly at Astraea. Themis immediately turned to him. "Do not for a moment think that I do not know your part in this altercation. You started it with your cruel words!"

Astraea suddenly realized why Themis's name was so familiar. She was a Titan seer, and back in ancient times on Earth, she had been the Oracle at Delphi, who passed along law and order to humans. It made sense that Jupiter would ask her to preside over Arcadia to keep order.

"I did not!" Cylus said. "She hit me first."

"After you teased Zephyr about her parentage. Then you called Astraea stubby-winged. You were both cruel and mean-spirited. I will not tolerate either in my school."

Her sharp eyes shot to Zephyr. "Nor will I tolerate violence. You must learn to curb that temper of yours if you plan to attend this school."

Zephyr also lowered her head. "I am sorry too."

"Now, this is all very new to us, so I will be lenient today. Instead of expelling you, which I should do, you will each serve a full week of detention. During that time, if there is any more trouble, I will not hesitate to expel you."

"What's detention?" Astraea asked.

"What *is* detention," Themis corrected. "It is where each of you will stay after school and perform whatever tasks I assign you. If you try to escape this punishment, the next punishment will be worse. Now do I make myself clear?"

Astraea and Zephyr nodded while Cylus shrugged. Seeing this, Themis rose from her stool and was over to him in a flash. "Did you just shrug at me?"

The hair on Astraea's arms rose and she felt tingling down her spine. The fine hairs of Zephyr's mane also started to float. It seemed the angrier Themis became, the more energy she gave off.

"I am sorry," Cylus said quickly, not daring to look at the principal. "Yes, I understand, I will be here for detention. There will be no more trouble."

Themis calmed and the static electricity in the air abated. She returned to her stool. "Fine. Now, Zephyr and Cylus, go rejoin the lines outside to receive your classroom assignments." Her eyes moved to Astraea. "You stay here for a moment."

Astraea looked over to Zephyr as her friend slowly moved to the door.

"And no more fighting!" Themis called as they disappeared into the outer office. "I am watching you both."

When they were gone, Themis stared at the marble floor for some time before looking back up at Astraea. "I have a special assignment for you." She looked over at the silver-skinned boy. "Come closer, Trynulus."

He was so still and silent that Astraea had forgotten he was even in the room. But when he stepped forward, he seemed to glide. There was a gentle calmness around him as he stood silently beside her.

"Astraea, I would like you to meet Trynulus. He will be joining us at school to further his education."

Astraea looked at the strange boy beside her. When his eyes landed on her, she was once again struck by the colors inside them.

"Trynulus," the principal continued, "Astraea will be your guide until you find your way around."

"Me?" Astraea cried. "Forgive me, Themis, but how can I be a guide when I don't even know my own way around? I expect to spend most of my time lost!"

For the first time since she'd arrived in the room, Themis smiled and laughed lightly. "Then you will learn together." The principal's eyes settled on Trynulus. "I appreciate that Titus is a big change for you. Xanadu is a wonderful place, but it is wild and untamed. Here we are more ordered. But I am sure in time you will come to love it. There is much to see and do. Just remember, you are the first of your kind to come here. If this works, more will follow. So you must consider yourself a diplomat."

"I understand," he said softly.

"Xanadu?" Astraea looked over at the silver-skinned boy. "Are you really from Xanadu?"

"Yes," he answered.

Themis left her stool and walked closer to them. She smiled at Trynulus before saying to Astraea, "Trynulus's father was from Earth and his mother is Rhean, a unique race rescued by Riza and Emily Jacobs when their world's sun went supernova. His mother's people now live on one of the new continents of Xanadu."

"Wow," Astraea said. "That's so cool."

"Cool?" Themis frowned. "I do not think so. Xanadu is a warm world."

"Sorry," Astraea said. "I mean that is very exciting."

"Yes, it is," Themis said. "So of course, you can understand how difficult the transition will be for Trynulus. I want you to help him adjust to life here on Titus."

"Sure," Astraea said. "Zephyr and I can show him all around."

Themis sighed. "Ah yes, Zephyr . . . Please do not let your friend lead him astray. We both know how . . . spirited she can be."

Astraea smiled. "I understand. We'll be careful."

Themis reached into a hidden pocket in her robes and pulled out a small piece of paper. She handed it to Astraea. "Here is the class schedule for you and Trynulus. You may go on to your first class now. Just remember to return here this afternoon to start your detention."

Astraea frowned. "I thought showing Trynulus around was my detention."

Themis shook her head. "No, showing Trynulus around is just good manners. You will still do a week's detention for fighting."

"Oh," Astraea sighed. "Of course."

Themis smiled at Astraea but held out both her hands to Trynulus. "Welcome to Arcadia. I'm sure you will soon fit right in."

5

ASTRAEA WALKED WITH TRYNULUS THROUGH
the confusion of Arcadia One. Around them were
other students looking just as perplexed as they
tried to figure out their schedules and locate their
classrooms.

Along the halls were doors, and each one had
a number on it. Astraea soon worked out that the
four buildings of Arcadia were numbered One
to Four. Within each building, classrooms were
also numbered, and the floors of the buildings
had names. Their first class was in Arcadia One,
room 3 on Prometheus level. She just had to figure
out which level was Prometheus.

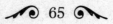

"How long have you been here?" she asked as they made their way to the stairs.

"A few days," he said.

"Where are you staying while you're here?"

"There is something called a dormitory—it's where the students stay who come from too far away to go home each night. But in my section, there's only me."

Astraea looked at his strange silver face and saw no emotion there. He didn't look around him and didn't ask her any questions. If she didn't speak, he remained silent.

They climbed the stairs to the next level. A sign said it was Prometheus. "Here we are, Trynulus. We just have to find room three."

Trynulus stopped. "May I ask a favor?"

"Sure."

"Would you please call me Tryn? My mother only ever calls me Trynulus when I'm in trouble. I prefer Tryn."

"I prefer it too," Astraea said, finding it hard to believe he would ever get into trouble.

By the time they arrived at their first class, everyone else was inside. There were desks, benches, and standing areas to accommodate every shape of Titan or Olympian. Astraea was disappointed to see Cylus standing with several other centaurs, and even more upset to see that Zephyr wasn't there.

Minerva stood at the front of the class. "Come in," she said, ushering them in. "Find an empty seat and sit down. We are about to get started."

Astraea knew that Minerva was known as a powerful Olympian warrior and Jupiter's favorite child. The class schedule said this was supposed to be ancient history. If so, why would a warrior teach it?

The answer had revealed itself by the end of class. Technically speaking, Minerva *was* teaching history—the history of the ancient battles between the Titans and the Olympians. Astraea realized that if the point of Arcadia was to bring the Titans and Olympians together, this was the worst possible class to do it. Minerva spent most of the time going into details about the Titans' attacks on Olympus. Not once did she discuss the Olympian return attacks on Titus.

When the bell finally rang, Minerva called out, "We are starting in the classroom, but soon we will take our lessons outside, where I will introduce you to the weapons we used and how to use them."

Astraea was seated beside Tryn and looked at him. "Weapons? Really?" Her eyes went to the back of the room, where the centaurs were laughing, pushing and shoving each other. Cylus's eyes landed on her. He made a motion as though he was holding an invisible bow and arrow. He drew back the arrow and fired it at her.

"Oh, great," she said. "I can't believe they put us in the same class as Cylus and his friends."

"Does he worry you?"

"Worry? No. But he does bother me. He's a trouble-maker."

Astraea waited for Tryn to say something else, but he looked down at his hands and remained silent.

"I guess we should look for our next class," Astraea finally said. She pulled out her schedule and sighed. "This day just keeps getting worse. We have black-smithing taught by Vulcan. Why do I need to know about metalworking? It's not like I want to build weapons."

A trace of a smile lit Tryn's face, then vanished. "I

know Vulcan well. He spent time on Xanadu helping us. He did not make weapons—he helped design and build our homes."

"Oh," Astraea said. "That was really nice of him. What's it like on Xanadu? I heard it's beautiful."

"It is."

Astraea waited for him to say more, but he said nothing. She watched him from the corner of her eye and noticed how sad he looked. When he glanced over to her, she looked down at the schedule again. "Um, it says Vulcan's forge is in Arcadia Three, at the back. Let's see how long it takes us to find it."

The first day at school sped by as Astraea and Tryn moved through their classes. There were blacksmithing, art, dance, astronomy, and Earth studies taught by the human-turned-sphinx Tom. Astraea shared that class with Tom's daughter, Seneka, and found she enjoyed it the most.

But through all the classes and even between them, Tryn said very little. Unless Astraea started the conversation, he said nothing at all. She decided by the afternoon that he was either very shy, indifferent or didn't like her—which made her especially grateful when she shared two afternoon classes with Zephyr.

When the final bell sounded and the day ended, Tryn just nodded and walked away.

"Well, good-bye to you too . . . ," Zephyr called as she and Astraea watched him slip through the crowded halls without a glance in any direction but down. Zephyr looked at her friend. "He's a ball of fun, isn't he?"

Astraea followed Tryn's departure. "He is quiet, I'll say that for him. I think he feels really out of place."

"You think?" Zephyr said. "Look at him. He's silver. Of course he's out of place. I bet he even glows in the dark."

"You're one to talk," Astraea teased. "I can read by the glow you give off."

"That's different," Zephyr replied hotly.

Astraea laughed as they slowly made their way back to the principal's office.

Themis was there, waiting for them. "You are late," she chastised.

"But we were at Arcadia Three for dance class. That's a long way away," Zephyr said. "And since

Astraea can't fly yet, we had to stay on the ground."

"That is no excuse." Themis walked over to the window and picked up a broom lying against it and large bucket with a dustpan. She handed the broom to Astraea and put the bucket before Zephyr. "For the rest of this week, you two will sweep the halls of Arcadia One. When you finish, you may return home."

"What?" Zephyr cried. "That's not fair! Cylus started the fight. What's he doing for his detention?"

"If you must know, because he started the trouble, Cylus is cleaning Arcadia Four—by himself."

Zephyr snorted. "It's still not fair. Why should we sweep the floors when you have cleaners to do that? Let the night dwellers do it when the school is closed. We shouldn't have to."

Themis's eyes darkened. "Do you believe you are better than the night dwellers? That they alone should do this kind of labor?"

"I didn't say that," Zephyr said. "But they do work at night when others have gone to bed. They like that kind of physical labor."

"So because they generally work in the nectar

orchards, they should automatically work here as well?"

"Well . . ."

Themis nodded and took the broom away from Astraea. "All right. For today you do not have to clean the halls—"

"Great!" Zephyr turned and began to clop out of the office.

Astraea saw the growing anger on Themis's face as Zephyr started to leave. Her best friend was getting them deeper into trouble and didn't even know it.

"Stop!" Themis commanded. She waved her hand in the air, and the double doors slammed shut in front of Zephyr, who whinnied and reared in fear.

"I am not finished with you yet," Themis said. "Come back here."

Zephyr looked from the doors to Themis and back to the doors again. "How did you do that?"

"The 'how' does not matter. What does is what will happen if you test my patience further."

When Zephyr returned, Themis shook her head sadly. "Since you believe you are so much better than the night dwellers and that they should do all the physical labor, I want you to experience what they do in the orchards. For your detention today, you will both go into the East Arcadian Nectar Orchard and collect two urns of fresh nectar. It's getting late and the flowers will be opening soon."

"You want us to collect nectar?" Astraea gasped.

Themis nodded. "You will each fill an urn. Then tomorrow morning before class, you will deliver the nectar to me and tell me what you thought of working in the orchards."

Zephyr snorted, "But I don't have arms. How am I supposed to do it?"

"You are clever, Zephyr," Themis said. "I am sure you will figure it out."

"I can't do it."

Themis advanced on her. "If you learn nothing else here at Arcadia, learn this. The words 'can't' and 'cannot' do not exist. You can do it if you believe in it. And I firmly believe you will go into the orchards and collect nectar and deliver it to me tomorrow."

"And if I really can't?"

"Failure is not an option." Themis's eyes moved

over to Astraea as well. "It would not be good for either of you."

Astraea jumped forward. "Of course. We understand and we won't fail."

Themis looked at Astraea doubtfully. "See that you do not." As she started to move away, she turned back quickly and pointed to Zephyr. "Do not try to trick me with nectar from home. I want it fresh and will know the difference. Do you understand?"

Zephyr dropped her head. "Yes, Themis. I still don't know how I'm supposed to do it with hooves and no hands, but I understand."

Themis moved back to her three-legged stool and sat down. "Fine, you may both go now. I will see you back here tomorrow morning."

"Yes, tomorrow," Astraea said. She caught hold of Zephyr's mane and the two walked out of the office.

6

JAKE MOANED AND OPENED HIS EYES. HIS head was pounding and every muscle in his body ached. Reaching up, he felt a golf-ball-size lump on the back of his head. "Oooouuuuchhhh . . ."

He was lying on soft grass in some kind of well-groomed but totally weird orchard. Sitting up slowly, he frowned. The trees had large gold flowers that looked like giant teardrops, and the green-and-gold oval leaves were bigger than his head.

A bee the size of his fist was buzzing around the flowers, and when it landed on a bud, the flower opened and the bee crawled inside.

"What the . . ." Jake climbed slowly to his feet and

approached the nearest tree. He tentatively touched one of the flowers. It opened, and a few drops of a thick, honeylike liquid poured into his hand. He lifted his hand to his nose and sniffed the liquid's sweet fragrance.

On the ground beside him were his backpack and skateboard, but his sister was nowhere to be seen. "Moles?" he called. "Where are you?"

All he heard in response was a strange birdsong that seemed to be repeating his words back to him in a high-pitched voice.

"Whoa, how hard did I hit my head?" He took a few more steps, staring in wonder. Nothing looked familiar or remotely normal. The sky above was clear and the bluest he'd ever seen. There was no yellow haze of Los Angeles pollution and no bad smell to the air, which was sweet, fresh, and warm—not hot. He couldn't see or hear any cars, and there was no one around.

The last thing Jake remembered was falling off his skateboard after . . . after what? Why did he fall off his skateboard? He hadn't taken a spill in ages. The last time was at the skate park, when he tried to do a triple twist. But he hadn't been at a skate park. He and Molly were heading to . . . to . . . the Santa Monica Pier!

He remembered that much. It was the rest that was gone. "Moles!" he called again. "Are you here?" Jake's initial shock was fading and being replaced by panic. Where was he? Where was his sister? What happened to Los Angeles?

Jake bent down, collected his things, and started to run. He didn't know where, only that he had to find his sister. He passed through row upon row of the strange trees with the weird bees. They seemed to go on forever.

When he couldn't run any farther, Jake slowed to a walk. He was out of breath, his head throbbed, and he was more frightened than he'd ever been in his life. What was happening?

As he moved forward, he thought he heard the sound of a soft, light voice. There were other sounds with it. It almost sounded like a horse neighing. The sounds were coming from a few rows away.

Following them, Jake passed through several more trees before coming to a full stop. Up ahead was the most beautiful girl he'd ever seen in his life. Her hair was almost as golden as the teardrop flowers on the trees and hung long down her back. Her face was smooth and clear and she was dressed in a . . . a Greek costume?

Jake took a few more steps, then stopped as his mouth fell open. If the beautiful girl in the pale blue costume was shocking, the large white horse with the big black blaze that approached her was impossible. Someone had glued white feathered wings to it. But the horse didn't appear to care as it carried a bucket in its mouth and offered it to the girl. When she took it, she bent down to pour the contents into a jug at her feet.

Jake stood in stunned silence. He couldn't be seeing what he was seeing. It was all wrong—it was impossible. But the trees, the strange flowers, the beautiful girl—all of them were forgotten when the horse stood taller and opened its wings in a large stretch.

The pity he felt for the abused horse with the glued-on wings vanished—the instant Jake realized the wings were *real*.

7

"I STILL DON'T THINK IT'S FAIR," ZEPHYR complained after Astraea took the bucket of nectar from her. "Cylus started the fight. He should be here doing this, not us."

Astraea laughed. "We're here because you opened your mouth again. All we had to do was sweep the floors of Arcadia One, but you had to speak up and say the night dwellers should do it. If you had kept quiet, we'd each be home now."

"So you're saying this is my fault?" Zephyr said.

"Isn't it?"

"All right, so maybe I might be a little responsible," Zephyr admitted. "But seriously, this is going to take

all night. I never knew it took so many flowers to fill one bucket."

Astraea carried her own empty bucket over to the tree she was harvesting. She gently caressed a gold blossom and held the bucket under it as it released its nectar. "We'd get through this faster if you stopped complaining and actually did some work."

"That's easy for you to say. You've got hands. I have to lick the flowers to get them to release the nectar. How can something as delicious as nectar come from a flower that tastes so bad?"

Astraea chuckled as she moved from flower to flower. But as she worked, she had the strangest feeling they weren't alone. She walked slowly back to Zephyr and lowered her voice. "Call me crazy, but I have the feeling we're being watched."

Zephyr snorted. "I've been feeling it too. . . ." She lifted her head high in the air and sniffed. "I smell something strange." She looked around. "Over there. What's that thing in the trees?"

Astraea turned and saw a large, dark shape dashing away from them. It moved strangely and made odd sounds as it ran. "What is that?"

"Let's find out!" Zephyr bolted after the fleeing creature.

Astraea dropped her bucket and raced behind her friend. As they sped through the orchard, she got only fleeting glimpses of the creature. It was big and black and moving incredibly fast as it barged through the trees as though they were no obstacle at all.

"You stay on the ground. I'm going up!" Zephyr flapped her large wings and took off, climbing high over the treetops.

Astraea was running faster than she ever had in her life, but still the dark figure was getting away. It darted from side to side and then circled back in the direction they had come. Astraea whooshed past their buckets and urns and was about to enter another row of trees when she saw a boy stopped in the row directly in her path. She was moving too fast to stop or even change direction.

She plowed into him at full speed, knocking him backward so hard that he tumbled to the ground and somersaulted several times before coming to a halt on his stomach. Astraea also crashed to the ground and

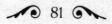

slid across the grass and bashed her knees on a large tree root growing over the surface.

"Astraea!" Zephyr cried. She landed on the ground and charged up to her friend. "Are you all right? Did it attack you? Do you want me to kill it?"

"No it didn't attack me. It just stood in my way and I couldn't stop." She sat up and inspected her bleeding knees. "Ouch . . ."

Across from her the boy groaned and rolled over. He sat up and shook his head. "What hit me?"

"I think that was me," Astraea said. "Why didn't you move before I hit you?"

"I—I didn't have time. You—you were running too fast."

Astraea looked at him and started to frown. The boy was dressed so strangely and smelled completely different from everyone else. His hair was long at the sides but short and spiky on the top of his head. A strange hat lay on the ground beside him, and his clothes were unrecognizable—if anything, he looked more like the man her grandfather had caught earlier in the day. He looked—human!

The boy's wild eyes flicked between Astraea and

Zephyr, who was pawing the ground and snorting. "This is getting too weird," Zephyr said. "I'm sure that a creature was watching us, and then this boy appears out of nowhere smelling like—what is that smell? He stinks."

"He doesn't stink," Astraea said. "He just smells different." She climbed painfully to her feet and looked around. "Where did the other one go?"

Zephyr snorted. "I don't know. It was moving incredibly fast, and then it just vanished."

"What do you mean, it vanished? How can something just vanish?"

"I don't know. Next time I see it, I'll ask," Zephyr said.

"Who—who are you?" the boy asked.

"I was just about to ask you the same thing," Astraea said as she peered closer at him.

"Careful, Astraea, we don't know what it is."

"Actually, I think I do know what he is." Astraea said to the boy, "You're human, aren't you?"

The boy looked at Zephyr with wide, frightened eyes and nodded.

"Human?" Zephyr cried. She reared and flapped

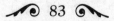

her wings. "Astraea, get back! They're dangerous and carry diseases!"

"No, they're not," Astraea said.

The boy pointed a shaking finger at Zephyr. "What is that thing?"

"Thing?" Zephyr cried. She landed on the ground again and stomped forward. "Did he just call me a 'thing'?"

"Zephyr, calm down. I'm sure he didn't mean it." Astraea looked at the boy. "You didn't mean to call Zephyr a 'thing,' did you?"

His eyes were still huge as he looked at Zephyr. "I—I . . . um . . ."

"Okay, you're right," Zephyr snorted. "He's not dangerous, he's just an idiot."

"He's frightened, that's all." Astraea focused on the boy. "What's your name?"

The boy's eyes were fixed on Zephyr. "I—I'm Jake. Can—can you understand it?"

"It!" Zephyr fumed. "First he calls me 'thing' and now 'it.' Astraea, stand back. I'm going to stomp him into a puddle."

"Zephyr that's enough. Besides, you called him 'it'

first." Astraea rose and stood next to her friend. She said to the boy, "If you value your life, you'd better apologize to Zephyr."

"For what?"

"For calling her 'thing' and 'it.' She's very sensitive about name-calling."

Jake climbed slowly to his feet and approached Zephyr. "You're not trying to tell me she can understand us. I mean, not really."

"What's he think I am?" Zephyr snorted. "Stupid or something?"

Astraea looked back at the boy. "Of course she can understand us. She's not stupid, you know, but she does have a temper. So you'd better apologize to her before she loses it and stomps you."

Jake shrugged. "If you say so." He looked at Zephyr. "I'm sorry I called you 'it.'"

"That's better," Zephyr said. "Now, where do you come from?" When he said nothing, Zephyr moved closer. "Well?"

"You'd better answer her," Astraea warned.

"Answer what?" he said.

"Her question," Astraea said.

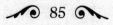

"But she didn't ask me anything."

"Yes, she did. She asked where you came from."

"No, she didn't. She just neighed at me like a horse."

"Horse?" Zephyr shrieked. "Tell me he didn't just call me a horse! That's it. There's only so much I can take. Stand back. I'm going to stomp him."

"Zephyr, please." Astraea caught hold of Zephyr's mane and held her down. She looked back at the boy. "And you stop too."

"Stop what? I didn't do anything!"

"You called her a horse."

"She is a horse!" he insisted.

"No, she's not!" Astraea insisted. "Horses are very different."

"How?" he cried.

"Just look at her. She looks nothing like a horse."

"Apart from the wings—which by the way are impossible—she's exactly like a horse." Jake looked down and started to shake his head. "This is insane! A horse that isn't a horse, a girl in costume who runs superfast, and these crazy trees." He walked a few paces and then stopped. "Wait a minute . . . I know,

I'm dreaming." He looked back at them and started to laugh. "That's it! This is just some whacked-out dream." He scratched his head. "That makes sense. I fell and I hit my head and . . . and now I'm dreaming. . . ." He started pacing again. "No, wait . . . not dreaming—it's a coma! I hit my head really hard, and now I'm in the hospital in some kind of coma and this is all a hallucination."

Astraea watched the boy talking to himself as though she and Zephyr weren't there. He was saying things she didn't understand. "What is a coma?"

He looked at her and grinned. "Oh you're good, you're really good. Asking me what a coma is when you're part of it. That's a trick question, isn't it?"

"Is it?" Astraea said.

Zephyr stood beside her and leaned her head closer. "I think he's crazy," she whispered. "We'd better stand back before we catch it from him."

"I'm not sure what he is," Astraea said. She stepped closer to the boy. "And we really don't know what a coma is."

He grinned again. "Okay, I'll play. A coma is when you're hurt and unconscious for a long time.

Sometimes you never wake up. I hit my head really hard, and now I'm in a coma. You're just part of what's happening in my damaged brain."

"Ah, that explains it," Zephyr said. "He's brain damaged!"

"Maybe," Astraea mused. She frowned at Jake. "So where exactly do you come from?"

"Where do *I* come from?" He laughed. "Nope, this is my coma. I get to ask the questions. Where do *you* come from?"

"Here," Astraea answered. "Titus."

"Oh, Titus. Of course, I should have known," he laughed again. "I'm from LA."

Astraea looked at Zephyr and then back to Jake. "Where is La?"

He laughed harder. "Not La, LA. That's Los Angeles—as in California."

Astraea shook her head and looked at Zephyr. "Have you ever heard of Los Angeles as in California?"

"Never," Zephyr said.

"We've never heard of it," Astraea said back to him.

"Of course not," Jake laughed. "That's because you're in my coma."

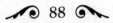

"This is getting us nowhere," Zephyr said. "Let's just tell someone there's a human here and go home."

"We can't. They'll take him away," Astraea said. "Besides, we still have detention. We have to collect nectar for tomorrow."

Jake started to frown. "Zephyr just said something to you, didn't she?" When Astraea nodded, his frown deepened. "If she's part of my coma, why can't I understand her?"

"Because you're an idiot," Zephyr said.

Jake looked at her. "What did she say?"

Astraea looked at Zephyr and then back to him. "She can't understand it either. Everyone here understands her."

"I didn't say that," Zephyr insisted. "Astraea, you're such a liar!"

"There are more people here?" Jake said.

Astraea nodded. "Of course. Titus is filled with Titans and Olympians."

"Hey, Titans and Olympians. I know them!" Jake cried. "They're from the movies." He looked around. "I'm dreaming about being in a movie! How cool is that!"

"You're not dreaming!" Astraea said. "This is real."

"Yeah, right," Jake laughed.

Zephyr shook her head. "He's giving me a headache. We've got enough nectar. Let's just go."

"We can't leave him here. Grandfather will take him away."

"So?"

"So it would be wrong."

Jake started to point at them and laugh harder. "You two are so funny. You're in my head but you're arguing."

"We're not in your head!" Astraea insisted. "We're very real, and unless you start to take this seriously, you're in a lot of danger."

8

ASTRAEA WATCHED JAKE WANDERING around the orchard. He approached a flower and touched it. He sniffed the nectar that the flower released and then licked it. This made him chuckle. "Honey from a flower—how cool is that!"

"He is completely insane," Zephyr commented.

"No, he's just confused. He still doesn't believe this is real."

Zephyr looked up. "It's about to get very real. The sun is going down. In a short while the night dwellers will arrive. I'd love to see what he does when he gets a look at them."

Astraea looked up at the blazing pinks and red

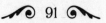

flashing across the sky as the sun started to set. Zephyr was right. It wouldn't be long before the orchards were full of nectar gatherers. "We have to hide him."

"Why?"

"I told you already. Something strange is happening here. Yesterday my father saw a human with my grandfather, and then today, during the ceremony at Arcadia, I watched another one being caught. Now we find Jake here in the orchard. The routes to Earth are all sealed, but in two days three humans have arrived here. How many more have come? How are they getting here and why?" She looked back at Jake. "And he's part of it, whether he believes it or not."

Zephyr looked over to Jake and nodded. "Three humans in two days isn't normal. But we can't expect any answers from him. He still thinks this is a dream."

"That's just shock. Once he realizes the truth, he'll help us figure it out."

Zephyr nodded. "I hope so. But where can we hide him until then?"

"I'm not sure," Astraea admitted. "But I was speaking with Tryn today. He said he was staying at Arcadia in a dorm. He's by himself there. . . ."

Zephyr gasped. "You want to hide a human at Arcadia?"

"Can you think of a better place? It's got a lot of kids there. He won't be noticed."

Zephyr shook her head. "There is no way anyone will believe he's a Titan. If we want to keep him safe, no one can see him."

Astraea grinned. "So you're going to help me?"

Zephyr whinnied. "Of course I am. I may not like humans, but you're my best friend. If you want to help him, so will I."

"Thanks, Zeph." Astraea walked over to Jake and touched him on the arm. "We have to go."

He smiled brightly. "Where are we going?"

"I'm not really sure. But you can't stay here or they'll catch you and lock you away."

"For what?"

"For being human," Astraea said. The smile on his face still suggested he didn't believe any of this. She had a thought. "You still think this is a dream, right?"

He nodded. "Duh! 'Course it's a dream."

"Well, it's about to turn into a nightmare if you

don't trust us. Please, just do as I ask and come with us."

Jake walked over and picked up his baseball cap, backpack, and skateboard. "Why not? Let's go."

All thoughts of detention and the two jugs of nectar they had to deliver to the school the next morning were forgotten as they made their way out of the orchard and onto the quieter paths of Arcadia.

Zephyr used her height and all her senses to warn them whenever anyone was around. When Zephyr gave the alarm, they hid behind trees or large statues and waited for them to pass.

Each time a Titan or Olympian walked past, Jake tried to meet them. It was only Astraea holding him back that prevented the three of them from being discovered. It was the same for buildings and statues. Jake would gaze at them with a huge smile on his face.

"This place is totally awesome!" he said. "I sure hope I remember it all when I wake up."

His constant denial was starting to grate on Astraea's nerves. She looked over at Zephyr, and her best friend chuckled. "He's in for a big surprise when he finally realizes this is real."

Jake stopped and looked at Zephyr and then Astraea. "What'd she say?"

This time, Astraea didn't lie. "She said you're in for a surprise when you realize this isn't a dream!"

Jake patted Zephyr on the neck and laughed. "Ha-ha, that's a good one!"

"Glad you like it," Zephyr said back to him.

"She said she's glad you like it," Astraea repeated.

When they approached Arcadia, Jake stopped and stared in wonder. "Whoa, who'd have thought I could dream up a place like that? It's awesome."

"You didn't dream it up!" Astraea insisted. "Those are the four buildings of Arcadia, our school. It just opened today."

"That's a school?" Jake cried. "It looks like a museum or library or something like that. . . . Is that where we're going?"

Astraea nodded. "There's a place inside called a dorm. I hope we can hide you there until we figure out how you got here."

"Wait." Jake stopped again and started to laugh.

"Didn't you say you both got detention? On your first day at school? What did you do?"

Astraea looked at Zephyr and then shrugged. There was no reason not to tell him. "We got into a fight with a centaur. He called Zephyr Pegasus's daughter and then said I had stubby baby wings."

"Wings?" Jake said, looking at her. "You don't have wings."

"Yes, I do," Astraea said. "They're small because I'm still young. But when I grow up, they'll be large enough for me to fly."

"No way!" Jake cried. He came closer and tried to look at her back. "Let me see them."

Astraea suddenly felt very self-conscious and moved so he couldn't get behind her. "Not now. We have to get you to safety first."

"Yeah, right, that's coz you don't have wings."

"Yes, I do!" Astraea insisted.

"Prove it."

"Astraea, just show him," Zephyr suggested. "It's the only way to get him to shut up. And it might help him believe this is real."

Astraea sighed heavily and lowered her head. "If

I show you, will you promise to take this more seriously? Your life is in very real danger, but you just keep laughing like you don't care."

"I promise." Jake grinned. He crossed his hand over his chest. "Scout's honor."

"I don't know what that is. But if you promise . . ." Astraea hesitantly undid the belt at her waist, reached up to her shoulders, and unclipped the flowing fabric that went down her back like a cape. When it fell away, she opened up her small wings. "See, wings."

Jake's hand went to his mouth and his blue eyes opened wide. "Whoa, that's totally rad. . . ." He touched the downy gray feathers on the long edge of her left wing. "It's so soft."

"All right, that's enough," Astraea said, pulling in her wings again. "You've seen them and touched them. Now do you believe this is real?"

"Yeah," he breathed. "Really cool."

"No, I mean this—Titus."

Jake laughed again. "I wake up in a place where horses have wings and can talk and you have wings too, and you seriously expect me to believe any of it?"

"Ugh!" Astraea threw her hands in the air and started to storm away. "I give up!"

Zephyr whinnied. "Now look what you've done. You've upset Astraea." She gave Jake a nip on the arm and trotted after her friend.

"Ouch!" Jake cried. "Hey, that really hurt."

He ran after Astraea and Zephyr. When he caught up with them, he showed Astraea his arm, where Zephyr's sharp teeth had nearly broken the skin. The area was bright red, and dark bruises were already forming. "Look what Zephyr did to me. You're not supposed to feel pain in a dream, but this really hurts."

Astraea finally lost her temper. "That's because this isn't a dream or a coma or whatever! It's real. Tell me, would you feel this in a dream?" Astraea shoved Jake in the chest. But not knowing how fragile humans were, she sent him flying backward. He crashed down to the ground several feet away.

Realizing what she'd done, Astraea ran over and helped him back up. "I'm so sorry! I didn't mean to do that."

Jake was gasping to catch his breath. He rose to his feet and bent over. "Wow, you're really strong."

"I'm a Titan. Of course I am."

When he could breathe again, Jake stood up straight and stared around as though seeing everything for the very first time. He walked over to Zephyr and lifted her wing and peered at where it joined her torso. He shook his head and his voice dropped. "This wing feels so real. But it can't be. . . ." A deep frown creased his brow. He walked over and felt the leaves on a nearby bush. "If this is real, what happened to me? How did I get here? Where is my sister?"

"You have a sister?" Astraea asked.

Jake nodded and continued to look around. His smile had vanished, to be replaced by a look of confusion and fear. "She was right behind me when . . . when . . ."

"When what?"

"I'm not sure," he said. He was standing beside a statue of Venus, touching the cool marble. He gazed up at the setting sun and followed a flock of colorful birds flying across the sky. The distress on his face was heartbreaking.

"I—I was with my sister . . . ," he started softly. "We had to go to the Santa Monica Pier to meet our dad. But it was so crowded that we took a shortcut. Molly was starting to irritate me, so I went ahead on my skateboard. Then she screamed, and when I looked back, I saw . . . saw something. It's impossible to describe. Then I fell off my skateboard and hit my head. . . ." He looked away. "I—I woke up here. Where is Molly?"

"I don't know," Astraea said gently. "She wasn't in the orchard with you?"

He shook his head and his shoulders slumped. "I was supposed to protect her and I didn't. That—that thing got her. . . ." His voice broke and he walked away.

"Whoa, he's taking it bad," Zephyr said softly.

"Wouldn't you, if you suddenly woke up on Earth?" Astraea said.

"Guess so," Zephyr agreed. She walked up to Jake and laid her head on his shoulder. "Tell him we'll figure this out. He's not alone. We'll find his sister."

Astraea nodded and approached Jake. "Zephyr says you're not alone. We'll help you find your sister."

His red eyes looked at her. "You really can talk to her?"

Astraea nodded.

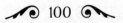

Jake reached up and gently stroked Zephyr's muzzle. "I'm really sorry I called you a horse—I didn't mean to hurt your feelings."

"It's all right," Zephyr said. "You're not too bad for a smelly human."

Astraea chuckled softly. "She says it's all right and that you're not too bad for a human."

Zephyr looked at her and her ears went back. "I said smelly human."

"Thanks," Jake said softly. "And you'll really help me find my sister?"

Astraea nodded. "But before we start to look for her, we have to hide you in the dorm."

"Why do I have to hide?"

"Because you're from Earth. All contact with Earth has been forbidden. Humans are banned from coming here."

"There's been contact with Earth? When? How? I've never seen anything like you before."

"But you knew about Olympians and Titans," Astraea said.

"Yeah, but that's just from the movies, they weren't real—"

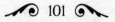

"But we are," Astraea said. "We used to have a lot of contact with Earth. But all of that's stopped now."

"Why?"

"I'm not sure. I know there was trouble between Olympus and Earth. After that, it was decided that it was safer if we never went back there or associated with humans again."

"So if contact is forbidden, who brought me here?"

"We don't know," Astraea said. "But I have to tell you, you're not the first human to appear. My father said my grandfather was with a woman yesterday, and just this morning, I saw a man. He was captured and taken away. I don't know where."

Fear rose in Jake's eyes. "If they found my sister, would they take her away?"

Astraea nodded. "Probably."

Jake looked around desperately. "We've got to find her first!"

"We will, but we also need to make sure that you're safe," Astraea said.

Jake shook his head. "I'm in serious trouble, aren't I?"

"Finally he's starting to understand," Zephyr said.

Astraea nodded again. "Yes, you are, but we're here

to help. Once we get you settled, we can work on who brought you here and why."

"And we find Molly?"

"Yes. If she's here, we'll find her," Astraea said.

Jake was almost overcome with fear. Suddenly he wasn't the smiling, playful boy who thought this was all part of a dream. Now he was vulnerable and frightened and realizing that his whole world had been turned upside down.

They crept closer to Arcadia, but there were still a lot of people milling around. The school was a novelty, and everyone was interested in seeing it. Astraea led them over to some bushes at the back of Arcadia One and pulled them open. "Jake, get in here. I'll go inside and find somewhere to hide you and then come back."

When he crawled inside the dense bush, Astraea straightened up. "Zeph, will you stay with him? I'm going to go see if I can find Tryn."

"You don't expect him to help us, do you? He doesn't seem to care about anything."

Astraea shrugged. "I know. But his father is human. I'm hoping that might count for something."

With Jake hidden in the bushes and Zephyr keeping watch, Astraea jogged over to Arcadia One. There was a line of torches set up outside, illuminating the front of the impressive building. She walked up to the doors and found them closed, but not locked, so she entered the main foyer. On the far right wall was a directory and a map that covered all the buildings of Arcadia.

According to the map, the dormitory was a small building attached by a covered walkway to the rear of Arcadia Two.

Making note of the directions, she started toward building two. Unlike Arcadia One, the doors to Arcadia Two were locked. But that wasn't enough to stop her. She walked around to the back and saw the covered walkway that led to her destination.

The dormitory was a white marble building, smaller than Arcadia Two, standing only three stories tall. But like all the school buildings, it had tall marble pillars out front. Unlike the others, however, the pillars here had been carved into the shapes of Titan and Olympian heroes. She recognized Prometheus, Phoebe, and Rhea, then Hercules, Perseus, and Diana. The primary pillars on each corner were carved into the shape of hero Nirads who had fought to save Olympus. The Nirads, each with four powerful arms, appeared to support the whole dormitory.

Astraea realized everything about the school was in balance. If there were lessons on Titan heroes, there were an equal number of Olympian heroes as well. The teachers were also a mix between the two. She imagined that this was meant to help the students integrate, but if today was any indication, they had a long way to go. Despite the teachers' best efforts, Titan students mixed only with Titans, while the Olympians kept to themselves.

As Astraea pushed open the dorm doors, she realized just how difficult it must be for Tryn. He was neither Titan nor Olympian. He hadn't even been born on Titus, so no one wanted to associate with him.

Once inside the foyer, Astraea had hoped there would be some kind of directory. But there wasn't. If Tryn's room was here, she'd have to find it on her own. She started down the hallway of the main floor, knocking on doors. At every one she tried, she received no answer. But when she reached the very end of the hall and knocked on the last door, she heard movement inside.

"Who is it?" a familiar voice demanded from behind the door.

"Tryn, it's me, Astraea. I need to speak with you. May I come in, please?"

The door opened a fraction, and Astraea saw Tryn's face peering through the crack. "Are you alone?"

"Yes. Please open the door. It's urgent."

Tryn's eyes narrowed, but he backed away and pulled open the door. "Come in. I'm sorry it's a bit of a mess, but I don't like visitors."

"I'm not worried about that. . . ." When Astraea entered, she stopped. The room wasn't a mess, it was a disaster area. Somehow, she'd expected him to be super organized. But he was the complete opposite. There wasn't a clear surface in the whole room. Books covered the floor and the windowsills, while the bookshelves were cluttered with clothing and stale ambrosia cakes.

Tryn shoved a rock collection off a chair. The stones clattered to the floor, and some rolled under the bed. "Sit," he said. Then he sat on a pile of clothes on the side of the bed.

Now that she was actually here, Astraea didn't know what to say. She frowned. "Tryn, can I trust you?"

His face revealed nothing. Not shock, anger, or even curiosity. "Why do you ask?"

"Well, Zephyr and I have found something, and we don't know what to do. I mean, really, we should go to my grandfather, you know, Hyperion, because he's head of security. But if we do that, it will make things really bad for someone. So I was hoping that since your dad is human, you might like to help us."

A flash of curiosity crossed his silver face, but then he hid it under a passive expression. "I don't understand. Is this some kind of trick?"

"Trick? No, I promise it's not." Astraea rose and started to pace the small bedroom. She walked over to the dresser and picked up a book. The cover was made of some kind of metal, and the writing was unlike anything she'd ever seen before. She opened the pages and saw pictures of a red world. She looked back at Tryn. "Is this your old world?"

He nodded. "That was Rhean. It was a gift from my mother. That book was all she was allowed to take from her home world. It's a storybook." He rose and took the book away from her. "You didn't come here to discuss my origins, did you?"

"No," Astraea answered quickly. "I told you, Zephyr and I found something and we don't know what to do."

He nodded. "You start by telling me. If you really need my help, I have to know what you're talking about."

Astraea sighed. "All right. You know Zephyr and I got detention. Well, part of it was we had to go into the orchards to gather nectar. And we were doing great. But then we found . . . well, I mean we heard . . . or rather, we saw . . ."

"Yes?" Tryn prodded.

"Well, we found a human boy."

"What!" Tryn cried.

It was the first time she'd seen emotion from him. His face lit up and his eyes went wide. "Really?"

"Yes," Astraea continued. "His name is Jake. He doesn't know how he got here. But he's really scared.

His sister is missing too, but we don't know if she's here."

"Where is he?" Tryn demanded.

"He's with Zephyr, hiding in some bushes not far from Arcadia One. But we can't let anyone see him or my grandfather will take him away."

"Why would he do that?"

"You know why," Astraea said. "Travel between Titus and Earth is forbidden. But somehow, humans are being found here. Just yesterday my father saw my grandfather with a human woman, and right before the opening ceremonies, I saw my grandfather and his security people capture a man. He was taken away, but I don't know where and no one is talking about it. Tryn, something is very wrong. Humans shouldn't be coming here."

Tryn nodded. "And they shouldn't be taken away. I want you to take me to him."

"So you want to help?"

"If he's human, I have to help. It's my duty."

Astraea wanted to ask what that meant, but Tryn was already rushing to the door. He looked back at her. "Are you coming?"

"Yes, of course," Astraea said, joining him. "It's getting dark out. The first thing we need to do is find him somewhere to stay."

"I know where he can stay."

"Here?" Astraea said.

Tryn opened his door. "Not really. I'm alone in the dorm, but it's regularly patrolled. A human would be discovered. But I do know another place he can go— somewhere that no one ever goes."

"Where's that?"

For the first time ever, Tryn grinned, and his smile was stunning. It lit up his whole face. "In the labyrinth beneath Arcadia Two."

9

BY THE TIME THEY CROSSED THE PLAYING field, night was falling. But Astraea could see exactly where they were going because Zephyr, just like her father and Pegasus, gave off a glow. "Over there," Astraea said, pointing. "You can see Zephyr. That's where Jake's hiding."

They ran the rest of the way, and when they stopped, Astraea looked around to ensure they were alone. "Is he still here?"

"No," Zephyr teased. "I sold him to the Muses when they were walking by. Of course he's still here!" She poked her head into the bushes and called, "Jake, it's safe to come out now."

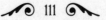

But Jake stayed where he was.

Zephyr pulled her head out and sighed. "This language barrier is getting on my nerves."

Astraea stepped closer and pushed into the bushes. Jake was hugging his backpack. "I'm back. Come out, I want you to meet someone."

Jakes eyes were still fearful. "Are you sure it's safe?"

Astraea nodded. "We're alone."

Slowly he rose and climbed out of the bushes. When he did, he gasped. "Zephyr, you're glowing."

"Yeah, I know, it kinda happens. You really notice it at night," Zephyr said.

Jake looked back at Astraea, "What did she say?"

"She says it happens at night." She caught him by the arm and led him forward. "Jake, this is Tryn. Tryn, this is Jake."

As big as Jake's eyes had been when he saw the glow around Zephyr, they were huge when they landed on Tryn. He gasped. "You're the Silver Surfer!"

"I am what?" Tryn asked.

"The Silver Surfer, you know, from the Fantastic Four." Jake leaned closer to Tryn's face and ran his finger down his cheek. "Does it come off?"

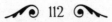

Tryn frowned and backed up. "Of course not. It's my skin. I don't shed it like a lizard any more than you do."

"Jake," Astraea said quickly, "Tryn is half Rhean and half human. His father is from Earth."

"Really?"

Tryn nodded. "He's from Ohio. He fought for Olympus many years ago, and then he helped save my people and get them to Xanadu. He lives there with my mother. Where are you from?"

"I was born in Detroit, but we live in Los Angeles now."

Tryn's expression brightened. "LA? My father has told me all about it. He used to work there. He said the Pacific Ocean is beautiful."

Jake nodded. "It is. I love to go down to the Santa Monica Pier and go skateboarding with my friends."

Tryn gasped. "He told me about skateboarding too. It is wheels on a board, isn't it?"

Jake pulled his skateboard out of the bushes. "Here's my board. It came with me." He handed it to Tryn.

"This is amazing!" Tryn started to inspect every

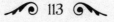

inch of the highly decorated and polished board. "How do you use it?"

"Let me show you. . . ."

Jake had just put the board down on the grass when Astraea stepped forward.

"*Ahem*, have you forgotten the danger? We're out in the open here. Look, there are others entering the field over there. What if they come this way? We just don't have time for you two to play. We have to get Jake under cover before he's discovered. Remember, humans aren't allowed on Titus."

"It will only take a moment," Tryn said.

"We don't have a moment to waste."

Zephyr was shaking her head. "It must be a boy thing. Why anyone would be excited about a board with wheels is beyond me."

"I don't understand it either," Astraea agreed.

"You're right," Tryn finally said. He reached for Jake's backpack. "Come, I will take you to a safe place."

They waited for others to leave the playing field before they crossed it and headed back to the dorm. When they approached the doors, Astraea stopped.

"I thought you said he couldn't stay in the dorm because it was patrolled."

Zephyr snorted, "Why would they patrol a dorm if Tryn is the only resident?"

Tryn looked at her. "I never thought of that. I don't know why. But they do."

"So let's just take him to the labyrinth beneath Arcadia Two," Astraea suggested.

"It's still too early. I have seen cleaners and sometimes teachers coming out of the school this time of night. It's best if we wait in my room until later." He looked over to Jake. "Are you hungry?"

Jake nodded. "I guess. But I'm more worried about my sister."

"You go inside with Tryn," Astraea suggested. "Zephyr and I will go back to the orchard and look for her."

"But I should go with you. She's going to be so scared."

"I understand," Astraea said. "But you can't risk getting caught. Go with Tryn. I promise we'll bring Molly to you if we find her."

Jake hesitated but finally started to walk inside. At

the doors he stopped and looked back. "Please find her. She may be a pain in the neck, but she's the only sister I've got."

Astraea nodded. "I have four brothers, and they drive me crazy. But I would do anything to protect them."

Astraea and Zephyr watched Tryn lead Jake away. When he was gone, Zephyr said, "We're not going to find her, are we?"

"I don't know. Whoever is bringing humans here has to be very cruel—they're all terrified. If they brought Molly to Titus, I doubt they would put her in the same orchard with her brother. If she is really here, that poor girl is lost and completely alone."

10

AS THEY MADE THEIR WAY BACK TO THE orchard, Astraea frowned. "Did you get a good look at that thing we saw right before we met Jake?"

"Not really," Zephyr said. "I flew right over its head. At first I thought it was the Minotaur, because it kind of looked like him. But it didn't move like him at all."

"I wonder if we'll see it again."

"Then what do we do?"

Astraea stopped. "I don't know. All I do know is that by the look of it, it doesn't belong here."

When they reached the orchard, Astraea stayed on the ground while Zephyr took to the sky. But after an

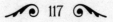

extensive search, they didn't find any traces of Molly or the creature. All they did find were some damaged trees.

Zephyr landed and pawed at one of the broken branches lying on the ground. It was as thick as her front leg. "I knew that thing was big. Look, it broke this like it was a twig."

They followed the trail of broken branches and damaged trees until it stopped abruptly.

Zephyr looked around. "The trail just stops. But I know it didn't fly away. I would have seen it. How is that possible?"

"This is getting so strange. First humans here and now this creature. What does it mean?"

"I don't know," Zephyr said. She lifted her head high and looked around. "Maybe someone else caught it and took it away like they are doing to the humans."

"Maybe. But who? We didn't see anyone else in here but Jake."

"Where are they taking the humans?" Zephyr mused.

Astraea rubbed her chin. "Well, it needs to be

someplace secure. Somewhere that people don't normally go."

"Where's that?"

An idea suddenly popped into Astraea's mind. "Of course, it makes perfect sense!" She looked excitedly at her friend. "Zeph, Dad has designed the new secure wing for the prison. It's all very hush-hush. But Grandfather asked him to do it a few weeks ago. I wonder if that's because they needed somewhere to house the humans they caught."

"They're putting them in prison?"

Astraea nodded excitedly. "It's the perfect place. Tell me, how much crime happens here?"

"Not much . . ." Zephyr paused and then started to nod. "So why do they need another wing on a prison that's hardly used?" She looked over to Astraea. "You're right, it has to be."

"There's only one way to find out."

Zephyr tilted her head to the side. "You want to go to the prison to look, don't you?"

"We have to."

Zephyr snorted. "How did I know you were going to say that?"

As they headed out of the orchard, the working night dwellers nodded and offered friendly greetings. Their dark eyes were shining, and their white hair almost glowed in the moonlight as they gathered the nectar from the flowers. Now that the stars were out, the flowers didn't need to be coaxed to open. In the darkness, they opened freely and released their nectar into the waiting jugs.

Two young night dwellers girls ran up to them. "Wait, please," they called softly. "You left these in the orchard."

Astraea was surprised to see the two urns that they were supposed to fill for detention. "Thank you so much. I forgot all about them. How did you know they were ours?"

The youngest night dweller grinned, showing all her sharp teeth. "We heard you were told to fill them for detention. I hope you do not mind, but we finished filling them for you."

"Really?" Astraea said, accepting the two urns. "Thank you. But who told you about us getting detention?"

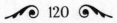

The night dweller smiled again. "Everyone is talking about it. You both got in trouble for fighting a centaur. We do not like Cylus or his herd. They are always making trouble for us."

Astraea shrugged. "They make trouble for everyone." She looked over to Zephyr. "Word sure does travel fast around here."

The night dwellers laughed and darted away.

"That was so nice of them," Astraea said, watching the two young girls run back. "And these give us an excuse for being out tonight. Let's drop them at home first and then go to the prison."

Judging by the moon's height, it was getting late. They hurried back to Astraea's home and hid the two urns of nectar at the back.

"You sure you want to go to the prison tonight?" Zephyr asked. "You're already in a lot of trouble after missing the ceremony this morning. How much more do you want to get in?"

"I don't think I could get in any *more* trouble," Astraea admitted. "So I might just as well stay out until after my parents have gone to bed. That way they won't know exactly when I got home."

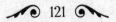

Zephyr shook her head. "You realize that doesn't make any sense."

Astraea grinned. "I know. Come on, let's go."

Walking through the empty streets, they saw very few people out except for the quiet night dwellers. Closer to the prison, they didn't see anyone.

"Have you ever wondered why darkness makes a place look creepy?" Zephyr asked.

Astraea stopped. "Are you frightened?"

"No," Zephyr said quickly. "I just don't like being out this late. Look around, there's no one here."

"That's good for us," Astraea said. "Look, there's the prison."

They reached the prison and stopped before the two-story building. What it lacked in height, it made up for in length. "Why did they make it so big?" Zephyr asked.

Astraea shrugged. "I don't know. Dad didn't design this part—it's been around since before we were born. Maybe it was meant to hold Olympians. The part Dad is working on is around the side."

They made their way along the length of the building. When it was finished, the prison would

form a large L shape, but it was obviously still under construction. There was a complicated spiderweb of scaffolding built up around the area, and a tall stack of huge, rough-cut blocks of marble lay nearby along with chisels and cutting tools.

"Remind me never to commit a crime," Zephyr said, gazing up at the imposing structure. "I don't want to end up in here."

Astraea paused. "Technically, we're about to commit a crime. We're going to break in there."

"What? You said you wanted to see it, not go in!"

"How else are we going to know who's inside?" Astraea stopped. "Zephyr, we both know something strange is happening here, but no one is saying anything. If Titus is in danger, I need to know. You don't have to come with me, but I'm going in."

"I hate it when you turn all detective on me."

Astraea grinned. "But you're going to come anyway, aren't you?"

Zephyr snorted. "Just shut up and lead on."

Astraea laughed lightly as they entered the construction area. "When Dad started working here late at night, I brought him his meals. There's a temporary door that the builders use to get in. It's never locked."

"Is it guarded?"

"I don't think so. It wasn't last time I came here."

Astraea's senses were on high alert as she crept closer to the construction entrance. However, as she got nearer, her heart sank—a large, complicated lock had been installed on the door.

"You said it wasn't locked," Zephyr said.

"It wasn't the last time I was here, and it wasn't *that* long ago. But look, that's no simple lock. Whoever put it here really doesn't want anyone to get in."

"Does this mean we can go home now?"

"You can, but I'm staying. This lock tells me that something special is inside—"

"Or something dangerous," Zephyr cut in.

"—that they don't want others to find," Astraea continued, ignoring her friend's interruption.

"And that includes us," Zephyr said.

Astraea's eyes twinkled. "Yes, but I know another way in."

"Would you please tell me how you know these things?"

"Well," Astraea said sheepishly, "I might have accidentally peeked at the plans when Dad wasn't working on them."

"You spied on your own father?"

"No, I peeked. You know how I am. The moment someone says something is secret, I have to know what it is. Are you coming?"

"Of course I am," Zephyr said. "I don't want to, every nerve in my body says not to, but still, I'm coming."

Astraea walked away from the construction site. "I noticed that they were building a secret access tunnel into the prison in case of emergencies."

"Emergencies to get prisoners in or out?"

"Both, I guess," Astraea answered. "It should be just ahead. On Dad's plans, it looked like a monument dedicated to those who fell when Olympus was attacked by the mutant Titans. It's in some kind of small park and didn't look very far away."

Relying on her memory, Astraea led Zephyr away from the prison and through the quiet, empty streets. Then she stopped suddenly. "This is it. The entrance tunnel should be in the center of the monument."

They left the pavement and crossed the grass. On

the far side of the park, night dwellers were working on the garden, trimming the bushes and planting more flowers. They moved like shadows, making no sounds at all.

"There it is." Astraea pointed to a small building with tall marble pillars out front. "The door down to the tunnel is inside at the back."

When they reached the monument, Astraea looked around. They were out of the sight line of the night dwellers, and she couldn't see anyone else around. "Let's go in."

The front doors were unlocked. Inside, an eternal flame burned on a tall plinth. A bronze plaque announced that the building was dedicated to the fallen in the "War to End All Wars" on Olympus.

"Hey, it's tight in here," Zephyr complained as she tried to maneuver around the plinth without knocking it over with her folded wings. "Next time I see your dad, I'm going to tell him how inconsiderate he is. He didn't think of those of us with four legs or wings when he designed it."

Astraea looked back at Zephyr and wondered if her friend would fit through the small door at the back.

That question was quickly answered when they reached it, found the hidden handle, and pulled it open.

"You've got to be kidding me!" Zephyr complained, staring at the tiny opening. "Seriously? You could hardly fit through there—there's no way I can. Look at it. It was built for starving satyrs."

"It is a hidden door. It's supposed to be small," Astraea said. "But you're right. You're not going to fit in there." She looked from the door back to Zephyr and to the door again, feeling very conflicted.

Zephyr sighed. "All right, go on. I'll keep watch out here. If anyone comes, I'll tell them I'm contemplating the tragedy of war."

"Zeph, you're the best!" Astraea threw her arms around Zephyr's neck. "I won't be long, promise."

"Yeah, yeah, you always say that. Just don't be *too* long. Remember, you will have to face your parents at some point."

"I'll just go look and see what they're hiding and then be right back." Astraea smiled at her friend and ducked down through the small entrance.

11

JAKE SAT IN TRYN'S ROOM, GAZING AROUND. The room itself wasn't that different from his bedroom in LA. There was the same kind of mess—clothes, shoes, and books thrown everywhere. But there was no television, no gaming console, and no computer. There were, however, amazing 3-D-type photographs in gold frames. He picked up one that showed more silver-skinned people. Another 3-D photo showed Tryn standing next to a man with dark curly hair and a beaming smile. Beside Tryn was an animal of some kind, but Jake had never seen anything like it. It was the size of a large dog with what looked like the head of a hippo and the fine legs of a giraffe, and it was covered in mottled gray fur, almost like a hyena.

"Is this your father?" Jake asked. He continued to move the picture around, fascinated by how the subjects' eyes followed him.

Tryn looked at the photo. "Yes. That was taken on my birthday."

"You look like him—I mean, except for the silver skin and all. But you have the same eyes and hair." Jake pointed at the strange animal. "What is that?"

"That is my manicox. Her name is Fiisha. I really miss her. I mean, I miss my family, but Fiisha and I used to spend all our time together."

"I've never seen anything like it before. Is she dangerous?"

"Is a manicox dangerous?" Tryn laughed. "They are the gentlest creatures in the universe, although they do drool a lot. But they're very loyal and loving. I'm really worried about her. Fiisha loves me absolutely, but I wasn't allowed to bring her to Titus with me. I hope she's all right."

"Can't you call home and ask?"

Tryn frowned. "How?"

"You know, with a cell phone or something."

Tryn's frown deepened. "I don't know what that is. But if you are talking about some kind of communication device, it wouldn't work. Xanadu is too far away."

"How far is it?"

"Light-years."

"What?" Jake cried. "What do you mean, light-years? Where is it?"

"Xanadu is almost at the other end of the universe. Even using the Solar Stream to get there takes ages."

"You mean it's like, another planet or something?"

"Of course. What did you think it was?"

"I—I don't know, I thought it was another country." Jake shook his head. "Wait, Astraea said this was Titus. I didn't ask, but does this mean . . ."

"Titus is a planet far from Earth."

"But—but that's impossible. I can't be on another planet!"

"I understand how difficult this must be for you," Tryn said sympathetically. "My father told me about Earth and how the farthest you have voyaged is your moon. Believe me, my people have been traveling in space forever. We had many worlds in our system and used to fly between them all the time. At least we did before our sun went supernova and destroyed everything."

Jake's heart was racing. Astraea and Zephyr had done their best to convince him this was real—everything about it *felt* real, but expecting him to believe in space travel was just asking too much. "Would you do me a favor?"

"If I can."

"Would you hit me, please?"

Tryn gasped. "I couldn't do that. My people are opposed to violence."

"It's not violence if I ask you to do it. Please. I need you to slap me really hard."

"Why?"

"It's an experiment. Just do it."

"I don't understand—"

"You don't have to." Jake stood up and walked over to Tryn. He leaned his face forward and shut his eyes. "Go on, slap me really hard."

"I have never struck another living being in my life, and I am not about to start now."

Jake could see the genuine horror on Tryn's face.

 131

"All right, you don't have to hit me." He walked over to the closet. He opened the door, put his hand on the inside of the frame, and then slammed the door shut on it.

"Ouch!" Jake howled and jumped around, rubbing his painful hand.

Tryn ran over to him. "What did you do that for?"

Jake was rubbing his bruised hand. Finally he looked into Tryn's silver face, and his shoulders slumped. "You're still here."

"Of course I am. What were you expecting?"

"I was hoping the pain would wake me up."

"Jake, you are awake."

"That's what I was afraid of." Jake looked around the strange room and sighed. "Molly missing, space travel, alien boys with silver skin, and girls and horses with wings . . . I really wish it were a dream."

"I am so sorry," Tryn said. "This isn't a dream. Someone has really taken you from Earth and deposited you here on Titus. The question is why."

He walked over to one of the bookshelves and pulled down a tray of ambrosia cakes. "Here, eat something. It might help."

"Cake for dinner?" Jake asked. "I'd rather have pizza and soda."

"I'm not sure what those are. But here, this is food. The Titans and Olympians need to eat it to stay healthy. I like other things too, but ambrosia isn't bad."

Jake reached for a cake square and took a bite. His mouth was flooded with sweetness. "Wow!" he cried. "This is awesome."

Tryn nodded.

As the two ate, they discussed their lives. Jake told Tryn about living in LA, how his parents were divorced and his mother and stepfather were about to have a baby. Then Tryn told Jake about his life on the wild world of Xanadu, and how he had a little sister who he missed very much.

Within a short time, they discovered that despite their different origins and appearance, they had more in common than they would have ever expected.

Jake was calmer than he had been, but now anxiety set in. He rose and started to pace the room. "You guys want me to hide, and I probably should. But how can I while Molly is still out there on an alien world? She's all alone and has got to be so frightened."

Tryn handed Jake another ambrosia cake and a cup of nectar. "I do understand and would feel exactly the same if it was my little sister. The best thing you can do for her right now is drink a lot of nectar and keep eating ambrosia. Humans have a distinctive odor—it's not bad, just distinctive. If you eat a lot, the food may cause it to fade, and then you might pass as a Titan and can go out looking for Molly." He frowned and rubbed his chin. "Though you will need to change your clothes. Titans don't dress like that." He rose and walked over to a pile of clothes, then pulled out a clean white tunic. "Here, put this on."

Jake's jaw dropped. "You're kidding, right? You really think putting on a dress will help me find Molly?"

"It's not a dress, it's a tunic, and it's how all the Titans and Olympians dress. If you want to stay safe, you will need to wear one too."

Jake accepted the garment. Tryn was wearing one, and apart from looking like he was from a gladiator movie, it wasn't half-bad. "Well, this is your world, not mine. If you say this is how they dress, then that's how they dress." He started to get changed.

"This isn't my world or how I normally dress," Tryn said. "But I have found it is often easier to go along with everyone instead of causing trouble."

When Jake finished changing, he pulled his baseball cap on again. Tryn looked at it and frowned.

"You can't wear that here."

"What? No way!" Jake held up his hands. "This is my lucky cap. You tell me that everyone here wears a dress and that I have to wear one too—that's cool, I'll wear a dress. But if you expect me to give up my cap, you're in for a big disappointment."

"If you wear it, you will stand out."

"No," Jake said. "I will be outstanding! Maybe I can teach you guys how to look rad."

"From a prison cell?" Tryn asked. "Because if you are seen like that, they will lock you away."

"Look, I have lost my sister and woken up on this crazy world where horses have wings—"

"Zephyr isn't a horse."

"I know!" Jake cried. "Astraea keeps telling me. But give me a break. Everything I've known is gone. I can't lose my lucky cap. You got that? End of discussion." Jake reached for his pack. "Now are we going or what?"

Tryn shook his head and gathered together bedding and a pillow. He packed up extra ambrosia cakes and a bottle of nectar and handed them to Jake. Then he kneeled down, reached under his bed, and pulled out a sealed bag. "You remind me of my father." Tryn stood up and walked to the door. "He is just as stubborn as you."

They left the room and walked farther down the empty corridor. Tryn held up his hand. "Wait here. I'm going to make sure no one is by the doors or walkway."

He ran a few paces ahead and looked around. "It's all clear."

Jake ran forward and paused when Tryn kept walking. "Wait, aren't we going outside?"

"No," Tryn said. "I've been on my own for several days now. I've found all kinds of interesting things here. Come, it's this way."

Jake followed Tryn through the enclosed walkway that connected the dormitory to Arcadia Two. They stopped before the school doors, and Tryn grinned. "My father was with the CRU back on Earth and taught me a few tricks for getting through locked doors." He put down the bedding he was carrying and pulled a small tool kit out of a pocket in his tunic. "I keep this with me at all times." He removed a pick from the kit. "This is called picking a lock. It's actually a lot of fun."

"What's the CRU?" Jake asked.

Tryn stopped. "It was called the Central Research Unit. It was a secret agency on Earth that looked for extraterrestrials and anything strange. My dad was an agent with them for years until he met Emily Jacobs and Pegasus. After that, he joined the Olympians and helped my people leave Rhean. When he met my mom, he didn't return to Earth. But I think the CRU is gone now."

Jake frowned. "Who is Emily Jacobs? I kinda know the name Pegasus from movies—he's like a flying horse too, isn't he?"

"He's not a horse either," Tryn said. "Back on Earth, the CRU captured him and made a lot of clones of him. One of his clones is called Tornado Warning—he's not smart like Pegasus and can be very vicious and wild. He can't talk, either, but he's

Zephyr's father. So, technically speaking, Pegasus could be considered her father—just don't ever tell her that, because she's as fiery as Tornado Warning and hates it when people compare her to Pegasus. She even started a fight this morning when a centaur said Pegasus was her father."

"Good to know," Jake said. "And Emily Jacobs?"

Tryn shrugged. "She's about our age. She's from New York, but when she met Pegasus, that all changed. Now they're always together. They live on Xanadu with Emily's father, aunt, and friends. Emily helped to save my people."

"So there are humans who came here and didn't go back to Earth?" Jake asked.

Tryn nodded. "A few. We even have a teacher at Arcadia who was also a CRU agent, but then he got turned into a sphinx and now lives here." He went back to picking the lock.

"A real sphinx?" Jake asked. "Like, part person and part lion, like they have in Egypt?"

Tryn nodded. "But they have wings, too."

"Really? Whoa, they must be awesome to see."

Tryn paused and looked at him. "Actually, they are."

There was something so bizarre about watching the silver-skinned boy in a tunic breaking into the building. It didn't look right, just like seeing a dog playing tennis. It was wrong on so many levels. But within seconds, Tryn had the door open and was slipping through.

"Wow," Jake said softly, following him into Arcadia Two. "You gotta show me how to do that."

"It's easy once you know how." Tryn ran though the darkened halls of Arcadia Two. "Stay close. It gets dark from here."

"Gets dark?" Jake cried. "I can barely see anything now. How much darker can it get?"

"A lot," Tryn said.

The school reminded Jake of his own back in LA. Long halls with classroom doors lining both sides. But soon Tryn was leading him to the stairs, and when they descended, everything went black.

There was no light anywhere, and Jake had to hold on to Tryn to keep from walking into things. "I need a flashlight," he whispered.

"I've got something better. It's what I use when I go exploring." Tryn stopped and opened the bag he was carrying. "Here, just hold on to some of this."

"Some of what?" Jake asked. But before he could speak further, he saw a golden glow coming from Tryn's bag. "What's that?"

"Luminarus moss," Tryn said. He leaned closer, and his silver skin glowed golden in the light. "I brought it from home. It grows in some of the caves of Xanadu. I've always loved exploring, and this stuff is amazing for giving light when you don't have anything else. It never runs out of energy, and all you have to do is water it from time to time to keep it alive." He pulled a clump out of the bag, and the whole area was brightened. "Here, take some." Tryn paused. "But don't eat it or you'll start to glow. I made that mistake when I was a kid and glowed for ages. Oh, and try not to hold on to it too long with your bare skin, because it will make your hand glow, and the warmth from your body will make it glow brighter."

Jake received a clump of the moss and held it up. "This stuff is sick!"

"No, it's healthy. I watered it a few days ago."

Jack laughed. "No, I mean it's cool, great."

"Sick means great?"

"Yeah, sometimes. It's an expression."

Tryn nodded. "I've not heard that before. But I like it."

With the lighting problem solved, Tryn led Jake into the bowels of the school. At the end of one corridor, they turned to the right and entered another. "Be careful while you are down here. This is a large labyrinth, and you could very easily get lost."

Jake's eyes were huge as he took in the vastness of the area. "How big is it down here?"

"Too big for it to just be a school," Tryn said. "I am certain there are tunnels that connect all the buildings together, but I haven't found them yet. I can't figure out why they built it. I haven't seen anyone down here, so it seems illogical to have all these tunnels and hidden rooms. Up ahead, this corridor splits off into more tunnels, and there are lots of small rooms. At first I thought perhaps some night dwellers lived down here, but they don't. It's just big, empty, and mysterious."

The area had a really creepy feeling to it, and the last thing Jake wanted to do was spend any time down here—especially alone. "Are you sure I can't stay in your dorm with you? This place gives me the creeps."

Tryn stopped. "I wish you could, but there are cleaners who come in every day, even though I ask them not to. If you were to stay with me, you *would* be found. This is the only place I can think of for now. But I promise, I'll look for somewhere else tomorrow."

"So it's just for one night?"

Tryn nodded. "I hope so."

Even one night down here felt too long, but under the circumstances, what choice did he have? "All right, I guess one night won't kill me. . . ."

They continued deeper into the labyrinth beneath Arcadia Two. After a while, Tryn stopped before the entrance to a particularly narrow corridor. "I found this last night. It's really narrow, so not many Titans or Olympians can fit through it. At the end it opens up into two rooms. You can stay in one of them."

When Tryn said it was narrow, he meant it. Jake was tall and lean, but even he had a hard time fitting through the passage. "Do they have earthquakes here? I'd hate to be in here if that happens."

"Earthquakes?"

"Yeah, you know, everything shakes because the plates beneath the ground are moving? LA gets them all the time."

Tryn stopped. "I've never heard of them happening here or on Xanadu." He paused. "Wait, yes, we do on Xanadu, when Emily and Riza are enlarging the planet or making a new continent. Then the whole planet shakes."

"Wait, two people can't make continents. That's impossible."

Tryn shook his head. "It's not impossible for the Xan."

None of this made any sense to Jake, and it didn't help ease his discomfort while they were moving through the narrow passage. Finally it widened at the end, and they stepped out into a kind of antechamber that spilt off into two different rooms.

"Here we are," Tryn said. "I'm sure you'll be very comfortable."

"That's not the word I would use," Jake said as he investigated each room. They were small, dark, and unfurnished. They also didn't have doors. But at least they were private. He picked one of them and put his things down in the corner. Holding up his hand with the moss, he saw the roof was high above them.

"What is going on here? I doubt even the biggest school back home would have all this beneath it."

"I don't know," Tryn said. "But I can't ask anyone, as no one is allowed down here. I'm sure I'd get into trouble if I were caught."

"At least they wouldn't lock you away because of what you are," Jake said as he started to put Tryn's bedding down to build a sleeping area. "I still can't believe what's happened. I'm in danger just for being me."

"I know," Tryn said. "I don't understand it either. I might try to find out more tomorrow."

"Just don't get into trouble," Jake said. "If anything were to happen to you, I'm really stuck. You're the only one who knows that I'm down here, *and* who knows the way out."

"I'll be careful," Tryn said. He started to walk out of the room. "So, you have food, something to drink, and a place to sleep. Get some rest. I'm going back up to try to find you somewhere better to stay. For now, just keep quiet and don't go wandering around. It's too easy to get lost. I'll be back as soon as I can."

As Tryn started to leave, Jake trotted to the doorway. "Hey, Tryn," he called. When Tryn turned, Jake tilted his head. "Thanks for everything, dude."

"You're welcome. Maybe tomorrow you can teach me how to skateboard."

"After we find my sister, you can count on it."

Tryn turned and disappeared back down the passage.

Alone in the small room, Jake sat down. Tryn had left him half the bag of glowing moss, so he did have some light to drive back the darkness. But it was the silence that disturbed him most. He could hear his own breathing and the beating of his heart, because there was nothing else to hear.

Leaning against the wall, Jake had never felt more frightened or alone. Nothing made sense. He shut his eyes and tried to remember what he'd seen on that street in Los Angeles.

Molly was walking behind him, saying something, but he wasn't paying attention because he was on his skateboard. Then he heard her scream. He turned

back and saw . . . saw . . . he gasped. Jake remembered what he'd seen and it was terrible.

He reached for his backpack, looking for a pen and paper to draw it while it was still fresh in his mind. He pulled out one of his school notebooks. But when he reached in again to find a pen, something stabbed his hand.

Pulling it free of the bag, Jake screamed. A small, colorful snake was dangling from the side of his hand by two sharp fangs piercing his skin.

Jake jumped to his feet and flicked the snake off, then watched it disappear into the darkness. Heat from the bite was rushing up his wrist and into his arm. The sensation kept spreading until it was coursing through his whole body and he broke into a full sweat.

He fell to his knees, clutching his head as his brain caught fire. Each beat of his heart was an enemy, forcing the burning poison throughout his body.

Breathing became difficult, as though someone was standing on his chest. Soon all his thoughts merged into a jumbled confusion. His sight faded and he collapsed and passed out.

12

ASTRAEA MADE HER WAY THROUGH THE tunnel leading under the prison. There were torches on the wall, giving off plenty of light. She also noticed there was no dust on the floor—which meant it was either used more often than she imagined or it was being regularly cleaned. But if so, why? Was this the route they used to deliver humans to the prison—if there were indeed humans being held in the new wing?

Curiosity drove her into a run. To add more speed, she opened her small wings and started to flap them furiously. Astraea was racing along and reached the end in a matter of moments. Once again she used her wings, but this time as air brakes. She stopped just a few paces before a set of stairs leading up.

Every nerve in her body was on alert. She stood still, listening for the sounds of footsteps or movement of any kind. Hearing nothing, she climbed the stairs and reached a door at the top. Much to her surprise, it wasn't locked.

She opened it a crack and listened again. This time she heard something. From the right end of the corridor came the sounds of light snoring, while to her left she heard soft weeping.

Entering the corridor, she saw the first cell on her right. There were golden bars across the front. A small cot with a lump under the covers was located near the back wall, while a tray on the floor held the remnants of a meal and a pitcher of water.

Astraea walked quietly toward the sound of weeping. It was filled with such despair that she felt her own heart breaking. Each cell she passed along the way held an occupant. Most of the prisoners were asleep, but then she reached the cell from which the sounds were coming.

Astraea stopped and gasped. A young woman not

much older than her was sitting on the side of a cot. Her head was down in her hands, and her shoulders shook as she wept.

"Are you all right?" Astraea asked softly.

The woman looked at her with a face that was the picture of misery. "Go away. Just leave me alone."

"Are—are you from Earth?"

"Here we go again," called the man in the opposite cell. "Yes, we're from Earth. Yes, we're human. No, we don't know who brought us here or how they did it. And no, we're not part of some kind of invading army. When will you people stop with all the same stupid questions and take us home in your spaceships, or—or whatever it was you freaks used to bring us here."

Astraea turned and saw one of the oddest-looking men she could imagine. At least, he sounded like a man, but he sure didn't look like one. His face was painted white, while his eyes were outlined with red and black. His mouth was also painted red and black. He was dressed in a puffy, brightly colored single-piece outfit with large dots all over it, big fluffy buttons, and ruffles around the neck and cuffs. Extremely large shoes had been tossed in the corner of the cell, and a clump of curly red hair was on the cell's only table, along with what looked like a red ball.

Astraea frowned at the man and walked over to him.

"What are you looking at?" he demanded. He called over to the weeping woman, "This alien ain't never seen a clown before."

"Alien?" Astraea said.

"Yes, you, alien," the clown repeated. "What, you think we don't know what you are or that we've been abducted and brought here against our will? I'm just wondering when the experiments will start."

His comment caused the woman to moan and weep harder.

"I—I'm not an alien. I'm a Titan, and we'd never experiment on you—that would be wrong. I am sure they're keeping you here so you'll be safe until they can find a way to send you all home."

"Yeah, right, like I'm going to believe you."

"I have no reason to lie," Astraea said. She looked around at the others, who were waking and approaching the bars of their cells. Some were curious; others exhibited anger. "How long have you been here?" she asked the clown.

He gave a single sarcastic snort and looked around. "Hello? No windows? How the heck should I know? I don't even know if it's day or night."

"It's night," Astraea said softly.

"Well, whoop-de-do, ain't that a revelation," he said. "So are you finally going to let us out of here? I have two birthday parties and a parking lot opening to attend. Those kiddies aren't going to be happy if Mr. Bo-Bo doesn't show up."

"Who is Mr. Bo-Bo?"

The strange man looked around in stunned wonder and lifted his gloved hands. "Hello? Do you see any other clowns in here? Because I sure don't. I am the great Mr. Bo-Bo."

"Oh," Astraea said. She peered closer at the lock. "This needs a special key, and I don't have it. I'm sorry, but I can't release you."

"Well, what good are you then? Get outta here."

Anger was coming from him in waves of white heat. "I am sorry that you are so angry. I had better go."

When Astraea turned to leave, she saw movement

in the corner of her eye. Suddenly the man's arm thrust through the cell bars and wrapped around her neck, slamming her back against the bars. "Okay, kid, you're gonna let me out right now or I'll break your scrawny neck."

"Ow! My wings!" Astraea cried.

"What are you talking about?" he demanded.

Before Astraea could pull away, she felt the man's free hand grab hold of one of her wings. "What the heck is this?"

"Let me go!" Astraea reached up and easily unhooked his arm from her neck, then moved away from the cell. She looked back and saw him holding a handful of her downy gray feathers. Opening her right wing, she felt stinging from a bare patch on the top where he'd ripped out the feathers. "Look what you've done! It's bad enough only having down feathers. You didn't have to tear out what little I've got."

The man let the soft gray feathers drift down from his hand. They landed silently on the floor. He looked over to the others. "This alien's got wings! Don't that beat all? I thought some of the others were bad, but she's the freakiest yet. So what are you?"

"I'm angry, that's what I am!" Astraea spat. "Why did you do that?"

"Because we want out of here and we want out now! You can't just keep us all locked up and not expect us to try to escape. I've got family and obligations."

"And I've got a sick baby," the weeping woman called. "Please, take me back home to her. She needs me."

Astraea gasped and crossed to her cell. "You left your child?"

"I didn't leave her," she wept. "You took me from her."

Astraea was stunned. Whoever abducted her had left her child behind. "You have no cause to believe me," she started. "But I promise you, we didn't take you from Earth. Someone else did, and I'm trying to figure out who. What do you remember?"

The weeping mother shook her head. "I—I don't remember anything. I went to get my baby's prescription and then—then I woke up here."

"I was out jogging," a voice from a neighboring cell called. "Then wham, I wake up here. I have no idea how I got here or even where here is."

More and more people were calling out. An older woman from the cell beside the clown asked softly, "This really isn't Earth, is it?"

Astraea looked into her pleading eyes. "I'm so sorry, but no, it's not. Earth is a long way away."

She turned in a circle, looking at all the people standing in their cells. Why were there so many? What was happening? They were all reaching out to her, begging to be released. She also realized that some had to have been here long enough to realize and accept that they weren't on Earth anymore. It took hours to get Jake to believe it.

"Hey," the clown said. "You seem like a nice enough kid. Why don't you get the key and let us out?"

"Everyone, please, listen to me," Astraea said. "Right now you're safer in here than anywhere else. And I can promise you that there are people trying to figure out how to send you back home."

"If they got us here, why can't they send us back?" asked the jogger.

Astraea walked up to his cell. He looked close in age to her oldest brother. He had dark skin and eyes and a friendly face. "Earth is a quarantined world.

We're forbidden to go there or bring anyone here. It had to be someone else who brought you."

"So what happens now?" the jogger asked.

"I don't really know," Astraea admitted. "But I'm going to try to figure out how to get you all back home." She looked around at everyone in their cells. "I had better get going. Please don't tell anyone that you've seen me. I don't want them to stop me from coming back. I give you my word. The moment I figure out how to get you all home, I will return."

"What if you can't?" the clown asked.

"I must," Astraea finished. "Failure isn't an option for any of us."

Astraea walked back down the corridor toward the stairs leading to the hidden tunnel. Just before she entered, she heard more noises coming from behind another door.

She knew she had to get back to Zephyr, but these sounds were different, she had to find out what was there.

Astraea opened the door slowly and was overwhelmed by the noise—growling, barking, squeaking,

and some sounds she'd never heard before. Then there was the smell . . . an awful stench that made it hard to breathe. Animals and unimaginable creatures filled the cells lining the space she was now in. In the one nearest her was a large . . . cat. It was as blue as the sky on a really clear day. Its head was almost too big for its body, and it had so many eyes that they seemed to go all the way around its head.

The moment Astraea entered, the cat lunged at the bars, thrusting one paw through and slashing at her with the longest claws she'd ever seen.

In the cell beside it was an even stranger creature. It had a glistening red surface and almost looked like a large worm. At each end of the long, thin body was a head with dark yellow eyes. The worm-creature glided closer to the bars, and the two heads rose up to Astraea's height.

Astraea backed away. But after two steps, she felt something tickling her ankle from behind. When she looked down, she saw a long, black, ropelike thing tightening around her leg. Before she could react, the rope wrenched back, pulling her leg out from under her and knocking her to the floor.

Looking up into the cell, Astraea had to fight to keep from screaming as she gazed into a large, gaping mouth. The black rope wasn't rope at all. It was a tongue, and that tongue was dragging her toward the cage.

13

ASTRAEA USED EVERY OUNCE OF STRENGTH
she had to stop the tongue from dragging her across
the floor. Its power was unimaginable. As she neared
the golden bars, she put her free foot against them to
brace herself.

It worked, but only temporarily. The tongue was
much stronger than she was. As it constricted around
her leg, she felt her bones creaking. Every moment
the pain increased.

"Child, claw it," two soft voices called. "Use your
nails. It is very sensitive."

Astraea sat up, which weakened her brace against
the bars but enabled her to reach forward. She stiff-

ened her fingers into claws and, with both hands, raked them along the length of black tongue.

With each swipe of her nails, she felt its grip loosening.

"That's it, keep at it," the voices hissed as one in their singsong style.

By the third pass, the tongue had loosened enough for her to pull her leg free. She scurried back and watched it recede into a head.

Astraea gasped. With its gaping mouth shut, the creature looked exactly like a boulder. It was big, gray, and round. There were no eyes, as far as she could see, and no nose. Any trace of the mouth was hidden in the rocky surface.

Astraea backed up farther as the boulder rolled to the rear of its cell.

"It won't come after you again until its tongue heals. You are safe. . . ."

Astraea turned. The voice seemed to be coming from the two-headed worm.

"It pleases us that you will live," it said.

"You saved me. Thank you." Astraea rubbed her painful leg. A dark, angry bruise was already starting

to show. "But why would you do that when everyone thinks I'm one of your jailers?"

"You are a child. We know you are innocent. And we heard what you said out there to the others. You are going to find a way to send them home. Will you send us home?"

Astraea approached the bars but stayed back a safe distance. She'd had enough violence for one night. "I'm going to try," she said. "Where are you from?"

"A world called Minder. We were brought here as everyone else was—against our will, with no recollection of how we came here. We want to go home."

"I promise you, I won't rest until I find a way to get you all home." She looked back at the Titan-eating rock. "Even that thing."

"We are Finan and Nanif, and we will hold you to your promise. Now it is time for you to go. The guards will be back soon to check on us. They must not find you here."

Astraea nodded. "Have you spoken to the others here?"

"No," the two heads said as one. "We don't trust them. We trust only you."

"Thank you, but why me?"

"Because we can feel your emotions, and you are speaking the truth. We are uncertain about the others."

"That's probably why they put you in here, because they don't know you're intelligent."

"Here or in there with the humans makes little difference to us. A cage is a cage. We will stay until it is time to go home."

"Then I'll find a way to send you home," Astraea promised as she limped to the door. "I will be back."

"We will be waiting . . . ," the two-headed worm said.

Astraea's mind was spinning as she hurried back to Zephyr. That had been the strangest and scariest experience of her life. In the brief time she'd spent in the cells, she had seen things she had never dreamed possible. She pushed through the small door at the monument and was grateful to see her best friend standing there.

"Well?" Zephyr demanded. "What happened? You were gone for ages."

Astraea closed the door behind her and leaned

against it. "You wouldn't believe what's down there. It's worse than I could ever have imagined."

"Were there humans?"

Astraea nodded. "Oh yes, humans—lots of them. They're all scared and don't know how they got here. But . . ."

"But what? What else did you see?"

Astraea took a deep breath and moved away from the door. "There are other things down there too. Really scary things." She lifted up her tunic and showed her bare leg.

"What happened to you?" Zephyr cried.

"I was attacked by a rock."

"A what?"

Astraea told Zephyr about all the strange things she had seen in the new wing of the prison.

"A talking worm . . . ," Zephyr said.

Astraea nodded. "A talking, two-headed worm that saved my life. That rock was so strong, I'm sure it would have pulled me through the bars if they hadn't told me what to do."

Zephyr snorted. "Astraea, this is bigger than we thought. We're not prepared to deal with it."

"We have to," Astraea said. "I promised that we would help. They're all counting on us."

"That prison is full of monsters," Zephyr said. "Just like that dark thing we chased in the orchard."

"Exactly!" Astraea agreed. "Zeph, there had to be at least thirty, maybe forty humans down there, not to mention the other creatures. I couldn't count them all, but there seemed to be even more of them."

Zephyr pawed the ground. "What is going on here? Why haven't we seen them before now?"

Astraea shrugged. "I guess my grandfather's people are good at their jobs. They've caught the strangers and hidden them away without anyone knowing about it."

"But why are they coming here?"

"I don't know. No one I spoke to seemed to have any idea how they got here. It's like they've had their memories erased." Astraea paused, haunted by the memory. "Zeph, there was one woman in there crying. She was taken away and her baby is sick."

"We have to find a way to send them home. But how? We're forbidden to use the Solar Stream,"

Zephyr said. "If I'm just like Pegasus, then I can fly fast enough to enter it, but then what? I don't know how to use it to find other worlds."

"I don't know either," Astraea mused. "But there is one thing we do know."

"What's that?"

"That we're going to school and being taught by instructors who used to use the Solar Stream all the time. We're students seeking knowledge. . . ."

"And?"

"And maybe I should ask them."

14

"MOM?" JAKE CALLED AS HE SLOWLY WOKE up. "Mom, I had the weirdest dream. . . ."

Opening his eyes, Jake saw the golden glow filling the small room. He sat up quickly and looked around. Where was he? What happened? Then it all rushed back to him. He wasn't home anymore. He was in a strange place called Titus. His right hand was still stinging, and the final piece of the nightmare slipped into place. He'd been bitten by a snake.

Jake backed up as his wild eyes sought the snake. "Where is it?" he cried aloud.

"*Where isss what?*" a small voice said.

Jake wasn't sure whether he'd heard the voice for

real, or if it was just in his head. Either way, he was terrified. "Who said that?"

"*I did.*"

"Who?"

"*Me.*"

Jake became aware of a light weight around his neck. When he put his hand up to see what it was, he felt something the thickness of his finger start to move. He tried to pull it away, but it wouldn't move.

"*You're hurting me!*"

His heart was racing and he was in a panic as he tried to wrench the thing away from his neck. Finally it gave, and Jake saw that it was the same snake that had bitten him. He threw it away. When it hit the floor, he heard it say, "*Ouch.*"

The snake rolled over and started to slither back to him. "*I am cold, you are warm,*" it said in its high, light voice. "*Pleassse let me be warm again.*"

Jake looked wildly around, hoping and praying for the source of the small voice. Because if he couldn't find it, there was only one thing it could be. But that was impossible. "Stay back!" he cried.

The small snake stopped. "*Pleassse, I am cold.*"

Jake knelt down and, in the dim, golden light, saw that the snake's head was off the ground, looking at him. Its tiny tongue flicked in and out of its mouth. "Would someone please tell me that snake isn't talking?"

"Pleassse, I am cold, you are warm. Help me."

Jake backed up farther until he was against the wall. "Oh no, no, no! I've seen Harry Potter at least five times. Talking snakes are not good."

"What isss Harry Potter?"

"Don't try that with me. You know exactly what it is."

"I'm cold. Pleassse help me."

"Help you? You bit me!"

"You hit me first."

"No, I didn't."

"Yesss, you did."

"This is insane. I'm arguing with a snake!"

"What is a sssnake?"

"You are."

"No, I am Nesso."

"No, you're a snake. See, you have a forked tongue that goes in and out, you have a thin body and sharp teeth that you bit me with."

"*Becaussse you hit me firssst.*" Nesso's tiny head drooped. "*And now I will die becaussse I am cold and you won't sssave me.*"

"Hey, don't die." Jake wasn't a fan of snakes, but he would never hurt one on purpose. "Seriously, dude, don't die."

"*Need heat to live,*" the snake hissed.

Jake started to shake his head. "I can't believe I'm going to say this, but if I pick you up and help you get warm, do you promise not to bite me again?"

"*Yesss . . .*" Nesso lay its head down on the floor.

Jake reached out and gently lifted the snake. Its smooth scaled body was ice-cold and limp. Its eyes were closed. "Hey, hey, little critter, don't die." He cupped his hands closed and blew warm air into them.

After a few minutes, he felt the snake moving in his hands.

"*I'm alive?*" Nesso's tiny voice called.

Jake was shaking his head. "Well, little dude, you're as alive as I am, because right now, I'm not so sure about either of us. Talking snakes? I mean, really . . ."

"*I don't undersssstand.*"

"Join the club." Jake looked down at the small, coiled snake in his hands. "So, why did you sneak into my bag?"

"I didn't sssneak into it. I entered it when you were in the treesss. You were warm. I hoped it would be warm too becaussse it isss cold here. But it wasssn't warm. Only you were."

"That's strange. It's warm here to me. Can I take you home?"

"Yesss, pleassse," Nesso said.

"A polite snake, go figure . . . So where do you live?"

"I don't know. I am lossst."

Jake leaned back against the wall and sighed. "I hear you, little dude. I'm lost too. I have no idea where I am or how I got here. All I do know is, I've been told that if I'm caught, I'll be in a lot of trouble."

"Me too, I think," Nesso agreed.

Jake was calming down and actually enjoying having someone to talk to—even if that someone was a snake. "I was going to draw a picture of the thing I saw right before I woke up. But I need my hands." He paused and peered into Nesso's red eyes. "Okay, so here's the deal. If you promise not to bite me again,

 169

I'll put you back around my neck so I can use my hands and you can stay warm."

"Promissse . . . ," Nesso said.

Jake pulled the snake closer, and it slithered off his hands and coiled around his neck. The cold, smooth scales tickled as Nesso's head made it to the front again and caught hold of its own tail. The snake settled down and sighed contentedly.

"Can this day get any weirder?" Jake mused.

"I hope not," Nesso said.

With his hands free again, Jake reached for his backpack. Right before he put his hand in, he paused. "Was there anyone else in there I need to worry about?"

"There wasss only me," Nesso responded.

Jake wasn't sure he could trust the snake—it was, after all, a snake, and could any of them be trusted? Still, he held his breath, shut his eyes, and reached into his bag, waiting for another stinging bite. Instead he felt his collection of pens and pencils at the very bottom. Picking one, he pulled it out and released his breath.

"I told you ssso . . . ," Nesso said.

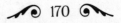

"Yeah, well, you're a talking snake. Forgive me if I don't trust you yet."

"And you are a sssilly big thing."

"Sorry, dude, you're not the first one to tell me that." Jake reached for his notebook and opened it to a clean page. He started to draw. After a few minutes, he was seeing the shape of the thing that had been going after Molly right before he fell off his skateboard.

"The head isss wrong," Nesso commented. *"And the beak wasss more pointed."*

Jake looked down at his picture of the monster. Nesso was right. The beak on the blackbird creature that he'd seen was longer and sharper. "How did you know that?"

"I have ssseen it too," Nesso said. *"It wasss before."*

"Before what?"

"Jussst before."

"Oh, that's helpful."

"I am sssorry, but what do you exssspect from me? I'm only sssmall."

"Size doesn't matter. It's what's inside that counts."

"That isss easssy for you to sssay. You are big. I am sssure

you could sssee where you came from. I live on the ground;
I can't."

"I hadn't thought of that," Jake acknowledged. With the help of Nesso, he kept working on the sketch of the creature he'd seen briefly before he fell off his skateboard and smashed his head. Jake remembered large black wings, a sharp, pointed beak, and the height: it had been tall, almost like a man in a bird suit. But even bigger than that and a lot more terrifying.

They worked together on the image and Jake was surprised at how detailed Nesso's memory was. When he finished, he felt shivers of fear coursing through him.

"Yesss," Nesso said. *"I sssaw that thing with the other oness."*

"What other ones? All I saw was this."

"No, there were othersss."

"What did they look like?"

"Big, like you. But dark, and I was ssscared. I tried to hide from them, but . . ."

"But what?"

"I—I wasss caught by the thing you drew. I thought it

wasss going to eat me. But it didn't. It put me in a dark placcce. Then I wasss here. . . ."

Jake was absently stroking its smooth body. It was warming up and seemed to sigh with each stroke. He looked at his finished sketch. "So what is it?"

"I don't know," Nesso said. *"But it isss bad. They all are."*

Jake studied the sketch, trying to remember more, but as he did, he thought he heard something coming from outside the small room. "Do you hear that?"

"Voicccesss," Nesso said. *"Coming thiss way. Ssstop the glow or they will find usss!"*

Jake looked over to the bag of glowing moss. He lunged forward and shut it tightly, throwing them into total darkness.

His heart was pounding and he held his breath as the voices came closer. They were speaking a strange language he couldn't understand. Soon they were passing the narrow corridor leading to his hiding place. Part of him wanted to go out and see who it was, but another part was too frightened to move. The warning from Astraea was ringing in his ears: if he was caught, he would be taken away.

Just as quickly as they arrived, the voices trailed

off, and Jake felt like he could breathe again. But he stayed quiet as he felt his way over to the entrance of the small room. When he reached the opening, he poked his head out.

"They are gone now," Nesso said softly.

"Tryn said no one comes down here."

"Maybe he doesssn't know."

Jake leaned back in but didn't reach for the bag again. He was too frightened in case there were others. His fears were justified. Just as he moved away from the entrance, more voices passed through the nearby passageway.

As much as he strained to hear, he still couldn't understand the language being spoken. But from the sound of it, there was a mix of men and women and . . . what? There were strange voices that were neither. But it was the final sound that really terrified him. Something or someone was being dragged along the floor, and Jake was certain he'd heard moaning.

15

BY THE TIME ASTRAEA GOT HOME, ALL THE lights were off. She was lucky that her parents had gone to bed. But she dreaded the coming morning and having to face them. Instead of entering the house from the front and risking waking them, she crept around to the back and climbed through her bedroom window.

Hiddles was on her bed and meowed when she appeared.

"Shhhh . . . ," she whispered softly.

Astraea listened for any sound that would indicate that her parents were still awake, but all was silent. She slipped into bed without removing her clothes.

At dawn Astraea got up, changed, went into the kitchen to grab some food, and left the house before her parents awoke. She knew the kind of trouble she was in and didn't want to face them just yet. At best, she'd be grounded; at worst . . . well, she didn't want to think about the "at worst." So she avoided it all.

She was wearing a long tunic to hide the deep purple bruises on her leg from the attack the previous night. But nothing could hide her limp. Her right leg was swollen, and it felt like the monster's tongue had cracked a bone. To ease the pain, she ate an extra-large quantity of ambrosia cake to encourage healing.

Astraea collected the two jugs of nectar they'd hidden the previous evening and limped over to Zephyr's home. Her best friend lived a short walk away. Despite her equine heritage, Zephyr preferred to live in a house like most Titans, while her parents were housed in the stable at the rear of the property. Because of the odd situation, Zephyr never told anyone where she lived. Astraea knew because they had grown up together, and for her, it didn't matter who or what her best friend's parents were.

Astraea arrived just as Zephyr was leaving the stable. "Morning, Zeph."

"Astraea," Zephyr called. "I've been thinking about you all night. How's your leg? Did your parents go crazy when you got home?"

Astraea put down the nectar and pulled up the hem of her long tunic.

"Ouch! That's impressive." Zephyr inspected Astraea's leg. "I've never seen such big bruises before. Does it hurt?"

"Well, it sure doesn't tickle!" Astraea said. "I think that thing cracked my bone. That's what really hurts." She looked around. "Can we go inside to talk?"

"Sure. I just finished feeding Mom and Dad. Come on in." She stood back and invited Astraea into the stable. "So, what did your parents say?"

"I haven't seen them yet. The lights were off when I got home, and I left this morning before they got up."

"Coward!" Zephyr teased.

"No," Astraea said quickly. "I just thought this was better."

Zephyr laughed. "You are going to be in so much trouble. They might think you never came home."

"They'll know I was home. I ate half the ambrosia cake in the kitchen. My brothers are working away from home, so it could only be me. But I'm sure I'll really be in trouble when I see them after school."

"I hope they don't make you stay in."

"I know." Astraea reached into a basket hanging on the wall and pulled out an apple. She held it out to Zephyr's father, Tornado Warning. "Good morning, Tornado."

It had taken him ages to get used to her. In the beginning, when she was young, Tornado Warning would rear and try to kick her, but with patience and a lot of treats, he finally accepted her. Now he greeted her with a soft whinny and gratefully took the apple.

Astraea stroked his muzzle and looked back at Zephyr. "If my mom and dad do ground me, I'll sneak out anyway. I gave my word to those people and creatures in prison. I said that I would try to help get them home, and I am going to."

"Well, while you were sleeping soundly last night, I went out again."

"You did?"

Zephyr nodded. "After you told me what you saw

in the prison, I couldn't sleep. So I went out to stretch my wings and look for anything strange. I found it at Arcadia. But I was glowing too much to get very close without them seeing me."

"What was it?" Astraea said. "Tell me!"

"I saw a group of people wearing dark cloaks—there had to be at least fifteen of them. They looked like they were dragging something heavy. I followed them as long as I could, but then they went into Arcadia Two. I waited ages for them to come out again, but they never did."

"Wait, Tryn was going to hide Jake beneath Arcadia Two?"

"Exactly," Zephyr agreed. "I wonder if they found him."

"I hope not. Maybe Tryn can tell us."

Zephyr pawed the ground. "Astraea, have you considered that Tryn might be part of it? We don't really know him, and we trusted him with Jake. What if we were wrong?"

Astraea considered for a moment and then shook her head. "I don't think so. He's too shy to be involved in anything."

"Just because he's shy doesn't mean he can't be corrupt. I really hope you're right."

"Me too." Astraea reached back into the basket of apples and handed several to Tornado Warning and then to Zephyr's mother, Lampos, in the neighboring stall. The black winged mare nickered in appreciation. "But there's only one way to find out: we have to ask Tryn."

They left the stable and made their way to school. Astraea was anxious to get to class to see Tryn, but before they could, they had to deliver the nectar to Themis.

After entering Arcadia One, they made their way to the principal's office. Astraea knocked, and they walked in.

Themis was in the inner office and called them forward. She was sitting on her three-legged stool, gazing out the large window. "So tell me, how was working in the nectar orchard?"

"Sticky," Zephyr answered. "And the flowers tasted awful."

Themis turned. "You are not supposed to eat them."

"I know," Zephyr said. "But I had to lick them to

get them to open and release their nectar. I can still taste them now."

Themis laughed softly. "So did it help you appreciate the hard work the night dwellers do for us?"

"Absolutely," Zephyr said.

"Good." Themis's gray eyes settled on Astraea. "You are very quiet this morning. Is there something you wish to tell me?"

"Not at all." Astraea held up the two jugs of nectar. "We did as you asked and brought these. It's fresh nectar. May we go to our classes now?"

The principal stood up from her stool and walked closer. Her eyes narrowed. "Are you sure there is nothing you wish to tell me? Did anything happen in the orchard?"

Astraea was instantly on alert. "Like what?"

"You tell me. The orchards can be a very mysterious place, especially after sunset. There is no telling what you might find in there."

Astraea looked over at Zephyr before answering. "All we found were the night dwellers, once they started to arrive. They were really nice and friendly. So we just collected your nectar and went home."

Themis stood still, staring at Astraea just long enough to make her very uncomfortable. "Um, is there anything else? We really should be getting to our classes."

Finally Themis moved back to the window and peered out. "You may go. Just remember that tonight you are sweeping the floors of Arcadia One."

"What?" Zephyr cried.

Astraea slapped her hand over Zephyr's muzzle. "Yes, of course. We have a week of detention and we're happy to do it."

"We *are* happy to do it," Themis corrected.

"We *are* happy to do it," Astraea repeated. She pushed Zephyr back toward the door. "Thank you, Themis. We will see you later."

Back in the hall, Zephyr whinnied. "What did you do that for?"

"I didn't want you to endanger our detention."

"So now you want detention?"

"Yes, and so do you." Astraea walked with Zephyr toward her first class on the main floor. "We have to stay late and clean the school, right?"

"Don't remind me."

"So what if it takes us longer to clean, and what if we accidentally clean Arcadia Two as well?"

"Why would you want to clean more than we have to . . . ?" Zephyr paused and then bobbed her head up and down. "Oh, wait, now I get it. *Yes*, we just might have to clean Arcadia Two as well, and it might take us all night."

"Exactly!" Astraea said.

Since their classes were on different floors, Zephyr moved on to hers while Astraea climbed the stairs to her first class. When she entered, she saw that Tryn was already there. She walked over and sat down. "Well?"

He looked at her, saying nothing.

She leaned closer and whispered. "So how is he?"

"He?" Tryn said. He frowned, then seemed to understand. "Oh, you mean Jake."

"Quiet!" Astraea hushed him. "No one is supposed to know about him."

"I don't know how he is," Tryn said softly. "I haven't seen him since last night. Though there is no reason he should be anything but fine."

Astraea stared into his eyes, searching for lies,

betrayal, or deceit. All she saw were the light flecks of silver in the deep blue. Other than that, he revealed nothing.

"I need to see him. Where did you hide him?"

"He is safe," Tryn said. "There's no need to disturb him."

Tryn's comment left Astraea worried. Could Zephyr be right? Could Tryn part of the mysterious happenings at Arcadia Two? "But I need to see him."

The arrival of Minerva cut off further conversation.

"Today we continue our discussion on the wars between the Olympians and Titans and how the peace was finally won." Minerva went behind her desk and pulled out several large marble friezes with sculptures on them, depicting ancient battles taking place on Olympus, Titus, and Earth. She set them up in a long row to form one long storyboard.

Astraea was only mildly interested until she saw that one of the friezes depicted Emily Jacobs standing on the battlefield. A very elderly looking Pegasus was floating behind her while a dog ran at her feet. Flames shot from her hands.

"That can't be right," she called to Minerva. "That

shows Emily Jacobs and Pegasus. But you said this was an ancient battle."

Minerva nodded. "It was, but she was there. That is what makes our shared history so interesting and important. This frieze is of Emily when she, Pegasus, and several others traveled back in time to our past and joined in the fight against the Shadow Titans."

Gasps filled the room, and students looked at each other in shock. The Shadow Titans, a mysterious army of living, hollow armor created by Saturn, were never spoken of and were entering the realms of myth. Though everyone had heard of them, the Shadows Titans were too terrifying to talk openly about.

"These are the Shadow Titans." Minerva pointed to another frieze showing several large, sculpted creatures that almost looked familiar, but were somehow more monstrous.

"Is that one with the beak supposed to be a harpy?" screeched a young harpy perched on a pole set into the classroom wall. Her feathers were red, brown, and black. They blended beautifully with the bronze skin of her smooth face. Her dark hair hung down in layers that looked almost like feathers.

 185

"No," Minerva answered. "The winged Shadows were not sourced from a harpy. That one was sourced using the essence of a large blackbird. The others were created from the Minotaur, a turtle warrior, and a dragon. The poor creatures were tortured, and in their suffering, the Shadow Titans were created. Those hollow monsters fought without pause or mercy and nearly defeated us. We thought we had destroyed them all long ago, until recently, when more were discovered on Earth. They were dispatched, and it is our hope that they have finally been eradicated from existence."

Astraea shivered as she gazed at the images of the Shadow Titans. She was glad they were extinct. They looked fearsome and unbeatable, and she would hate to meet one in person.

The rest of the history class proved more interesting than Astraea expected as they discussed Shadow Titans and the war, which finally ended with Saturn being defeated and the Titans being imprisoned in Tartarus.

Midway through the class, Minerva invited everyone outside. In the playing field at the back of the

school were a series of tables. Across the field a target range had been erected as well as fighting mannequins.

On the first table was a selection of swords, daggers, and spears. The second table held an array of bows and arrows fletched with colorful plumage. The final table, constructed of metal and not wood, contained a collection of swords. These caught the attention of everyone in the class. They weren't ordinary swords. Each blade had a deep groove cut into the length of it, and within the groove a flame burned, though it had no source or apparent fuel.

"These flame-swords are the actual weapons we used to turn the tide against the Shadow Titans," Minerva explained as she picked up a sword and swished it through the air. "They were designed by Vulcan and his human assistant, Stella. They were the only weapons capable of defeating the terrible Shadows. As you can see, the flames can't be extinguished—even after all this time, they still burn."

"How is that possible?" an Olympian satyr asked.

"There was a special mixture poured into the channel. It needs no fuel and keeps burning," Minerva said.

With her flame-sword held high, Minerva invited

each student to pick up a weapon. "Some of you may feel you are too young to handle these weapons, but believe me, we had warriors much younger than you fighting beside us."

Tryn took a step back from the tables.

"Is everything all right?" Astraea asked as she held up a flame-sword.

"My people do not believe in weapons."

Astraea frowned. "Your father is human and they fight with weapons. I've heard Earth has had many wars. We've only had two."

"My mother's people don't fight, and they have never had a war. I do not like weapons, and fighting is pointless." Tryn said no more and walked away.

Astraea watched him go but didn't try to follow. He was the strangest person she'd ever met. It had nothing to do with his shiny silver skin or speckled eyes. Tryn himself was a mystery.

Cylus clopped up behind her. The centaur was holding the flame-sword aloft and staring at Tryn with a threatening expression. "I wonder what this would do to silver skin. Do you think he can be burned?"

"Stop it, Cylus," Astraea warned. "Leave Tryn alone."

Cylus looked down at Astraea. "Oh, really? Why do you care what happens to him?"

Astraea felt the color rush to her cheeks. "I don't care. I just don't like bullies."

"This is not bullying, but I'll show you what is." The centaur trotted up to Tryn and shoved him. "Hey, silver boy, are you too good to use a sword?"

Tryn looked at the centaur but didn't say anything. He started to walk away again.

"Where are you going?" Cylus challenged, trotting after him. "Did I say you could leave?"

"I don't need your permission," Tryn said softly.

Cylus's face turned red with rage. He wasn't used to others not being frightened of him, and by the look of it, he didn't like it one bit. "You are going to regret that."

The bully went back to his friends but kept staring at Tryn and muttering. His friends laughed and patted Cylus on the shoulder.

Astraea realized that Tryn had just made a terrible mistake. Cylus had a lot of friends who were ready to do anything for him. Whether Tryn realized it or not, he now had an enemy.

After history class, Astraea made her way through the rest of her morning without incident. At lunch she met up with Zephyr and told her friend about what had happened between Tryn and Cylus. "Tryn is an idiot," Zephyr said. "Doesn't he realize how dangerous Cylus and his herd of centaurs are?"

"I don't think he cares."

They were eating in the gardens in front of Arcadia One, sharing the ambrosia cake Astraea brought from home. A fountain with trickling water was nearby, and marble benches were dotted across the grounds so the students could sit and enjoy their meals.

Astraea stood up and gazed around. "Speaking of Tryn, have you seen him lately?"

Zephyr raised her head. "Nope, and I can't see him here. Maybe he's still in the school."

"I hope so," Astraea said. "But by the look on Cylus's face in class, I wonder if he's done something."

"That wouldn't be good."

"I know, especially as Tryn's the only one who knows where Jake is hiding."

16

JAKE SAT IN HIS ROOM BENEATH ARCADIA Two. As the long hours ticked away, he found himself more and more grateful for the snake's presence. Sitting quietly in the dark, he stroked Nesso's soft scales and actually found it comforting.

At one point, they heard the strangers go back the other way. This time, though, neither he nor Nesso heard the sound of something being dragged.

"I don't like it here," Nesso hissed softly.

"Me neither," Jake agreed. "I don't care what Tryn, Astraea, or Zephyr says. We are not spending another night down here."

 191

"Thank you," the snake said politely.

Fear kept Jake from opening up the bag of glowing moss. Without its light, he had no concept of time's passage. Leaning back against the wall, he dozed off but rarely stayed asleep long.

"Jake, wake up. I hear sssomething." Nesso squirmed around his neck.

Startled awake, Jake strained to listen. It was several more heartbeats before he could hear what the snake heard. Someone or something was moving around in the corridor. Soon he saw a soft golden glow and heard the sound of footsteps in the narrow passage outside his room.

"Jake, are you still here?"

"Tryn?"

Tryn entered the room. "I left you moss. Why are you in the dark?"

"Why?" Jake cried. "You said no one ever came down here. But this place was busier than the Santa Monica Pier! There were loads of people here." He checked Tryn's wrist for a watch but found nothing. "What time is it?"

"It's midday," Tryn explained. "I've come during

my lunch break. What do you mean it was busy here last night?"

"I mean, there had to be at least twenty people down here. They came in two groups. It sounded like the second group was dragging something heavy—something that groaned."

"Did they find you?"

"Uh, considering I'm still here, I guess the answer is *no*!" Jake said angrily. "But they scared the day-lights out of me."

Tryn frowned. "I've been down here many times and have never seen anyone."

"Yes, but have you ever been here all night?"

"No, I haven't."

"Well, I don't plan on spending another minute down here. This place really creeps me out. Let's go back to your dorm room. I'm hungry and thirsty, and I really need a shower."

"We can't leave, at least not yet," Tryn said. "It's still light out and the cleaners are in there. We have to stay here for a bit. Do you remember which direction the strangers went?"

"Pleassse don't go looking for them," Nesso cried.

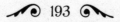

"Don't worry, we won't," Jake said. "There still may be someone down here."

Tryn frowned. "Worry about what? What are you talking about?"

"I don't want to go walking around down here in case anyone else is here."

"I have excellent hearing. I would know if anyone else was down here with us. We are alone."

Jake's eyebrows rose. If Tryn was so good at hearing, how could he not hear Nesso? He hadn't even mentioned the snake. But then again, in the dim light, maybe he couldn't see it.

"Why are you looking at me like that?" Tryn asked.

"No reason," Jake said. He grabbed his things and followed Tryn into the corridor.

They walked in the direction of the sounds from the previous night. But after a while, Jake stopped. "I don't know where they went from here." He looked down at the snake. "Did you hear where they went?"

"I don't know where they went," Tryn said. "You heard them down here, not me."

"I wasn't talking to you," Jake said. "I was talking to Nesso."

"Yesss, they went to the left. . . ."

"Who is Nesso?" Tryn asked.

"This is." Jake pointed to the snake at his neck. "I found—um, him? Her? It?—in my pack last night."

"Her, if you don't mind," Nesso said indignantly.

"Sorry, I found *her* in my pack. Actually, she bit me."

"I told you, you hit me first," Nesso argued.

"I didn't hit you intentionally. But you bit me on purpose."

Tryn frowned and looked closely at the snake around Jake's neck. "Can you really understand her?"

"Of course. I mean, all the animals here talk, don't they? Look at Zephyr. Okay, so I can't understand a thing she says, but you and Astraea can. Just like me and Nesso. We understand each other perfectly."

Tryn shook his head slowly. "This is not the same at all. Not every animal here is capable of speech, but those that can talk are understood by everyone—except for strangers not raised around them. I have never seen a snake like that before, let alone heard one speak. Where did she come from?"

"Here," Jake said. "She climbed into my pack at

some point after I arrived here. I know for sure I didn't bring her from LA."

Alarm rose on Tryn's silver face. "Jake, I assure you, there are no snakes like Nesso here or on Xanadu."

"Where else could she be from?" The words were just out of his mouth when Jake remembered Nesso saying she was cold and how the bird monster put her in a dark place before she was here. "Wait a minute." He looked down at the snake. "Nesso, in your home, are there other big people like me or Tryn?"

"No. There are other big thingsss, but nothing like you. I have never ssseen anything like you before."

"Uh-oh," Jake said. "Houston, we have a problem. . . ."

"My name is Tryn, not Houston."

"It's an expression. It means we have a really big problem. Nesso has never seen anyone like us. It means that whoever brought me here must have brought Nesso from somewhere else."

"How can that be, when you speak the same language?" Tryn asked.

"It wasn't alwaysss like that," Nesso said. *"When I*

firsst came here, I couldn't underssstand anyone. But then I bit you and now I can."

"Really?" Jake said. He frowned. "She says she couldn't understand any of us until she bit me. Then she could."

"Fascinating," Tryn said. "Perhaps when she bit you, it broke some kind of barrier between you." He held up his hand to the snake. "Maybe if she bites me, I could understand her."

Jake pushed Tryn's hand away. "Trust me, you don't want to do that. When she bit me, it was like every part of me was on fire. My heart raced and I couldn't breathe. I thought for sure I was going to die, and I know I passed out. Even now my hand really hurts." He held up his hand, revealing the swollen fang marks and dark bruising around them. "She might even be poisonous to you."

"Good point," Tryn agreed. "But her being here is really bad. It means whoever is bringing humans to Titus is also bringing others. The question is, who and why?"

"Well," Jake said, bending down and reaching into his backpack. "I can't answer why, but I can show you who." He pulled out his notebook and opened it to the sketch. "This is what I saw grab Molly before I fell off my skateboard. Nesso says she was caught by the same thing right before it put her in a bag or something. But she says she saw other dark things too."

Tryn looked at the sketch and gasped. "Is this really what brought you here?"

Jake nodded. "I remember it was big and black. It kinda looked like a giant bird."

Tryn was shaking his head and his eyes were wide. "That was no bird. Jake, this is a Shadow Titan!"

17

ASTRAEA PUSHED THE HEAVY BROOM DOWN the empty hall of Arcadia One, while Zephyr worked beside her, dusting off shelves and windows with a flash of her long white tail.

"This isn't so bad," Zephyr said. "It's better than licking flowers to get nectar."

"That's easy for you to say. You don't have to push a heavy broom."

"They say a little hard work is character building." Zephyr moved on to the next window and sang aloud, "Swish, swish, swish," as her tail brushed against the glass. "All done, nice and clean . . ."

When Astraea reached the end of the hall, she

turned and pushed the broom back again. "Finally!" she said. "Now just pick this up and we can head over to Arcadia Two."

Zephyr trotted over with the dustpan gripped between her teeth. She bent down and held it to the floor as Astraea swept the dust and debris from the busy day onto the pan. It was then dumped into the trash receptacle.

Astraea picked up the broom and slung it over her shoulder, and they made their way to the ramps that led from the upper floors down to the lower ones. Students and faculty with legs and feet used the stairs. But for those with hooves and other means of transport, the ramps were ideal.

The sun was still shining overhead as they exited Arcadia One and started walking across the grounds toward the second building. The park area in front was filled with students. Some were sitting together, others were walking, or standing and talking. As Astraea looked at them, she noticed several Olympians speaking with Titans. They were laughing and shoving each other playfully.

In the field beside the school she saw a mix of

Olympian and Titan satyrs, Seneka the sphinx, some harpies, and a few centaurs playing a ball game. They were chasing each other as the ball was kicked toward the goal line. But at the last minute, one of the harpies swooped down from above and caught it in her clawed feet. Screeching loudly, she turned and carried the ball toward the other goal line. Before she could get it into the net, a harpy from the other team knocked the ball from her claws. Everyone cheered as it fell to the ground, and a blond centaur took control and maneuvered it back to the net. Seneka was the goalkeeper and tried to block the centaur, but he turned and kicked the ball. Seneka roared in fury as it whooshed past her and into the back of the net.

"Hey, Zeph, are you seeing what I'm seeing?" Astraea said. "You don't think this crazy idea of a school is really going to work, do you? I mean, look, those are Titans playing with Olympians."

Zephyr watched the new friends and nodded. "Maybe they were right. Maybe Arcadia will bring everyone together."

"Just in time for it to be ruined by whoever's bringing strangers here."

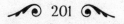

"Aren't you cheery," Zephyr commented.

They made it to the front of Arcadia Two and waited while a couple of teachers stood at the entrance chatting. When they finally left, Astraea charged forward. "If we're going to do this, now's our chance."

Astraea held the front doors open as Zephyr passed through them. Since Astraea had two classes in this building, she knew where the stairs were, but not the ramps. "How do you think you'd do with stairs?"

"Why?"

"Because I don't know where the ramps are or if they even go down into the lower level. Tryn said Jake is hiding below."

"Well, there's only one way to find out." Zephyr clopped forward and headed into the stairwell.

If the situation weren't so serious, Astraea would have been in hysterics watching Zephyr trying to get down the stairs. Each step was shallow, and she looked like she was walking on tiptoes. Twice she slipped and nearly fell. But with Astraea helping, they eventually made it to the lower level.

Zephyr glared back at the stairs and snorted, "I am

not doing that again! Once we leave here, I'm never coming back."

Astraea nodded. "I wonder if the designer didn't want Titans and Olympians like you to come down here."

"Why would they do that?" Zephyr asked. "Was it your father?"

"You know Dad would never do anything like that. Besides, he's been too busy with the prison."

"Well, when we find out who it was, remind me to step on their foot."

"I will," Astraea chuckled. She looked around. "You know, it's dark down here. I have great night vision, but this is too much even for me. I'm sure glad you're here."

Zephyr's natural glow was enough to drive away the total darkness of the lower level—but not enough to remove the eeriness. "It's bigger than I thought," she said. "Why are there so many corridors? Which way do we go?"

Astraea shrugged. "I have no idea. Let's just look around and see if we can find Jake."

They made their way through the lower level,

looking and listening for any signs of Jake or the mysterious figures that Zephyr had seen entering the school the previous evening.

"I don't like it down here," Zephyr said softly. "It feels . . . wrong."

"It sure does," Astraea agreed.

Zephyr leaned closer. "Why are we whispering?"

"I don't know, but I'm not going to stop." Astraea was still carrying her broom. She turned it around and reached for one of the bristles, pulled it out, and laid it against the wall.

"What are you doing?"

"This place is a labyrinth. I half expect to see the Minotaur down here. The last thing I want to do is get lost, so I'm leaving us a trail to follow."

"Good idea."

They stayed close together as they wandered through the corridors. Along the way they passed multiple closed doors. Astraea tried each one and found them all locked. "Why would they lock them? What are they hiding?"

"Do we really want to know?" Zephyr asked.

Astraea looked at her best friend but said nothing.

The hair on the back of her neck was rising, and she had the feeling they weren't alone.

Zephyr's eyes were wide and her tail swished the air as her ears moved around. "I hear something," she nickered softly.

Astraea nodded and pointed forward. "It's coming from there. I wonder if it's Jake."

In that moment, Astraea was torn. Should they go forward and investigate the soft sounds? Or turn around and run? Every instinct in her body said run, but her feet started to move in the direction of the sounds.

"Astraea, wait . . . ," Zephyr nickered. "What are you doing?"

"I don't know," she admitted.

They approached a four-way junction. The sounds were coming from just ahead and seemed to be getting closer. Astraea was locked in the grip of fear but still kept walking.

As they reached the junction, they turned to the left and came face-to-face with two figures.

Astraea screamed.

18

"YOU SCARED THE LIFE OUT OF ME!" Astraea cried as she shoved Jake back.

"Me?" he cried. "What about you two, all glowy and mysterious? I thought for sure you were the strangers coming back. I've had the worst night of my life, and the last thing I need is you two sneaking around."

"Who's sneaking?" Astraea said. "We were looking for you!"

Tryn was standing back, trying to hide a smile.

"What are you laughing at?" Zephyr said to him. "Scaring us half to death isn't funny."

"I know," he said soberly, "though your faces are rather amusing."

"You want to know what would really be amusing?" Zephyr challenged. "Me stepping on your foot—that would be hysterical."

Astraea took a deep breath and calmed down. "I'm all right now. But seriously, you really scared us."

"It's this place," Jake said. He looked past Astraea. "Did you find my sister?"

Astraea shook her head. "I'm sorry, we couldn't find her. We searched until the night dwellers arrived to work in the orchard."

"Where is she?" Jake demanded. He looked back at Tryn. "I've gotta get outta here and look for her."

"You can't. You still smell like a human," Tryn said. "You'll be caught."

"Look, I'm going nuts down here doing nothing while my sister is out there somewhere," Jake said. "I've got to go. There are bad things going on that I want no part of."

"What things?" Zephyr asked.

Jake looked at her and frowned. "If you just said something, I can't understand you."

Zephyr shook her head and snorted. "This language thing is really getting up my nose!"

Astraea stroked Zephyr's head. "She wanted to know what bad things are going on."

Jake told them about the two groups of strangers he'd seen the previous night—and the sound of something heavy being dragged. He also introduced them to Nesso. Despite all attempts at communication, no one other than Jake could understand her—though she could understand everyone, including Zephyr.

"Isn't this just great," Zephyr fumed. "Jake can't understand a word I say, and none of us can understand what Nesso says *except* Jake. This is like a poor comedy from the Muses."

"Except it isn't funny," Astraea said. She peered more closely at the snake. "She is really beautiful. Her scales look like sparkling beads."

"Thank you," Nesso hissed. *"You are beautiful too— for a big thing."*

Jake passed along the message and added, "She's also very polite."

Astraea looked back at Zephyr. "I bet Nesso was brought here by the same people who brought all the other creatures and humans."

"What creatures?" Jake asked.

It was Astraea's turn to explain what she'd seen the previous night in the prison. "It's easy to get into, but some of the things in there were terrifying. They all have one thing in common, though. No one remembers how they got here."

"I can't believe they brought a clown here," Jake said.

Astraea nodded. "He's really nasty. I didn't like him at all."

"No one likes clowns, ever since Pennywise. My sister is terrified of them. I'm glad she's not in the prison with him."

"Who is Pennywise?" Astraea asked.

"You don't want to know," Jake said. "But he's terrifying."

"Still," Astraea continued, "the clown was better than that living rock that tried to eat me." She lifted the hem of her long tunic and showed them her leg. Even in the dim light of the golden moss and Zephyr's glow, the dark tongue marks were easy to see. "I thought for sure I was dead until the two-headed worm told me what to do to get away."

Jake was shaking his head. "For the last time, are you guys absolutely, positively, affirmatively, and completely sure I'm not in a coma? Because right now, that's starting to look awfully good."

Zephyr whinnied angrily, "Would you please stop all this ridiculous talk of a coma? This isn't a coma, it's real!"

"What did she say?" Jake asked Astraea.

Astraea's eyes flashed to Zephyr and then back. "She says it's not a coma, this is real. And she's right. It is."

Jake nodded. "Then we're really in trouble."

"We are," Astraea agreed. "Those creatures have been brought here from many worlds, not just one."

"Why?" Jake asked. "Why did they bring me from LA? And what did they do with my sister?"

"That isn't the biggest puzzle of all," Tryn said softly. "Jake, show them the picture you drew."

Jake pulled the notebook from his pack. "I drew this last night before the strangers came. Nesso really helped. She said the same thing took her."

Astraea gasped when she saw the sketch, while Zephyr snorted and pawed the ground.

"It's a Shadow Titan, isn't it?" Tryn said. "We talked about them in school today."

Astraea nodded. "But how is this possible? Minerva said they were all destroyed."

"Obviously not all of them," Zephyr added.

Tryn said. "When I saw this, I realized the danger is bigger than we thought."

"None of this makes any sense," Astraea said. "Saturn was the one who created them, but he seems fine with his sons ruling Titus. He's even become Jupiter's top adviser. He can't be the one creating them."

"So who is?" Jake asked. "I don't remember much, but I do remember it being big and scary."

"You were lucky to have survived," Astraea said. "From what Minerva said, they have no mercy. All they do is kill."

Tryn nodded. "Unless they have been instructed to do other things."

"Who would do that?" Zephyr asked. "I thought they couldn't be controlled."

"I don't know," Astraea answered. "But we're going to find out. I promised those people and creatures in prison that we'd get them home, and we're going to— even that awful rock monster that wanted to eat me."

"Then I guess the first thing we do is figure out

who was down here last night and why. Jake and I were trying to follow a trail. We think it's blood."

"Blood?" Zephyr cried. "Are you sure?"

"Where is it?" Astraea asked.

"This way," Tryn said.

He led them down the dark corridor. Halfway down, he stopped and pointed at the floor. "There. It's not a lot, but it looks like a few drops."

Astraea bent down and looked at the blood. "Zeph, you've got a great nose. What do you think?"

Zephyr harrumphed. "Are you saying my nose is big?"

"Did I say that? No, I said it was great," Astraea said. "You can smell things I can't."

"Oh, all right then." Zephyr lowered her head down to the floor, sniffed the dots, and shook her head. "Yuck, it's blood. I think I might be sick. . . ."

Jake frowned. "What did she say?"

"She said it was blood, and that she might be sick," Tryn repeated.

"I thought horses couldn't throw up."

Zephyr glared at him and pulled back her lips. "What—did—you—just—say?"

"It doesn't matter," Astraea said.

"Yes, it does! He called me a horse again!"

Astraea looked over to Jake. "Jake, please. I keep telling you—Zephyr gets really angry when you call her a horse. You've got to stop before she becomes violent."

"I'm really sorry, Zephyr," Jake said sincerely. "But I'm still not used to all this and you being—well, you know—you."

"What's that supposed to mean?" Zephyr challenged.

"Hey, look what we found," Tryn said quickly as he reached into his pocket and pulled out a wide bracelet. "I'm sure it's Vulcan's. I think that might be his blood."

Astraea looked at the bracelet. "How do you know it's his?"

Tryn was turning over the bracelet. "I told you he helped build our homes on Xanadu. He was always wearing it." He pointed to a mark on the polished metal. "Look here, I was there when he scratched it putting up a wall."

Astraea looked at the mark. "So you think it could

have been Vulcan that Jake saw being dragged down here last night."

"I'm afraid so," Tryn said.

"Wait, no, it can't be," Zephyr said. "I saw Vulcan today in class. He was teaching us about metalworking. It couldn't have been him down here last night. There were no wounds on him."

"I'm not lying," Tryn said. "This is Vulcan's bracelet!"

Astraea nodded. "We'll see him tomorrow at school and look for it. But there is something else to consider. Perhaps Vulcan was down here. But maybe that isn't his blood at all. Maybe he was one of the cloaked people Jake saw dragging the big thing."

A flash of doubt crossed Tryn's face but disappeared just as quickly. Finally he said, "Perhaps. But the Vulcan I know would never be part of anything where people were hurt."

"Or just maybe," Zephyr suggested, "you don't know him as well as you think you do."

They continued to search the labyrinth beneath Arcadia Two and were able to pick up the blood trail and follow it through several corridors. But it mysteriously stopped at a stone wall at the end of a remote hall.

"This is impossible. It can't just stop here." Astraea's eyes searched the area, looking for any other clues. "It's like they've gone right through the wall. There has to be a secret passage or something."

Astraea, Jake, and Zephyr inspected every inch of the rock. After several minutes they finished, and Astraea scratched her head. "Nope, I can't figure it out."

"I fear I may know what happened," Tryn offered.

"Finally he speaks!" Zephyr said. "You know, you could have helped us search."

"There was nothing to find," Tryn said. "Had I told you, you wouldn't have believed me."

Astraea approached him. "Believed what? Do you know what happened here?"

He shook his head. "Not *this* in particular, but I do believe I have an idea. I have seen it before—on Xanadu."

"What are you talking about?" Zephyr said.

"There are several ways to open the Solar Stream. One can fly very quickly to enter it, or there are certain gems that can open it. All you need do is either

place it on a wall or wear it, and with a command, the Solar Stream will open and you can venture to other worlds."

"That's impossible!" Jake cried. "Nothing could do that."

"I'm sorry, Jake, but you're wrong," Tryn said. "I have seen such gems with my own eyes. In fact, Emily Jacobs wears a ring with a Solar Stream gem, though she doesn't really need it. She can open the Solar Stream by herself, or Pegasus can fly into it."

Astraea frowned. "I've never heard of gems that can open the Solar Stream."

Tryn shrugged. "Probably because they've all been gathered up and are stored on Xanadu. There's only one missing, and that's lost somewhere on Earth."

"And this is the first time you thought to tell us about all this?" Astraea cried.

"I didn't think of it until now."

Astraea could hardly believe her ears. "So if someone had one of those gems, they could travel anywhere and bring anything back." She looked back at Zephyr. "That's why they gathered them all together on Xanadu—to stop it."

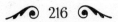

"Then they did a rotten job of it," Jake added. "Look at me and Nesso, and maybe Molly. How else did we get here from our worlds? Or the others you saw in the prison."

Zephyr pawed the ground. "This just keeps getting worse and worse."

Tryn moved away from the group and walked back down the corridor. He stopped halfway and stood before a door. It was locked. So he pulled out his lockpick set and adeptly opened the door.

"In here," he called.

Astraea followed him into the room. It was filled with stacks and stacks of crates. Tryn pulled down a wooden crate from the top of a pile and opened it.

"What is that terrible smell?" Zephyr called.

"Something stinks!" Jake choked out at the same time. At his neck, Nesso was hissing and slid around until her head was hidden under the back of Jake's tunic. "It smells worse than roadkill!"

"It's this." Tryn held up what looked like a freeze-dried animal. It was thin and wide, but there was no mistaking a head and limbs.

Astraea pinched her nose and approached the

dried animal. "What is that? I've never seen anything like it before."

"I don't recognize the species, but it looks freeze-dried. Look how many crates there are." He glanced down the corridor again. "I wonder if there are more rooms like this."

"What's it all for?" Astraea asked.

"Your guess is as good as mine," Tryn mused. He put the animal back, sealed the container, and returned it to the stack. "But I have an idea how we can find out." He squeezed through the maze of crates. "Jake, come here."

Jake followed him and disappeared behind the crates.

"What are you doing back there?" Astraea asked.

Tryn reappeared with Jake behind him. "I was checking to see if we could both fit back there. We can."

"And?" Jake said. "Please don't say what I think you are going to say."

"I was going to suggest we hide in here tonight, and if we see the strangers return, we can discover what they are doing."

Jake sighed. "He said it."

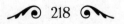

By the time they finished exploring as much as they could of the labyrinth beneath Arcadia Two, the sun was setting. Instead of leaving the school by the front, Astraea and Zephyr carried their cleaning supplies with them back to Tryn's dorm room.

Tryn's room was small for one person, tight for two, and uncomfortable for three. But there was no way Zephyr could also fit in with them. She had to remain in the corridor outside with her head sticking in.

"We'd better get going," Astraea said. "I'm already in so much trouble at home that if I'm late again, my parents won't just ground me, they'll kill me. Are you sure you want to go back down there tonight?"

"No," Nesso hissed.

"Me neither," Jake agreed. Then he had to tell the others what Nesso said.

"Well, I'm going back," Tryn insisted. "I need to know for certain if they are using one of the gems."

"Then what?" Zephyr asked. "Once we know, what do we do about it? Who do we tell?"

Tryn said, "For now, I suggest we don't tell anyone. Not until we figure out who is doing this and why."

Astraea nodded to Zephyr. "He's right. We need to know more, and the only way is to find out what's going on down there." She looked back at Tryn. "I wish I could go with you."

"I don't!" Zephyr said. "That place makes my feathers curl. And we haven't even seen all of it. What about the other buildings at Arcadia? Do they have labyrinths as well?"

Tryn shrugged. "I don't know for sure, but it would seem logical that they do. I haven't found the passage that connects them yet, but that doesn't mean it's not there."

"But what's it all for?"

"That we won't know until we find out who is bringing strangers here," Tryn said. "With luck, we should be able to get some answers tonight."

19

ASTRAEA AND ZEPHYR LEFT JAKE IN TRYN'S room. It was getting late, and Astraea was feeling the pressure to get home.

"I'm coming with you," Zephyr said. "Your mom likes me and won't yell if I'm there. Besides, I want to ask your dad a few simple questions."

"Like what?"

"I want to know who designed Arcadia. Someone had to draw up the plans for that labyrinth. Maybe if we find out who it was, we can ask them why they built it."

Astraea considered. "Good idea. Why don't you stay for dinner? You can ask him then."

They hurried back to Astraea's home. When they walked through the door, Astraea called, "Mom, I'm home. I'm so sorry about yesterday. I—"

"Astraea, stop," Zephyr said. "She's not here. The house is empty."

"But she's always home when I get home. . . ."

They walked through to the kitchen and there was no sign of her mother. Dirty dishes in the sink suggested that at least one of her brothers had been in for a visit—but then left.

Astraea started to fill the sink. "If we do the dishes, and get dinner ready, Mom and Dad might not be so mad at me, and maybe we can go out tonight."

"To do what?"

"Watch the front of Arcadia Two. I want to see if the strangers come back."

Zephyr nodded. "We'll let Jake and Tryn watch from the inside, and we'll take the outside."

"Exactly."

The plan was set, but as the sun went down, there was still no word from Astraea's parents, and they were starting to worry.

"This is getting strange," Astraea said. "Mom's

never gone this late, and Dad really should be home by now."

Food was forgotten as they sat outside and waited for Astraea's parents to return. Others walked by and waved, and Astraea even asked a few passing friends if they had seen her parents, but the answer was always the same—not since the morning.

"Did they say they had somewhere to go tonight?" Zephyr asked. "Is Jupiter or Saturn having an event that they might be invited to?"

Astraea shook her head. "No—anything like that and I'm usually invited too."

"I'm sure it's nothing," Zephyr said lightly—though the alertness in her eyes told a different story.

"Me too," Astraea agreed, lying to herself. "I sure they're fine and will be back soon." She heard herself speaking the words that even she didn't believe.

20

JAKE WAS GRATEFUL TO HAVE A SHOWER and get cleaned up after the long night and day in the labyrinth. Before bathing, he tried to get Nesso to let go of her tail so he could put her down, but she refused. Jake finally had to shower with Nesso still wrapped around his neck.

This was the first time in her life Nesso had experienced hot water, and she loved the feel of it beating on her scales.

"I am warm!" she cried joyously.

"And I'm clean!" Jake said as he turned off the water and reached for a towel. He dressed in another of Tryn's tunics and walked back into the bedroom. "I guess it's too much to ask for a hair dryer?"

"A what?"

"Thought so," Jake said. He sat down on the edge of the bed and pulled a comb out of his pack. "So what do you want to do now? Do you think I might pass for a Titan and we can look for my sister?"

Tryn shook his head. "I'm sorry, not yet. Dressed in my tunic you look like a Titan, but you still smell very human." He pulled out a plate of ambrosia cakes and fruit. "The cleaners always leave more food for me than I need. Eat some more, it might help. I was also kind of wondering if you might teach me how to use your skateboard."

"Really? You want to learn to skateboard? I mean right now, with all this going on?"

Tryn nodded. "Why not? The trouble will still be here whether we do or not. But we have time to spend before tonight. It might be a way to relax."

Jake said. "But you said I still smell human. How can we go out?"

"We're not going out."

"Where are we going then?" Jake asked.

Tryn grinned. "The long corridors beneath Arcadia Two."

Jake enjoyed a meal of fruit, ambrosia cakes, and nectar. He handed up small pieces of fruit and cake to Nesso and was surprised when she ate them.

"With those teeth, I thought you'd eat small animals or bugs."

"I eat anything," Nesso said. *"Thisss isss ssso good."*

"And very messy," Jake laughed as he looked at the snake's face, covered in red fruit juice and cake crumbs.

Tryn remained silent through most of the meal. Finally he said, "I'm really sorry, but I think I've made a terrible mistake."

"With what?"

"With you," he said. "Astraea said she saw what the prisoners were fed in prison. It was fruit and baked breads. No ambrosia or nectar. I've only just realized what I've done. . . ."

"What's that?" Jake stuffed another ambrosia cake into his mouth. The sweet yellow cake reminded him of pound cake, and nectar was like drinking thin honey.

"Well, um," Tryn continued. "Remember I told you my father was human? Well, back in the war he was badly hurt, so Emily forced him to eat ambrosia so she could heal him. But he didn't want to, because he knew ambrosia would make him, um"—his voice softened to a whisper—"immortal."

"What!" Jake cried, spitting out crumbs. He looked at the remains of the cake. "Are you saying this stuff makes people immortal?"

Tryn nodded. "I'm really sorry, Jake! I was so focused on helping you not smell like a human that I didn't even think about how it would change your physiology. Titans and Olympians are immortal—but they get weak and sick if they don't keep eating it. My mother is a scientist and says she's never seen anything like it and that it's changed us, too. I'm as immortal as you are. I'm sure that's why they aren't feeding it to the prisoners. I probably shouldn't have given to you, either."

"Well, it's a little late now, isn't it?" Jake cried, holding up a cake. "I've been eating these like potato chips! Immortal, really? Like living forever and not dying?"

Tryn nodded. "I don't know how it works if some-one were to kill you. Perhaps if they cut off your head, you would die and stay dead."

"Hey, I've grown really attached to this head. It's my favorite! No one is going to chop it off."

"Of course not," Tryn agreed. "I was just thinking that I shouldn't have given you ambrosia or nectar."

"I really can't believe you're telling me this now."

"I'm really sorry," Tryn said. "But at least you and Nesso can live together forever."

"That pleasssesss me," Nesso said.

Jake stroked the snake but didn't speak. He could hardly believe what Tryn had said. Immortal? Really, like forever? It was just too much to think about at the moment. Not with Molly missing and monsters running amok and abducting people. But when this was over, he had a lot to think about.

In the meantime, since the damage was done, Jake reached for another piece of ambrosia.

After they finished eating, they were ready to set off again. Jake carried his skateboard, while Tryn brought the bag of glowing moss.

"I want it on the record right now that I don't think going back down there is a good idea," Jake said. "When this goes south, and it probably will, you'd better hope I'm in a coma, because if this is real and we get killed, I'm really gonna get mad."

"You won't be killed. You're immortal now, remember?"

"Well, if they chop my head off."

"Don't worry, I'll protect you."

Jake laughed as they left Tryn's room. "Seriously, dude, you're half my size. I don't think you could protect a dandelion if it was threatened by a caterpillar."

"I am stronger than I look."

"Yeah, right."

Tryn stopped. "You don't think I can protect you?"

"Nope," Jake said.

Tryn lunged forward and grabbed Jake. With no effort at all, he hoisted him in the air and spun him around as though he weighed nothing.

"Hey, hey, put me down!" Jake cried.

"Not until you acknowledge that I am stronger than you."

229

"Okay, okay, you're stronger than me. I just ate! Put me down before I hurl!"

Tryn stopped spinning Jake and lowered him gently to the floor. "My people are very strong—stronger than Titans and Olympians. We just don't like to show it."

"Well, you showed it pretty good just then," Jake said, running his hand through his hair and hoping his meal would stay down.

"That's because it was necessary to prove a point. I would appreciate it if you didn't tell Astraea or Zephyr what I did."

"Why?"

"Because we do not like to draw attention to ourselves."

Jake burst into more laughter. "Dude, have you looked in the mirror lately? You're bright silver with speckled eyes. Trust me, you're already drawing attention to yourself."

"I have no control over that. But this I do. Please Jake, say nothing of this."

"Sure, if that's what you want. I have no idea why, but I won't tell anyone."

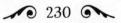

"Thank you."

They traveled under the covered walkway toward the rear entrance to Arcadia Two. Just like the previous evening, Tryn used his lockpick to get inside. As they made their way to the stairs, Jake stopped. "This is a school, right? I mean, like, there are kids here during the day?"

Tryn nodded.

"Then why does it feel so creepy? I've been to lots of schools, and none of them ever felt like this."

"Perhaps it's the mystery of what's happening beneath us that makes you feel like that."

"Seriously, dude, don't you feel it?"

Tryn paused and looked at Jake for several heartbeats. Finally he nodded. "Yes, I feel it too. Something is very wrong here."

"Exactly," Jake agreed.

They took the stairs down into the darkened corridors beneath the school. Even though Tryn opened the bag of moss to drive back the darkness, Jake shivered as he looked around.

"I don't like it here," Nesso complained.

"Me either," Jake said. He put his skateboard down

and automatically jumped on. It gave him a sense of normalcy in the midst of the insanity. He kicked his foot and felt the board glide like a hot knife through butter on the marble floor. "At least it's great for boarding down here."

Tryn jogged up to him. "May I try?"

"Sure." Jake climbed off and reached into his backpack. He pulled out his helmet and handed it to Tryn. "Put this on. I usually don't wear it, but my mom worries, so I keep it with me."

Tryn frowned at the helmet.

"It's in case you fall and smash your head."

"Like you did," Tryn said.

"Exactly. See, if you don't wear it you could fall, hit your head, and end up in a weird world full of talking animals and cakes that make you immortal."

"I doubt hitting your head has anything to do with that."

"Maybe," Jake agreed. "But put it on anyway."

Tryn pulled on the helmet. "Is this right?"

Jake nodded. "Now, the first thing you need to work on is balance." He moved the skateboard until it was sitting horizontally in front of Tryn. "Practice climbing on and off, using the leg you want to push with. . . ."

Tryn followed Jake's instructions and climbed easily on and off the skateboard. Next he learned to keep one foot on and push with the other. Soon he was gliding short distances.

As the time passed, Jake was so engrossed in teaching Tryn how to skateboard that he forgot to be afraid. "Yes!" he cheered, punching the air as Tryn managed his first, simple trick. "You're a natural! We could have you competing in no time. I bet you would win loads."

Tryn jumped off the board and handed it back to Jake. He was beaming and his silver skin shimmered with excitement. It was the first time Jake had seen him looking genuinely happy.

"That was wonderful," Tryn said. "I must make myself a board. Perhaps Vulcan can help. There is nothing he can't build."

"Tell you what—you can have my board if you help me find Molly and get us home."

A flash of regret crossed Tryn's face, but he hid it quickly. "Of course, you must both get home."

Jake nodded. "But what's to stop you from coming back with me for a visit?"

Tryn shook his head. "I don't look human. I'd be captured."

"Not if we put makeup on you," Jake offered. He reached for Tryn's hand and looked closely at the skin on the back of it. "Obviously the silver doesn't come off. But my mom has terrible skin and she uses loads of stuff to cover it up. You could do the same."

"Really?" Tryn said. "You think we could? I would love to see Earth. My father has told me so many stories."

"Sure we could. So when I go back, you can come for a visit."

"Thank you," Tryn said sincerely. "I would like that. But first we have to find out how."

They continued deeper into the labyrinth, toward the corridor where the blood trail ended. Tryn used his pick to get into the storeroom with the smelly flattened animals.

"I was dreading this," Jake said as they squeezed in behind the stacks of containers.

"I wasn't looking forward to it either," Tryn admitted. "The stench is foul, but it's the best place we could be if the others return. Especially since the blood trail ended at the wall just outside this room."

"I hope it doesn't take too long," Jake said. "I don't want to spend a minute longer down here than we have to!"

21

JAKE AND TRYN SAT IN THE DARKNESS OF the tight space behind the crates. The door was closed and locked again, so they had to remain silent to hear anything happening outside it. As though sensing Jake's fear, Nesso slid down from his neck and curled herself in his hands.

"She's very sweet," Tryn noted. He reached over and gently stroked the snake.

"You can see her?"

"Yes," Tryn said. "Not as good as in daylight, but I can see well enough."

Jake started to stroke the snake. "I wish I had your eyes. All I see is black."

"*All I sssee isss you glowing with heat,*" Nesso said. "*You both are warm, but Jake isss much hotter than Tryn.*"

"Really?" Jake asked.

"*Yesss.*"

"What did she say?"

When Jake repeated what Nesso had said, Tryn nodded. "My mother's world was very hot because our sun was going to supernova. Over generations, our silver skin developed to reflect the sun's heat away from us. Of course, this now means we feel the cold a lot more intensely."

"*Me too,*" Nesso agreed.

"Then you'll really like LA. It's hot—especially in the summer."

"Is it summer now?"

"Yes, it's just—"

Tryn's cool hand slapped over Jake's mouth. "I heard something," he whispered tightly. "Voices. Coming this way."

Jake nodded to let Tryn know he could remove his hand. His breathing quickened, and suddenly he needed to go to the toilet. But he couldn't move. Terror rooted him to the spot.

"They're coming," Tryn said in barely a whisper. "Don't make a sound."

Jake wanted to say that it was Tryn making all the noise, but he didn't. He was too scared. Instead he sat still and hoped he didn't scream. In that instant, Jake realized he wasn't built for this type of suspense. Skateboarding? No problem at all. Dangerous tricks? A piece of cake! But this was enough to make him cry.

Before long, he too could hear the same soft voices he'd heard the previous evening. But this time they were much closer, just outside the door. Then the voices stopped, and they heard the sound of a key being fitted into the lock.

Jake ducked down farther as the door opened and light shone in. He went from trembling to absolute quaking. From his position, he couldn't see who or what was there. But he could hear the voices, speaking a language he couldn't understand. This was followed by the sound of the containers being opened.

The stench from their contents was almost enough to make him sick. He looked over and saw Tryn's nauseated face. His silver hands covered his mouth and he looked like he might throw up.

Jake couldn't see how many were in the small room, but it had to be at least three—maybe even five. They were moving and opening the crates. Then the sickening sound of crunching and chewing started, and it took all Jake's willpower not to vomit. He didn't have to see it to know that whoever was there was eating the flat animals, raw.

New voices entered and left the storage room as crates were opened and their contents devoured. Time stood still as Jake and Tryn remained hidden, listening to the disgusting sounds. Finally all the crates were resealed, and the strangers exited the room—leaving the door open and a torch burning.

Jake looked over at Tryn. The silver of his friend's face was reduced to dull gray and had lost all its shimmer. His eyes were huge and frightened. Then Jake realized that from Tryn's angle, he could see out between the crates. Whatever he'd seen, it had been enough to terrify him.

The sounds of quiet conversation continued down the corridor toward the wall where the blood trail had ended. Beside him, Tryn started to stand.

Jake caught his arm and shook his head. He held

up a finger and pulled Nesso closer. "Can you go out and see if anyone else is coming?" he whispered.

"Yesss," Nesso hissed. *Put me down. I will look.*

"Be careful. . . ." Jake lowered the snake to the floor and Nesso slithered out of his hands. She slid easily through the cracks between the containers and to the door. Moments later she returned to Jake's hands.

"There are many big thingsss out there," she hissed. *"They are all at the wall. There are two other big thingsss that are ressstrained with coversss over their headsss. They look very weak. There wasss no one elssse."*

Jake nodded and returned Nesso to her place around his neck while he repeated the message to Tryn.

Tryn nodded and stood. "I must see."

"Are you nuts?" Jake whispered.

But Tryn kept moving. He motioned for Jake to stay put. But even if he wanted to, Jake couldn't. He stood and started to follow Tryn out from behind the crates.

The doorway was just ahead. If anyone walked past, there would be no way to avoid being seen.

Tryn lowered himself to the floor and crawled. Jake did the same thing as the two of them approached the open door.

Tryn was first to gaze out toward the wall. Jake saw something bright reflecting on Tryn's silver skin as the sound of whooshing started. Unable to hold back, Jake rose above him and peered out.

His mouth fell open as he saw a large group of cloaked strangers standing before the wall. There was a blinding white light coming from the wall itself. As he watched, he saw the strangers haul two people, bound and with their heads covered, to their feet. They staggered and moved as though they had been drugged.

One of them broke free, and Jake nearly gasped aloud as a set of large white wings unfolded and started to flap to break free of the restraining arms. "Please let us go," a woman's voice cried. "Who are you? Why are you doing this to us? We have a family—you must stop!"

"Silence!" a man's voice said harshly. "It will be over soon."

Jake watched as several of the cloaked figures

tackled the woman. One removed a glove and touched her wing with a bare hand. She cried out once and became still.

"Do not kill her yet!" one of the figures commanded. "Just get them out of here."

The others stood and pulled the unconscious woman to her feet and dragged her into the blinding light. The second figure was shoved through right behind them.

Moments later, others arrived from the light, carrying containers just like the ones in the storage room.

"You three," the cloaked man commanded, pointing at the new arrivals. "Wait here for the others. When they arrive, get them into position. Soon it will be time to make our move."

The speaker started to turn to leave. Jake and Tryn dashed back inside the room and barely had time to make it to their hiding spot before he and several other cloaked figures crossed in front of the open door and walked back down the corridor.

"That was too close," Jake panted. "What was that light?"

Tryn's eyes were wild with terror, and he was shaking his head. "That was the Solar Stream," he said softly. "They're using it to take people away."

"What people?"

"Titans!" Tryn's frightened eyes settled on him. "Jake, I'd know that voice and those wings anywhere. That was Aurora—Astraea's mother."

22

ASTRAEA AND ZEPHYR REMAINED OUTSIDE the house, waiting for her parents to return. As the long night dragged on, Astraea was finding it difficult to stay awake. She settled down on the grass, leaning against Zephyr, and slowly drifted off to sleep.

At dawn she awoke. Titans were walking past her house and chuckling at the sight of her and Zephyr sleeping on the damp grass.

"Zeph, you awake?"

"I am now," Zephyr moaned. "I ache all over. Whose bright idea was it to sleep outside?"

"We weren't supposed to sleep at all." Astraea climbed slowly to her feet, yawned, and stretched her stubby wings. She looked back at her house. "Come on in for a bit. I need to clean up and change my clothes. Then we should go over to my grandfather's and tell him about Mom and Dad."

Zephyr scrambled to her feet and opened her wings wide. She gave several long, powerful flaps that lifted her front end off the ground. When she finished, she settled them into position on her back. "I can't believe we fell asleep."

"I know, but we have had a few long nights lately. I feel more tired now than last night."

They walked into the house, and Astraea's nostrils were immediately on alert. The smell of baking was making her mouth water. She looked at Zephyr and ran through to the kitchen. Her mother was standing at the counter, cutting up a freshly made ambrosia cake.

"Mom?"

Aurora looked up and nodded at Astraea.

"What happened?"

"What happened with what?" Aurora asked.

"You! Last night you and Dad weren't here. We waited up all night for you. But you didn't come back."

"Of course we did," Aurora said. "We just went

out for a walk. Your father and I are entitled to a little private time on occasion."

"But—but—didn't you see us out there waiting for you?"

"We saw you two sleeping on the grass and didn't want to disturb you. Now, breakfast is almost ready. Go clean yourself up, and then you can eat." Aurora stepped up to Zephyr. "Isn't it time you went home?"

Zephyr looked over to Astraea. "Um, yes, of course, Aurora." She took a few hesitant steps toward the door and looked back. "See you later, Astraea. . . ."

"Mom, I invited Zephyr to breakfast."

"I'm sorry, not this morning. You can see each other later."

"Don't worry about it, Astraea," Zephyr said softly. "I'll see you at school." Zephyr's head hung low and her wings drooped as she walked to the front door.

"Mom, you hurt her feelings," Astraea said, watching Zephyr leave.

Aurora stopped cutting the cake. "She'll be fine. But I do want to talk to you about her. Astraea, I don't like Zephyr spending so much time around here."

"You *don't* like it?"

"No, I don't. If you want to see her, you can go over to her house. You know your father has a lot of work to do. You and Zephyr constantly underfoot is a distraction he just doesn't need."

Astraea felt like she'd been slapped. Her mother always said she loved Zephyr like a daughter. Now she and her best friend were a distraction? "Does that mean I can spend the night at her house?"

"Of course."

"But—but I thought I might be in trouble."

"Trouble? Why, have you done something wrong?"

"I did stay out a bit late these past couple of nights."

Aurora kept cutting the same piece of ambrosia cake. "Oh, that. Don't worry about it. We all stay out late at times. Now go get cleaned up and ready for school."

Hiddles came into the kitchen, meowing and rubbing against Astraea's legs, looking for attention. But when the kitten saw Aurora, it started hissing and ran away.

Aurora watched him go. "Take that thing with you when you leave for school."

"Hiddles?"

"Yes, there is a new rule in the house: no more animals. If you insist on keeping him, take him to Zephyr's house. You can visit him there."

Astraea could hardly believe her ears. Her mother had given Hiddles to her for her birthday and now she didn't like him? It just didn't make sense. She ran to her bedroom, changed her clothes, and brushed her hair. She didn't want to stay in the house a moment longer.

Hiddles was hiding under her bed. When Astraea caught him, the fluffy rainbow kitten's eyes were huge with fear and he was trembling. "Mom didn't mean it," she said, petting him gently. "We'll go to Zephyr's and have a nice time there."

Astraea went back downstairs. The kitchen was empty, so she grabbed several slices of ambrosia cake and left the house.

"Zeph!" Astraea called, entering her friend's house without knocking. "Are you here?"

When there wasn't an answer, Astraea ran around to the stable and received the surprise of her life. Tryn and Jake were standing with Zephyr in one of the stalls.

"Astraea, I'm so glad you're here!" Jake called. "You wouldn't believe what happened last night." He stopped and stared at the kitten in Astraea's hand. "What a freaky-looking cat!" His eyes flashed to Tryn. "Look at it. It's got wings!"

"Hiddles is not freaky," Astraea said. She marched over to Tryn. "What are you doing here? Don't you realize how dangerous it was to bring Jake here?"

"He's wearing my clothes, and from a distance he could pass for Titan. Believe me, coming here is a lot less dangerous than staying at Arcadia."

Astraea frowned. "But how did you know where Zephyr lives?"

Tryn shrugged. "I just did."

Zephyr came forward. "Astraea, how he knew doesn't matter. We have to talk. It's about your mother."

Astraea patted Zephyr on the neck. "Zeph, I'm so sorry about the way Mom treated you this morning. She's acting so weird. She just told me to get Hiddles out of the house and not to allow animals in again. And she didn't even care that I've been staying out at night. I just don't understand it."

"We do," Tryn said. "And it's not good."

"That's impossible!" Astraea started to pace. "I just saw my mother. It couldn't have been her being taken through the Solar Stream."

"I'm sorry," Jake said softly. "But we saw a woman with big white wings. Her head was covered, but Tryn recognized her voice and her wings. He's certain it was your mother."

"It was her," Tryn insisted. "I met her and your father when I first arrived here. It was at your grandfather's house. Hyperion is the one who arranged for me to come to Arcadia. I'm certain it was your mother being taken through the Solar Stream. A short time later, others in cloaks returned. They walked past the door where we were hiding, and when they did, this fell." Tryn held up a long white feather.

Astraea took the feather and frowned. It was a primary flight feather. These were the hardest to grow out. "I always know when my mother is going through a molt—especially flight feathers. But she isn't going through one now."

"Maybe they hurt her feathers when they tackled her," Zephyr suggested.

Astraea inspected the feather and then sniffed it. She frowned. "This isn't hers. My mother always perfumes her wings, but this doesn't even smell like a feather. It doesn't feel like one either." She looked back at Tryn. "That wasn't my mother you saw."

"It was," Tryn insisted. "At least it was your mother who was forced through the Solar Stream. Perhaps it wasn't her who came back."

"That doesn't make sense. Who else could it be?" Zephyr asked. "There aren't *that* many winged Titans."

Astraea was shaking her head. "If it really was my mother, what about my father? Where is he?"

"There were two being taken through. I wouldn't be surprised if the other was your father," Tryn said.

"Why?" Astraea cried.

"I don't know," Tryn acknowledged. "But what I saw last night is going to haunt me for the rest of my life. Those creatures in cloaks—they had pale grayish skin that looked like it was melting. You could barely see their eyes because of the folds of skin over them. They didn't have noses, and they could open their mouths really wide. They were eating those flat, dried animals whole."

Jake nodded. "They were going through them like

251

they were chocolate chips. I couldn't see them, but I could hear them. It was disgusting."

Astraea shook her head. "But if there were creatures like that here, I'm sure we would have seen them already. Or at least I would have in the new prison wing. But there was nothing like the things you described."

"We know what we saw," Tryn said. "Those things weren't Titans or Olympians. But judging by all the food they have stored down there, they've been here for a while."

"Tell them about the guy we heard talking," Jake suggested.

Tryn nodded. "All but one of them spoke in a language we couldn't understand. But there was one we could. We didn't see his face, but by the way he spoke, he sounded exactly like a Titan. When your mother tried to escape, one of the cloaked figures touched her with its bare gray hand and she stopped moving. It was like she passed out. The Titan-sounding man told them not to kill her yet. Then, after they dragged your parents through the Solar Stream, he said to the others who stayed behind, 'When they arrive, get them into position. Soon it will be time to make our move.'"

"Position," Jake repeated. "Kinda like an invasion or something—like they are putting their people in strategic positions. When the others arrived, one of them dropped the feather."

"He said not to kill her yet?" Astraea repeated in a haunted voice. "They plan to kill my mother? Why? Who are these people?" She shook her head. "No, it's not possible. There has to be some other explanation. The woman I saw this morning looked and sounded just like my mom. And she knew me and Zephyr. She was making ambrosia cakes and everything. How could an imposter know us?"

"I don't understand how it all works," Tryn said. "All I know is that last night we saw genuine monsters forcing two people who I'm convinced are your parents through the Solar Stream. After that, more came back through, including one with this feather. I don't know who they are or why they're here, but they scare me."

Astraea was more than scared. Her mother hadn't been herself that morning. The woman in her house had been cold and cruel. And . . .

"What is it?" Tryn asked. "I can see it on your face that you know something. You must tell us."

"I don't know what I know," Astraea said softly. "But—but my mother wasn't behaving like herself. She said something really strange. She said, 'I don't like Zephyr spending so much time around here.'"

"Wow, that's harsh," Jake said.

"No, you don't understand. First, my mother loves Zephyr. But more than that, she never speaks like we do. She's very formal and is always correcting us. She would never say 'don't.' It's always 'do not.'"

Zephyr snorted. "You're right! She said, 'I'm sorry' . . . she didn't say, 'I am sorry.'"

Astraea nodded. "And she didn't care about me being out late at night. Plus, she didn't wait to kiss me good-bye."

"What?" Zephyr whinnied. "That's definitely not your mother. She's always there when you leave and is the kissiest person I know."

"It sounds like someone is mimicking her but isn't doing it quite right," Tryn said.

"Mimicking?" Astraea repeated.

Tryn nodded. "It's a word my father uses. To mimic means to copy something or someone, or behave the same way."

"But how could they mimic my mother? It looks just like her."

"What if the creatures are shape-shifters or something?" Jake suggested. "I've seen lots of sci-fi movies and shows. They're always having stories about shape-shifting monsters."

"It's impossible," Astraea insisted.

"No, it's not," Tryn said. "Jupiter can change his shape, and so can a few other Olympians. Maybe those creatures can do the same."

"If that's true, why would they take my parents?"

"I don't know. . . ." Tryn rubbed his chin. "But your parents are very powerful people. Maybe they have been replaced to get close to Hyperion. Or even the Big Three."

"What?" Zephyr cried. "That's insane."

"Is it?" Tryn said. "If someone wanted to invade and take over Titus, it would be next to impossible because our leaders and people are too powerful. But what if they were quietly coming here and secretly replacing important people with their own?"

A cold chill ran down Astraea's spine. "Could it be possible?"

"I don't know for certain," Tryn said. "But it makes sense."

"We must tell someone," Zephyr said.

"Who?" Tryn challenged. "Who can we trust? If this is really happening, then anyone could be one of those things."

"What, a mimic?" Jake asked.

Tryn nodded. "Yes. It's the only explanation, and I think that's what we should call them. The Mimics."

"All right," Astraea said. "So how do we prove these Mimics exist? If they have really taken my parents, I need to get them back—and I need to warn my grandfather about them."

Tryn shook his head. "We can't tell anyone, at least not yet, because we don't know who we can trust. Think about it. If this is really happening, it is more dangerous than any war. It's insidious, silent, and maybe the greatest threat we have ever faced, because the takeover will happen without anyone realizing it until it's too late."

"That's heavy duty," Jake said.

Tryn nodded and looked at Zephyr. "Who else lives with you at this house?"

"Just me and my parents," Zephyr said. "No one comes here but Astraea."

"Good," Tryn said. "Then Jake can stay here."

"What?" Zephyr cried. "You want me to hide a human in my house?"

"That's a great idea," Astraea said. "Jake can't stay beneath Arcadia Two, not after everything he and Tryn have seen down there, and he can't stay in Tryn's room either. This is the perfect place for him. He can take care of Hiddles, too. Please let him stay."

Jake walked up to Zephyr and patted her on the muzzle. "Please, Zephyr. I can't go back there—it's too scary."

Zephyr shot a withering look at Astraea. "All right, he can stay, just as long as he cleans out my parents' stalls and feeds them."

Astraea repeated the message.

"Clean the stalls?" Jake cried. "Are you nuts? You can't expect me to go into Tornado Warning's stall. He tried to kill me when we got here! That stallion is wild!"

"That's because he doesn't know you yet," Astraea said. "Give him a few apples and he'll be fine."

"That's easy for you to say," Jake said. "He seems to like you."

"All right," Zephyr said. "You don't have to clean the stalls. Just don't make a mess."

Tryn told Jake what Zephyr had said, then turned back to her. "Actually, if it's all right with you, Zephyr, I might spend some time here too. We are going to need a safe place to meet and figure out what's happening."

"Yes," Astraea agreed. "Mom said I could spend the night here too."

"Did she?" Zephyr asked.

Astraea nodded. "I don't think she wants me home anymore. She said you and I were a distraction to my dad."

Zephyr snorted. "That's the proof right there. There is no way Aurora would ever call us a distraction."

"Or not punish me for being out late . . ." Fear settled in Astraea's eyes. "But if all this is true, we have to find my mother and father before they do what that man said and kill them."

Jake nodded. "We'll add them to the list of missing people: your parents and my sister, Molly."

23

"I DON'T WANT TO GO BACK TO THAT place," Astraea said as she, Zephyr, and Tryn walked slowly to school. "Arcadia isn't a school. It's the birthplace of an invasion."

"That is precisely why we *must* go back," Tryn said. "We must behave like we don't know anything. Besides, I need to go back and find something out."

"What?" Zephyr asked.

"I need to be sure that this is really happening before we plan our next move."

"So how do we do that?" Astraea asked.

"I have some ideas, but nothing solid at the moment. I'll let you know when I come up with something."

Astraea put her hand on Zephyr's neck as they walked. "My parents have been abducted, and he says he'll let us know. . . ."

"Great," Zephyr said sarcastically. "I can't wait."

They arrived at the school, and even though the sun was shining brightly, the trees were in bloom, and students milled around chatting, Astraea felt it had changed completely. Arcadia was now a place of mystery, suspicion, and darkness. Who could they trust? Were people actually being replaced by Mimics? Was this really a silent invasion?

Astraea said good-bye to Zephyr as she and Tryn went into their first class, ancient history, together. Once again they were taken outside as Minerva explained in great detail how to use the various weapons.

As she listened, Astraea started to wonder why Minerva constantly talked about the war and was trying to teach them to use weapons to defend themselves. Did she suspect something and wasn't saying? Was she trying to arm the students without them knowing it?

The morning passed in a blur as Astraea tried and failed to focus on learning. After lunch, she walked with Tryn and Zephyr to Vulcan's workshop, as they all shared the same class. They entered the workshop and took their seats at the rear. Vulcan entered, looking just the same as he always did. His clothes were filthy and worn. His face was haggard and pockmarked with scars, while his hands were gnarled and black from working at his forge.

Vulcan took his place at the front of the room and held up a piece of metal. "Today we are going to learn to craft jewelry."

Tryn leaned closer to Astraea. "See, he's not wearing his bracelet. There isn't even a mark on his arm where it was. But he never goes anywhere without it."

"What does that prove?" Astraea asked.

"That he's not the real Vulcan."

"Tryn," Astraea whispered, "if that's all you are basing your theory on, we're in trouble. Look at him. He looks just like Vulcan—dirty and messy as ever."

"That is not Vulcan, and I'll prove it." Tryn stood up. "Vulcan, I need to get a drink of water."

Vulcan's pockmarked face screwed up in a scowl. "Not now, Trynulus."

"But you know my problem. It's urgent."

Astraea touched his arm. "What problem?"

Tryn looked at her and gave a tiny shake of his head.

When Astraea understood, she called, "Yes, Vulcan, you know his problem. He needs a lot of water or—or he gets very dehydrated."

Everyone turned to look at Tryn, including the centaur Cylus, who was across the room with his friends. He started to laugh. "Poor Tryn, he has a problem. . . ."

Vulcan stood still, watching Tryn for a moment longer. "All right. Go ahead, but come right back. We are going to be heating metal, and you will not want to miss this."

"Thank you." Tryn looked back at Astraea before walking away from their table. Instead of going straight up the aisle to the front, he went around the back and then up the aisle where Cylus and his herd were standing.

When he walked past Cylus, he poked the centaur's rear flank with a sharpened pencil.

Cylus yelped and bucked. "You stabbed me!" He reared and kicked out his front hooves, striking

Tryn in the chest. Tryn was knocked backward and started to stumble and fall. He tried to catch himself but overcompensated and spun around, staggering toward the front of the room. He finally lost his balance completely and fell onto Vulcan, knocking him down to the ground and landing on top of him.

"Get off me!" Vulcan howled as his arms flailed out.

The class erupted into laughter as Tryn rolled away from Vulcan and climbed to his feet.

"What do you think you are doing, boy?" Vulcan demanded.

"Cylus kicked me," Tryn said softly.

"Not before you poked him with your pencil! Get out of my class this instant and go to the principal's office. I will deal with you there shortly."

"It was an accident," Tryn insisted as he stole a look back to Astraea and Zephyr and left the room.

"What was that all about?" Zephyr asked Astraea softly.

"I really don't know," Astraea said. She knew Tryn was opposed to violence—so why had he stabbed Cylus?

They didn't see Tryn again all afternoon. But when classes ended and Astraea and Zephyr had to report to the principal's office for their afternoon detention, they saw Tryn sitting in the corner of the outer office. His head was down and he didn't even look at them.

"Come in," Themis called.

When they entered the inner office, they saw Themis standing at the window. Her back was to them when she asked, "Do you two wish to tell me something?"

"Like what?" Zephyr said.

"You tell me," Themis countered.

"Well, we've had a good day at school and learned a lot . . . ," Zephyr said.

"That is not what I am talking about."

Astraea watched Themis closely. The tall woman's shoulders were tight, and her calf muscles looked knotted. If there was ever a visual definition of stress, Themis was it.

"I'm sorry," Astraea said. "What are you talking about?"

Themis turned, and her face was as tight as her

calves. Her eyebrows were together in a deep frown. "Perhaps you wish to explain why you were both seen entering Arcadia Two late yesterday afternoon."

Astraea remembered seeing the teachers hovering outside the school. They must have told Themis about her and Zephyr being there.

"Well?" Themis demanded.

"Well," Astraea started, "Zephyr and I finished here. But then I remembered seeing a mess on the third floor of Arcadia Two. It was outside Tom the sphinx's class. So I suggested we go and clean it up, since we had the broom and all."

"You saw a mess in another building and wanted to clean it up. Is that what you are telling me?"

"You said we shouldn't assume the night dwellers would always do it, so we did it instead," Astraea said.

Themis nodded, but the hardness never left her face. "So if you have energy enough to clean a mess in Arcadia Two as well as One, perhaps you should continue to do both buildings for the duration of your detention."

"What?" Zephyr cried. "That's not fair. We did

that as a favor to the night dwellers, but now we're being punished for our good deed."

Themis's eyes became stormy. "No, Zephyr, you and Astraea trespassed on property you were not authorized to enter. But if you are so set on doing it, then why shouldn't you clean both buildings?"

"Because it's not fair."

"Making you do all the buildings of Arcadia would not be fair," Themis said. "But it will happen if you do not stop arguing with me!"

"But—but no!" Zephyr cried.

Astraea slapped her hands on Zephyr's muzzle. She loved her best friend like a sister, but if Zephyr didn't stop soon, their detention would never end. She looked back at Themis. "We were wrong to go into Arcadia Two without permission, and we're sorry. If you want us to do both buildings, we will."

Zephyr was struggling to speak beneath Astraea's hand as her head bobbed up and down. But Astraea wouldn't let go and grasped Zephyr's muzzle tighter with both hands. "She's fine," Astraea said to Themis. "She just wants to thank you for your understanding."

"All right, but you won't be working alone tonight. . . ." Themis called into the outer office. "Trynulus, get in here."

Tryn entered the room with his head down. "Yes, Themis," he said formally.

"You should be ashamed of yourself, attacking Cylus like that. What will your parents say when they find out?"

"I am truly sorry," Tryn said.

"Sorry is not enough. Consider yourself on detention. Starting tonight, you are going to help Astraea and Zephyr sweep the floors of Arcadia One and Two." Themis's eyes settled firmly on Zephyr. "And *only* Arcadia One and Two—no more adventures. Do you understand?"

Tryn's head remained bowed. "Yes. Again, I am sorry."

Themis returned to her spot by the window and kept her back to them. "You may go now and get to work."

They left the room together. Astraea started to speak, but Tryn shook his head tightly and looked around as if to say they were being watched.

Astraea nodded. "The brooms are this way."

They remained silent the whole time they cleaned Arcadia One, moving from floor to floor until the marble shone. It was only when they walked outside and headed toward Arcadia Two that Tryn said his first words.

"Vulcan is a Mimic."

Astraea stopped. "What?"

"How could you tell?" Zephyr said. "Apart from tackling him, which I must say was really impressive, I didn't see anything to suggest it wasn't really Vulcan."

"How well do you know him?" Tryn asked.

"Not very," Astraea said. "I've seen him a few times."

"Did you know he has deformed legs?"

"Really?" Astraea said.

"Yes," Tryn said. "When he was a boy, he made new legs for himself so he could walk as well as the other Olympians and be as tall as them."

"All right," Zephyr said. "Good to know. Thank you for sharing that with us."

Tryn shook his head. "You don't understand.

When I tackled Vulcan today, I felt his legs through his long tunic and forge apron. They were soft flesh. But the Vulcan I know forged his legs from iron and gold. They are not flesh at all."

Astraea's mouth hung open. "So . . . so Vulcan is . . ."

"The real Vulcan is missing, and there is a Mimic who is pretending to be him. That's the proof we've been waiting for."

"So it's really true. My mother and maybe my father . . . ," Astraea mused.

"Have been replaced," Tryn finished for her. "I'm sorry. But I knew it was your mother I saw being forced into the Solar Stream."

"What do we do?" Zephyr said. "We have to get them back!"

"We will!" Astraea said. "We just need to figure out where they've been taken."

Tryn sighed. "I just wish I could talk to my dad. You know he was an agent with the CRU on Earth. He would know what to do."

"Yes," Astraea agreed. "He could help us. Maybe Emily can too!"

Tryn started to shake his head. "They can't. Emily,

Pegasus, and Riza returned to Xanadu right after the opening ceremonies and we can't get there."

"Why not?" Astraea asked. "If they can come here, we should be able to go there."

"Not anymore. After the first day at school, I went to Jupiter and told him this wasn't going to work for me. I asked him if I could use the Solar Stream arch to go home, but he said no."

"Really?" Astraea said. "You wanted to go home?"

"I know I don't fit in here," Tryn admitted. "I felt it was better for me to just go home. But Jupiter wouldn't let me."

Astraea felt terrible that Tryn was so unhappy he wanted to go home. She never imagined how difficult it would be for him to fit in. "Um, did Jupiter tell you why?"

"He said I had to grow up and learn to be independent and not run home whenever I had a problem. He said it was time Titus became fully independent, so he was going to declare that no one could use the Solar Stream anymore."

Astraea frowned. "What? That doesn't sound like Jupiter at all."

"I know. When he first said it, I didn't understand it. But now I think I do."

"Understand what?"

Tryn looked at both of them. "Jupiter is a Mimic too."

24

ASTRAEA COULD HARDLY SPEAK AS SHE, Zephyr, and Tryn cleaned Arcadia Two as quickly as they could. Knowing what lay beneath them, none of them wanted to linger in the school a moment longer than necessary.

When they finished, they returned the cleaning supplies to Arcadia One. Just as they left the school grounds, they heard voices shouting and hooves pounding the ground, charging right at them.

"Get him!" Cylus cried.

They were quickly encircled by Cylus and his herd of centaur friends. Zephyr reared and kicked out her hooves, driving some of the boys back, but there was no escape.

Cylus charged forward. His face was filled with rage and his arms were crossed over his chest. "If you think it was funny stabbing me today, freak, you have made a big mistake."

Tryn didn't seem that bothered as he faced Cylus. "I am sorry that I had to do that to you, Cylus. But I needed you to strike me."

Cylus frowned. "Wait. Is this some kind of trick? You wanted me to hit you?"

"I didn't want it, but I needed it," Tryn said. "I needed to learn something, and you helped me. Thank you."

"You planned that?"

"Of course," Tryn said. "You did exactly what I expected you to do."

That comment seemed to make Cylus angrier. "All right, freak, if you want me to hit you, fine. I'll hit you again!"

"Cylus, wait," Astraea called. "I know your mother—she's on the same council as my mom. What do you think she'd say if she knew you were threatening us?"

"She wouldn't care. These days she doesn't care

what I do or say as long as I leave her alone and don't distract her."

Astraea gasped. "Cylus, did your mother say you were a distraction? Is she acting differently?"

"Don't you talk about my mother!" Cylus said. "I don't care who you are, Astraea. No one talks about my mother."

"No, no, that's not what I mean!" Astraea said urgently. "Please, Cylus, I'm begging you to tell me. Has your mother changed? Does she prefer you out of the house and doesn't care where you go as long as you stay away? Because my mother doesn't want me around either."

Some of Cylus's gang were nodding their heads. "My mom has changed," one said. "Both my parents have," said another.

Cylus paused and raised a fist. "If you're trying to worm you way out of this, it won't work."

Zephyr reared high and then slammed back down to the ground. She moved in on Cylus. "Turn off your anger and listen to us! Something is happening here, and it's really dangerous for all of us."

Astraea joined Zephyr. "Cylus, we really need your

help." She looked at all the large, powerful centaurs. "We need all of your help. Titus is in genuine danger, and we don't know who we can trust anymore."

"You think you can trust us?" Cylus laughed. "You're stupider than I thought."

Tryn remained silent through most of the exchange. Finally he sighed. "I really didn't want to do this—I had hoped that we could reason with you, but you've left me no choice." He charged forward and wrestled Cylus to the ground. Though the centaur was much larger than Tryn, with four powerful hooves and two strong arms, there was nothing he could do to free himself from Tryn's grip.

Astraea was stunned at Tryn's strength. He managed to pin Cylus down with almost no effort at all, and no matter what Cylus did, he couldn't get up.

"Get off me!" Cylus cried. His hooves kicked air as he called to his friends, "Get him!"

As one of the centaurs moved forward, Zephyr jumped at him. "Oh no, you don't. This is between Tryn and Cylus. Let them settle it, and then we need to talk."

"Cylus, enough," Tryn said calmly. "You are wasting

precious time. I believe your mother has been abducted. Just like Astraea's parents, Vulcan, and several other Titans."

"What are you talking about?" Cylus continued to struggle.

Astraea knelt down beside Cylus while Tryn kept him pinned down. "Cylus, we are being invaded. If we don't stop them now, we could very well lose our world."

"Don't be so stupid," Cylus grunted. He was sweating as he continued to struggle. "Who would dare invade us?"

"We're calling them Mimics," Astraea said. "They're creatures that can change shape and look like us. If you stop fighting, we'll tell you more, because we really need your help to prove it."

"What do you want us to do?" one of Cylus's friends demanded.

Astraea looked at everyone. "Help us capture Vulcan."

Cylus finally stopped struggling, and Tryn was able to release him. When he gained his feet again, Tryn,

Astraea, and Zephyr explained their suspicions.

"That is why I hurt you," Tryn said. "So you would hit me and I could tackle Vulcan without raising suspicions. The real Vulcan has metal legs. The one in school today had flesh legs."

"You're all crazy," Cylus cried. He was rubbing his shoulder where Tryn had twisted his arm back. "That was Vulcan, not some stupid Mimic."

"Believe me, I know it sounds crazy," Astraea said. "But we've seen them. There is a huge labyrinth below Arcadia Two. There are rooms filled with containers of dead, dried animals. That's their food. We don't know how they're doing it yet, but they're taking our families through the Solar Stream and replacing them with other Mimics."

"And you seriously expect me to believe that my own mother is one of those Mimics?"

Astraea nodded. "Be honest with yourself. She has changed, hasn't she? You said she called you a distraction? My mother said those exact same words about me and Zephyr. We're distractions. She didn't care that I was out all night or that I'm going to stay at Zephyr's house."

Despite Cylus's angry outward demeanor, he was listening to them, and his expression revealed a trace of fear. Finally he said, "All right, so my mother has been acting weird for a while. That doesn't prove anything."

"It proves we're in trouble," Zephyr said.

Cylus shook his head. "But if that's not my mother, who is it and where's my real mother?"

"We don't know yet," Tryn said. "That's why we need to capture Vulcan so we can ask questions."

"Why Vulcan?" demanded one of the centaurs.

"Because I know the real Vulcan very well," Tryn said. "And I am one hundred percent convinced that the creature in class today wasn't him."

"And I'm convinced that it wasn't my mother this morning," Astraea added. "I haven't seen my father yet, which is also strange. He's always home for breakfast."

"Why are they taking our parents?" asked Cylus's best friend, Render.

"I don't know," Astraea admitted. "But my mother is on the council of advisers to Jupiter, and my father is the designer of the new prison."

"I heard about that," Cylus said. "Why do we need a bigger prison when there aren't any criminals here?"

"Exactly," Astraea said. "That's why I broke into the prison's new wing to see what was in there. It's filled with humans and creatures from other worlds."

"What?" Render cried. "Humans are here on Titus?"

"Yes," Astraea responded. "There were other creatures too, some really dangerous ones. I've seen them with my own eyes, and I've spoken to some of them. They don't remember being taken, just waking up here. I'm thinking they were brought here to keep my grandfather, Hyperion, and his security people distracted while the Mimics move in and take over."

Cylus paused. "I am not saying that I believe you, but I have seen some strange things lately."

"Me too," another centaur said. "My father is acting really strange."

"We've all seen strange things," Zephyr insisted. "But we can't tell anyone, because we don't know who to trust anymore. Anyone could be a Mimic."

Tryn looked at all of Cylus's friends. "I know you don't like me because I'm not a Titan or an Olympian, and that's all right. But you have to trust me. Tell me how many of you have noticed your parents behaving differently."

Four of the six centaurs raised a hand.

Tryn nodded. "Now I understand."

"Understand what?" Cylus challenged.

"Understand why some have been taken, and it's worse than I thought." He looked at Astraea. "Your mother and father are very influential because you are related to the Big Three. Your grandfather is Hyperion, and your father is the designer of the new prison, and Aurora is on Jupiter's council." He looked at Cylus. "Your mother is on the Big Three's ruling council as well." He looked at each of the other centaurs who had raised their hand. "And your parents are Jupiter's advisers."

"What are you saying?" Zephyr asked.

"Don't you see? The Mimics are taking the most powerful and influential Titans and Olympians first. This is how they're going to take over. They're quietly replacing our rulers one by one until there will be no one left to stand against them."

"You seriously expect me to believe this?" Cylus cried.

"Do you have another explanation?" Astraea challenged.

Cylus said nothing, but a member of his gang called Darek came forward. "I know something has happened

to my father. He's just not the same. He was teaching me how to shoot my bow more accurately. But lately he has no time for me. If you want to capture Vulcan, I'll help."

"Me too," said Render.

Finally Cylus came forward and poked a finger in Tryn's chest. "I don't like you, Tryn. I doubt I ever will. But I believe you." He looked at the others. "All right, we're in. Let's go get Vulcan."

They all headed over to Vulcan's forge but didn't find him there.

Astraea looked up to the setting sun. "It's getting late. He might be feeding beneath Arcadia Two."

"So what do we do now?" Cylus said. "Wait here for him to return?"

Astraea shook her head. "I've got a better idea. Why don't we all go to our homes and act like nothing is wrong? We can have our dinner and do all the things we normally do. After that, we can gather the supplies we need to capture Vulcan. Then we all meet up at Zephyr's house and go from there."

"I can bring a rope," Cylus offered.

"And I've got a big woven bag we can use if we have to," said Render.

 281

"I've got some chains," said another centaur.

"Excellent," Astraea said. "I guess we're ready."

Tryn stepped forward. "Remember, everyone, act normal. We can't let them know we suspect anything. If Mimics are really replacing our parents, *we* don't want to be replaced too."

Zephyr gave Cylus and his herd directions to her home. She stood with Astraea and Tryn, watching them leave. "I hope that wasn't a mistake. I don't like them knowing where I live—especially Cylus."

"It wasn't a mistake," Tryn said. "You saw his face. Cylus believed us. He doesn't like it, but he does. I just hope he doesn't mess up and let his mother know we suspect something."

"Me too," Astraea agreed. She looked at her two friends. "Why don't you two come to my house for dinner?"

Zephyr's ears went back. "But Aurora didn't want me there. Remember she called us a distraction?"

"Exactly," Astraea said. "Tonight will prove once and for all whether my parents have been taken and replaced by Mimics."

25

"MOM, DAD, I'M HOME." ASTRAEA LISTENED for a response, but just as on the previous evening, no one was there.

They walked through the house into the kitchen. The room was spotless—cleaner than it had ever been. On the marble counter was the ambrosia cake from the morning. The only pieces taken from it were the ones Astraea had grabbed on her way out. Neither her mother nor her father had touched it.

"Not home a minute and already this is weird." Astraea turned to Zephyr. "Have you ever seen our kitchen looking so clean and organized?"

Zephyr snorted. "Actually, no. Your family is

always so busy you eat on the run. No one has time to clean."

"Exactly," Astraea said.

She walked through the house, with Zephyr and Tryn following close behind. Everything was in its place, and there wasn't a speck of dust to be found. "I don't like this one bit," Astraea said. She led them through to her father's office, where he was working on the plans to the prison. But when Astraea tried the door, she discovered a lock had been put on it.

"This door never had a lock on it before," she said.

"Then it's good that I keep this with me." Tryn produced his lockpick set. He bent down, and within seconds the door was open.

"You've got a real knack for getting into places," Zephyr said. "Is there something you want to tell us, Tryn? Like maybe you're a thief or something."

Tryn's face remained calm. "I'm not a thief, but my dad taught me to always be ready for anything. Picking locks is only one of his tricks."

"Do we want to know the others?" Zephyr asked.

Tryn shook his head. "Don't think so."

They entered the office and Astraea's jaw dropped.

"Wow," she said, turning in a circle. "This isn't my dad's office. He's the messiest of all of us. This is way too organized."

"Astraea, get over here," Zephyr called. She was standing at the drafting table. "I don't think these designs are for the prison, but they look like cells."

When Astraea arrived, she saw plans laid out, but none she'd ever seen before. "You're right, that's not *our* prison, but it does look like one with all those cells." She peered closer and saw strange writing on them. "That's not Dad's handwriting—I can't read it."

Beneath the first page were similar pages filled with drawings of cells. Again, there was a lot of writing on them, but not in a language they could understand.

As they went through the plans, Tryn called, "Wait, stop! Go to the last page."

"Do you recognize this place?" Astraea asked.

"Maybe," Tryn said. "Just show me the last page."

Astraea lifted up the collection of pages and found the last one. The drawing showed narrow steps built along one wall and a long corridor that opened up into three massive cells.

Tryn groaned. "It's what I was afraid of."

"What? What do you see?" Astraea demanded as she studied the plan.

"Three immense cells on the bottom level."

"So?" Zephyr said. "Big cells for big prisoners."

"Yes," Tryn agreed. "The biggest. Those cells were built to hold the giant Hundred-handers."

"What? No," Astraea said. "The Hundred-handers were never in prison here. They were held in . . ."

Tryn started to nod.

"No," Astraea cried in a hushed voice. "It—it can't be."

"It is," Tryn insisted. He put the plans down and reordered them, then ushered Astraea and Zephyr out of the room.

"Hey, watch the feathers," Zephyr complained as Tryn shoved her to the door.

"Zephyr, move," Tryn grunted, pushing harder. "We have to get out of here right now, before they come home and find us." He closed the door after them and locked it tightly. "Astraea, you can't stay here tonight or any other night. Go to your room and grab some clothes. You're leaving with us."

Astraea started to move when Zephyr snorted loudly. "Stop! I am not moving another hoof until someone tells me what's happening. What were those plans?"

"Zeph, don't you remember your history?" Astraea asked. "The Hundred-handers were only ever imprisoned in one place. A horrible, wretched place—the worst place ever . . ."

"Let's pretend for a moment that I don't know what you're talking about, because I don't," Zephyr said. "What place?"

"Tell her," Tryn said.

Astraea took a deep breath. "The Mimics have taken my parents and everyone else they've abducted from Titus and are locking them up in *Tartarus*!"

Astraea's hands were shaking as she ran into her bedroom and started to pack a bag, while trying to make it look like she wasn't moving out. Zephyr was beside her, helping as best she could, while Tryn stayed outside keeping watch.

"Hurry!" Tryn called.

"I'm moving as fast as I can!"

Before Astraea could finish, they heard the front door open.

"They're back," Tryn called. "Hide your bag!"

Astraea tossed her bag out the window and ran out of her room, with Zephyr close behind her. Taking a deep breath, she, Zephyr, and Tryn walked through to the kitchen.

"Hi, Mom!" Astraea said lightly as her mother entered.

There was shock and a quick flash of dismay on her mother's face. "Astraea, I thought you were spending the evening at Zephyr's."

"I was—I mean, I am. I just came back to see if I could have some ambrosia cake for us." She walked up to the cake to cut a few pieces. "Mom, you remember my friend Trynulus."

Aurora frowned for a moment and then nodded. "Of course. Hello, Trynulus, it's lovely to see you again."

"Good afternoon, Aurora," Tryn said. "I hope you don't mind me being here."

"Not at all," Aurora said. "Astraea's friends are always welcome." Her eyes landed on Astraea. "But you know your father is due home any moment. I can't have you three distracting him while he works this evening."

"We won't," Astraea promised. "Once I get some ambrosia, we'll go."

"Take it all. I have already eaten and I'm sure your father has too." Aurora started to pack up the whole cake.

"Thanks, Mom," Astraea said. "Oh, I wanted to ask, are you starting to molt? I found a flight feather."

Aurora showed no reaction. "I don't think so."

"Maybe you should check. I thought it was mine." Zephyr opened her wings as wide as the kitchen would allow. "But it's not—they're all here."

Aurora looked at Zephyr and shook her head. She handed Astraea a container with the ambrosia. "Not now. I'll look later. Now run along and have fun."

"So it's still all right for me to spend the night at Zephyr's?"

"Yes, spend a few nights if you like. I know how close you two are." Aurora smiled, but it held no affection or humor.

Astraea nodded. "Great! So I'll see you later?"

"Yes, see you later." Aurora turned and left the kitchen.

Astraea stood watching her go. There was no hug or kiss good-bye. Her mother had just handed her the cake and left.

Astraea walked out of her house in a daze, followed by Tryn and Zephyr. She could hardly believe what had happened. If there was any lingering doubt in her mind that the woman she had seen in the morning wasn't her mother, this last encounter completely removed it.

"My mother has been replaced by a Mimic." Astraea spoke in a voice hushed by shock. The three of them went around to the back of the house to retrieve her bag from beneath her bedroom window. As they walked toward Zephyr's house, Astraea stopped. "They aren't going to get away with this. I won't let them."

"*We* won't let them," Zephyr insisted. "I love your parents as much as you do."

"Don't worry, we'll stop them," Tryn promised. "And we're starting tonight."

26

THEY ARRIVED AT ZEPHYR'S HOUSE AND found Jake sleeping on the bed that was usually Astraea's whenever she stayed over.

After getting Jake up, they gathered in the kitchen, and picked at the ambrosia cake while they told Jake what they'd discovered.

"Maybe that's where they've taken my sister. We have to go there to check," Jake said.

"We?" Tryn asked.

"Yes, we," Jake said. "If there's a chance that Molly is in that prison, I have to try."

Astraea was pacing the kitchen. "That's the problem;

I don't know how to get there. I know we need to use the Solar Stream, but I've never been in it."

"I have," Tryn said. "It was through the arch in Jupiter's palace. But now Jupiter won't let anyone use it."

Zephyr snorted, "If Jupiter is really a Mimic, that's how they're getting here. They're using the arch."

Tryn shook his head. "No, that's only for travel between Xanadu and here. They're using a different way in. Once we have Vulcan, we'll get him to tell us how they're doing it."

A knock on the front door stopped the conversation. "That must be Cylus and the others," Astraea said. She looked at Jake. "Stay in here until we're sure. We don't want anyone to see you."

Astraea and the others left the kitchen and headed into the living room. Astraea opened the front door and stood back to let Cylus and his herd in.

Cylus had a thick rope draped around his shoulder, while his best friend, Render, was carrying the large sack. "I hate to admit it, but you're right," Cylus said. "My mother has been replaced by a Mimic. I asked if I could stay out all night and she said yes. My real mother would never let me."

Several other centaurs were nodding. "My dad said the same thing . . . ," Render added.

Cylus puffed up his chest. "We're going to get Vulcan and he's going to tell us where my mother is or I'll kick the stuffing out of him."

"We think we know where they've taken our parents," Astraea said. "We just need to figure out how to get there."

"Where is she?" Cylus demanded. "What have they done with my mother?"

"She's in Tartarus with everyone else," Astraea answered.

Cylus reared up, and his face contorted with rage. "Tartarus! I'm going to kill Vulcan for taking her there."

The other centaurs snorted and pawed the floor with their sharp hooves.

"We're not killing anyone," Tryn insisted. "But we are going to ask him why they're here."

"And how to get to Tar-teer . . . Tar-tar . . . you know, that prison place." Jake entered from the kitchen. He stopped short when he caught sight of the centaurs. "Whoa, what—are—you?"

"Tartarus," Astraea corrected, coming up to him. "Jake, this is Cylus and his herd. They're centaurs."

Jakes eyes were huge as he walked all around Cylus. "You guys are totally awesome! I gotta take a selfie with you when this is over."

Cylus wrinkled his nose. "What are you? You stink."

Astraea said, "I told you the Mimics are bringing humans from Earth. Jake is one of them."

"This is a human?" Cylus cried. "A real one from Earth?"

"Yep." Jake nodded, still studying the centaurs. "I'm from Los Angeles. I was brought here a few days ago." He leaned closer to Cylus. "Are you for real? I mean, I've never seen anything like you before. You're like half man and half horse!" Jake reached for Cylus's chestnut back where it joined his torso, but the centaur caught hold of his arm.

"You touch me, human, and you will be pulling back a stump!" Cylus shoved Jake backward.

"Cylus, stop," Astraea said. "Jake didn't mean anything. He's never seen anything like us before and doesn't understand our ways." She looked at Jake.

"You must never touch a centaur unless they invite you to."

Jake nodded quickly and put his hands up. "Sorry, dude!"

"Dude?" Cylus said. "Is that an insult?"

"No, it's not! Cylus, calm down," Astraea cried. "We have more to worry about than your feelings. We're in trouble and we need to figure this out."

"What's to figure out?" Render said. "We're going to tie Vulcan up, put him in the sack, and then demand that he tell us how to get to Tartarus to free our parents or we'll thump him. It's simple."

Jake leaned closer to Tryn and whispered, "Are all centaurs this violent? He reminds me of the bullies back at my school."

Tryn nodded. "I've only ever met one that wasn't. He's a teacher called Chiron. The rest are as fiery as Cylus and his friends."

Cylus heard the remark and turned on Tryn. "Chiron isn't a true centaur and everyone knows it. He's a weak—"

"All of you, shut up!" Zephyr whinnied. "Cylus and Render, calm your tempers, and Jake, stop

asking stupid questions that annoy the centaurs. We have to plan our attack on Vulcan!"

"It's not me, it's him!" Cylus challenged.

"Yeah," Render huffed. "Stupid humans . . ."

Jake looked at Tryn. "What did Zephyr say?"

"She told you to stop asking questions that annoy the centaurs and that we have to plan the capture of Vulcan."

Jake nodded. "Sorry, Zephyr, you're right."

"Good!" Zephyr said. "Now, does anyone know where Vulcan is right now?"

Darek clopped forward. "Yes. Before meeting up with Cylus, I checked his forge. He's alone there now—but it's very open. If we're not careful, we are going to be seen interrogating him."

Astraea nodded and rubbed her chin. "Obviously we can't question him there. We're going to have to take him somewhere else."

"Bring him here," Zephyr offered. "No one ever visits me but you. We could keep him here and no one would ever know."

"And it's not too far from the forge," Darek offered. "Here is the best place."

"Well then, let's stop all this talking and go," Cylus said impatiently as he clutched the rope on his shoulder. "I want my mother back, and he is going to tell me how to do it!"

27

JAKE RELUCTANTLY AGREED TO STAY behind and prepare the stable to keep Vulcan while everyone else headed out.

"We'll meet you there," Cylus said, as he and his herd trotted off into the darkness the moment they were outside.

"It's all right," Zephyr called after them. "Don't worry about us, we'll be fine. Just leave us here and we'll catch up with you. . . ."

"That's centaurs for you," Astraea said as she, Zephyr, and Tryn took a different route to Vulcan's forge. "They don't want to be seen with us in case it tarnishes their tough reputations."

"Well, I don't want to be seen with them, either," Zephyr said. "I just hope Cylus doesn't do anything stupid before we get there. His hands and hooves work much faster than his poor little brain."

"He'll wait for us," Tryn said. "You saw the look in his eyes. Despite his angry exterior, he's genuinely frightened about his mother. He wouldn't do anything to endanger her."

The evening air was fragrant and warm as they walked down the quiet, tree-lined path toward Vulcan's forge. Night dwellers were out and nodded in greeting as they passed. Animals that only came out at night strolled through the parks, unbothered by their presence. An owl, almost as large as Astraea, swooped down from a tree branch and snatched away a large squirrel.

Up ahead a Titan couple was walking hand in hand and seemed to have eyes only for each other. Astraea stole a look at Tryn but looked away quickly when he caught her staring at him.

Zephyr watched their exchange and nudged Astraea playfully with her muzzle. "Something you want to say, Astraea?"

Astraea looked at her sharply, but then gazed around at the beauty of Titus and the people out walking, unaware of the danger they were facing. "It all looks so peaceful out here." She stopped and faced her two friends. "We're doing the right thing, aren't we? I mean, we're not crazy, something is happening here, right?"

"Oh it's happening," Tryn said. "I am absolutely certain—especially after what I saw beneath Arcadia Two. There's no doubt about it. This is just the calm before the storm, and if we don't stop it now, it might be too late."

"That's what I'm afraid of," Astraea said. "I don't know who to trust anymore. If we can't trust our own families, what's left?"

"I know," Tryn agreed. "When we get Vulcan, maybe we'll finally understand."

They walked the rest of the way in silence. It wasn't far to the forge, but they were drawing their journey out, hoping that by the time they grabbed Vulcan, the streets would be as empty as possible.

When the forge was just half a block away, the herd of centaurs appeared from the opposite direction.

"What took you so long? We've been circling this block forever," Cylus challenged. "Was it that smelly human?"

Zephyr snorted, "Hey, no one calls him smelly but me. You got that, Cylus?"

"Both of you, please," Astraea said. She looked at Cylus. "His name is Jake, and no, we're not late because of him. We took our time so the streets could clear a bit. We don't want to be seen."

"Oh . . . yeah, good plan," Cylus agreed. "We looked inside the forge. Vulcan is still there. We think he's alone."

Tryn nodded. "Good. I want to go in first and see if I can get him in the back area of the forge. Then you guys can come in and grab him from behind."

"Why do you get to go in first?" Cylus challenged. "Maybe you want to warn him or something." The centaur looked at his herd. "I don't trust this silver-skinned weirdo, do you?"

The other centaurs muttered and shook their heads.

"Well, you're going to have to trust me, because Vulcan knows me better than all of you. You saw for yourself in class, he knew my name. So even if he is a Mimic, he somehow knows me. I can distract him."

"Cylus, you're wasting time. Just shut up and let's get this done," Zephyr said.

"All right," Cylus said to Tryn. "But we're watching you. You do anything to ruin this and I'll stomp you into the ground."

A flash of anger crossed Tryn's face but vanished just as quickly. "You could try, but you wouldn't succeed." He nodded to Astraea and walked toward the forge. "Count to twenty and then come in."

When he was gone, Astraea stood before Cylus. "I know you don't like him, Cylus, but trust me, Tryn is strong. I mean *really* strong. He's already shown you that once. You'd have to be a big idiot to take him on again."

"Who are you calling an idiot?"

"You, if you don't realize Tryn is trying to help save Titus. Now come on, that should be twenty. It's time to go." Astraea stormed down the street, with Zephyr close beside her.

Halfway down they turned to the right, up the cobbled path that led to Vulcan's area. The big double doors were open, and they could see the massive hearth in the center of the forge. The flames were lit, but barely. That wasn't like Vulcan at all. He always kept his hearth roaring. How could anyone who knew him not notice?

Tryn was talking to Vulcan. When he caught sight of Astraea and the others, he walked deeper into the forge and invited Vulcan to follow.

"Let's go," Astraea said. She looked at the centaurs. "Cylus, you and your herd catch hold of him. We'll watch at the door to make sure no one comes in."

A dangerous grin lit Cylus's face. "Sure, we'll get him."

"Don't hurt him," Zephyr warned. "He can't tell us what he knows if you hurt him."

Cylus looked back at Zephyr and snorted. "We won't hurt him—not yet anyway. But I'm warning you, if he doesn't tell me what I want to know, I won't make any guarantees about how long he stays unhurt."

"That's fair," Zephyr said. She looked at Astraea. "It is. It's fair."

They quietly entered the forge. Astraea and Zephyr

remained at the doors and watched for anyone coming. "It's still clear. Go get him," Astraea whispered.

She split her attention between keeping guard at the doors and following the centaurs as they crept up on Vulcan. Nerves and doubt bunched in her stomach. She had never imagined in her life that she would be part of a plan to attack a senior Olympian.

Tryn was still standing with Vulcan, asking questions about how to use some of the tools in the workshop. Though he was talking to Vulcan, his eyes remained on the centaurs as they inched closer.

When they were close enough, Tryn nodded.

"Now!" Cylus cried. He threw his rope around Vulcan, pinning his hands to his sides as Render and another centaur, Panis, charged forward with the large sack. They pulled it over Vulcan's head and butted him forward to knock him to the ground.

"What is this madness?" Vulcan howled. "Release me this instant."

"We know you're not Vulcan," Cylus called as he wrapped more of the rope around the thrashing body.

"Don't be ridiculous," Vulcan shouted through the sack. "Of course it's me!"

Tryn moved down to Vulcan's legs and pulled up his trouser hem, revealing his bare skin. "Vulcan never wears trousers, even in the forge, and he doesn't have organic legs. You are not him! We know you have been replacing Titans and Olympians! Now we want to know who you are and why."

Vulcan stopped struggling and went still. "You don't want to know who we are, spawn," he said in a soft, threatening voice. "Now release me before I lose my temper."

"He's talking too much," Panis said. "Why don't we hit him with something hard to knock him out?"

"You do that and it will be the last thing you ever do—" Vulcan's hand shot out from under the sack and latched onto one of Panis's hooves. From her vantage point at the door, Astraea couldn't see his face, but she watched as the centaur collapsed on the filthy floor of the forge.

"Panis, no!" Cylus shouted. "Vulcan, let go!"

Astraea looked over at Zephyr. "Stay here and keep watch. I'm going back to help!" She ran deeper into the forge, only to discover a horrifying sight. Panis was limp on the ground, with the false Vulcan's bare hand wrapped around his pale hoof. When Render caught hold of the hand and tried to pull it away, he froze and also collapsed.

Cylus roared in rage and reared up. He crashed down on the sack with both front hooves, while Darek kicked at Vulcan's head and another centaur kicked his back. As Cylus rose up to do it again, Tryn dashed over to the workbench and picked up a cutting tool. He knelt down beside Render and, without touching Vulcan's hand, cut away the fingers wrapped around Panis's hoof.

Inside the sack, Vulcan howled and pulled back his arm just as Cylus came down on him with a second blow. After that, Vulcan went still.

Astraea knelt down beside Panis. She couldn't see the blond centaur breathing, so she lay her head against his chest to listen for a heartbeat. "No, no, it can't be!" she cried. "It just can't." Astraea looked up at the others. "Panis is dead."

28

SILENCE FILLED THE FORGE AS EVERYONE looked at the dead centaur. Cylus didn't believe Astraea and had to check for himself before he could acknowledge that his friend was really gone.

Across from them, Render came around and managed to make it to his hooves but was woozy. "What happened to me?" He was swaying on his feet, and his face had gone pale.

Tryn's voice was soft and filled with shock. "You touched Vulcan's hand while it was on Panis. It wasn't long, but it was enough to knock you out. Whatever these Mimics are, they're lethal to the touch. We have

to get Vulcan out of here before he wakes and tries to touch us again."

"Wait, we can't leave Panis here," Astraea said. "We have to tell his parents what happened."

Cylus's face was red, and he looked like he was on the verge of tears. "His parents aren't here. They have been taken too." He took a deep breath and looked up at his herd. "We have to hide him—Panis would understand, I know he would. Let's take him into the storeroom. Then Vulcan will tell me what I want to know or I will kill him!"

While the centaurs removed their dead friend, Tryn knelt down and looked at the fingers he had cut away. As he, Astraea, and Zephyr watched, the fingers seemed to melt into a pool of gray goo.

"What are you?" Tryn asked the unconscious Vulcan softly.

When the others returned, Tryn rose. He walked back to the workbench and picked up several pairs of the thick forge gloves that Vulcan and his assistants used when they were working with hot metal. He handed out the gloves and kept a pair for himself. "We have to be sure that none of us touch him

barehanded. I'm sorry, but we have to get going before Vulcan wakes up."

The journey back to Zephyr's house was one of the longest Astraea had ever made. She and Zephyr kept watch for anyone while the centaurs dragged the unconscious Vulcan behind them.

When they made it to the stable at the rear of Zephyr's house, they found that Jake had cleared out one of the stalls and set up a kitchen chair in preparation for their prisoner. They hauled Vulcan inside.

"I'll go get Jake," Tryn said. He looked back at Cylus. "Don't do anything until I'm back."

Astraea expected a sharp reply from the centaurs, but Cylus stayed silent and simply nodded as he watched Vulcan on the stall floor. When Jake and Tryn returned, Jake approached Cylus. "Tryn told me what happened. I'm so sorry about your friend."

"What do you know about it?" Cylus said angrily.

"Enough to know what it feels like when you lose someone you care about," Jake said. "I lost it when my grandmother died last year."

"I didn't care about Panis," Cylus said gruffly.

"Cylus, stop it," Astraea said. "We're all in this together. You don't have to hide your feelings from us. I know Panis was your friend, so why can't you admit that you're suffering?"

Tryn came forward. "Because to admit that would also mean admitting that this is very real, and it's frightening to all of us to realize that those Mimics can kill us."

"I'm not frightened of anything!" Cylus shouted.

"Then you're stupid," Zephyr said. "Because you should be frightened of them. We all should be if we want to survive this."

Jake frowned. "But I thought you guys were immortal because of all that sweet stuff you eat. How come Panis died?"

"We are," Astraea said. "Or at least we were until these Mimics came along."

Tryn reached for the sack and hauled Mimic Vulcan up into the chair. He undid the outer rope and pulled off the sack, but then tied him to the chair. Just as he finished, Vulcan opened his eyes.

"Are you happy now? Think you've got me nice and secure?" Mimic Vulcan asked casually. He looked around. "So, how many of you know the truth about us?"

"We're asking the questions," Cylus said, nearly spitting out the words. "You killed Panis, so I'm this close to doing the same to you. Now I know you've taken my mother. Tell me, how do I get to Tartarus?"

"So you know about Tartarus...," Vulcan mused. "Very interesting. Tell me, who told you about that?"

Tryn stepped closer. "No one told us. We figured it out."

Vulcan raised an eyebrow. "I hardly think so. You are just spawn. Who is your commander?"

"I told you, we ask the questions!" Cylus said.

Vulcan smiled, and it chilled Astraea to the bone. "All right, little spawn, ask your silly questions and I will answer. But know this: I have a few of my own."

"Where do you come from?" Astraea asked.

"Does it matter?" Vulcan answered. "If I were to tell you the name of our world, would it make any difference to you?"

"Try us," Tryn said.

Zephyr whinnied. "Or are you frightened?"

"Me frightened of you? Hardly. All right, we come

from Tremenz in the Zolcar system, and our queen is Langli. See, it means nothing to you—but everything to me."

"So why are you here?" Tryn asked. "If you come from Tremenz, what does your queen want from us?"

"She wants nothing from you. You have no value to us," Mimic Vulcan said casually. "It is Titus we want for ourselves. Soon you will be gone and Titus will be ours. The queen will divide and we will spread further."

"You want to take Titus?"

"No, we are *going* to take Titus, and you can't stop us." Vulcan looked past everyone as though he expected others to arrive.

Astraea followed his gaze. "What are you looking for? No one knows you're here."

Vulcan smiled at her. "Are you so sure, Astraea? If you must know, I am waiting for your commander. Talking to you is a waste of my time."

"We have no commanders," Cylus spat. "We figured out who you were all on our own. We know you've taken our parents."

"Foolish spawn," Vulcan said. "Do you think I

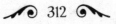

care what you think you know? I only let you capture me so you would bring me to those in charge. Now, who and where are they?"

"You didn't let us capture you," Darek said. "We overpowered you."

"No, I allowed you to capture me. I was awake the entire time and heard everything you said. Now answer me, who else knows about us?"

"Enough of us to stop you," Tryn said.

Vulcan studied Tryn and everyone in the stall for some time. He tilted his head to the side. "How strange that foolish little spawn have discovered our presence. I believe you, you have no commanders. But you also have no others with you—you are alone in your knowledge, and it will die with you."

"Why does he keep calling us spawn?" Render asked. The young centaur approached Vulcan. "What does it mean?"

Jake stepped forward. "Spawn means offspring, or in our case, kids. We are the spawn of our parents."

Mimic Vulcan's eyes landed on Jake. "I am surprised you are still free, human. We have kept Hyperion busy with all the visitors we've been bringing to Titus."

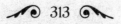

Jake nodded. "Sorry to disappoint you, but I'm still free and intend to stay that way."

"Not for long. After we take Titus, your world is next."

"You won't be taking Titus or Earth," Tryn said. "We will stop you."

"There is nothing you can do to stop us. You are just weak little creatures with no power of your own. Now that I know you have no commanders, I need not be concerned. This interrogation is over. . . ."

"I'll show you how weak I am!" Before anyone could stop him, Cylus launched an attack on the Mimic with both his gloved fists. He wrapped his hands around Vulcan's neck and started to squeeze. "This is for Panis!"

"Fools," Vulcan laughed. "You have no idea what you are up against. Now you will learn there is no opposing us. None of you will survive the night to warn the others."

Mimic Vulcan didn't so much break free of his bindings as melt through them as though he was made of soft dough. He stood and caught hold of Cylus's hands and tossed the young centaur across

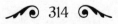

the stable. Cylus struck a stall door and crumpled to the floor in an unconscious heap.

Render charged the Mimic and punched his face with his gloved hand. But the hand went right through the flesh as though it was liquid. The Mimic's face then closed around it, locking his hand in place. Mimic Vulcan smiled and reached for Render's neck. He didn't squeeze—he didn't have to. With just the light grip, Render's eyes rolled back in his head and he collapsed.

"Let him go!" Tryn cried. But as he caught hold of Render, Mimic Vulcan's other hand shot out, clutching Tryn by the arm. Tryn gasped and crumpled to the stable floor.

"No!" Jake cried as Tryn fell.

"You should have stayed hidden, human; you might have lived a little longer!" Vulcan caught hold of Jake and in seconds, he too was unconscious on the floor.

Zephyr reared and called to the centaurs, "Everyone, fight before he kills them!"

As they charged, more hands sprang out of the Mimic's soft body and shot out toward the centaurs and Zephyr. As soon as the hands caught hold of

the attackers, they all froze and then dropped to the floor, unconscious.

Astraea watched in horror as her best friend crumpled under the Mimic's deadly grasp. Vulcan didn't have to do anything other than touch them, and the centaurs and Zephyr were defeated.

"Zephyr!" Astraea cried.

"Do not worry, Astraea. I have a hand just for you."

Another hand shot out, reaching for her. But Astraea was faster and darted away. She might not be able to fly with her small wings, but flapping them gave her the speed on the ground she needed to keep out of his reach.

"Release them!" she shouted, as she looked around for any kind of weapon to use against him. She saw a pitchfork against the stall wall and grabbed it. Just as she charged Vulcan, she caught sight of Nesso crawling onto one of the Mimic's hands. The small snake opened her mouth wide, and her two long fangs bit into the flesh of Vulcan's wrist.

The Mimic shrieked and pulled all his hands back into his body as strange, choking sounds filled the stable.

Astraea looked at the Mimic and screamed. He was staggering on his feet as his face started to melt and drip onto the floor. In fact, his whole body was melting into a pool of gray goo.

Astraea dashed forward and pulled Jake and then Tryn away from the spreading mess. After that, she struggled to get Zephyr away from it before it touched her. She was out of breath by the time she finished dragging all the heavy centaurs away as well.

The gurgling continued for several minutes until Mimic Vulcan had completely dissolved into a large gray puddle.

Astraea knelt and checked on Zephyr. She was breathing—they all were except for the fake Vulcan. The imposter had managed to bring them down with no effort—including Zephyr, the biggest of them all. If it hadn't been for the little snake, everyone would have died.

Jake was the first to stir. He shook his head, sat up, and looked around. "What happened?"

"Vulcan grabbed you and you collapsed," Astraea said. "No one could stop him until Nesso bit him. Then he just melted. That's what's left of him over there."

"Nesso saved us?" Jake reached up to his neck and frowned when he felt she wasn't there. "Where is she?"

"I—I don't know," Astraea said. "She was still biting Vulcan when he pulled his hands away." She gazed around and saw the bright colors of the snake lying in the middle of the gray puddle. "There she is."

Jake crawled over and prepared to pick Nesso up. She was covered in thick gray slime.

"Don't touch her with your bare hands," Astraea warned. "That stuff may still be lethal."

Jake pulled on the gloves from Vulcan's forge and reached into the puddle for Nesso. He wiped her off and looked closer. "Nesso?" His desperate eyes went to Astraea. "She's not breathing." Tears started down his cheeks as he cradled the snake. "Nesso, no, please, don't be dead. . . ."

It took several minutes for the others to recover. They clambered slowly to their feet and gathered around Jake. Tryn knelt beside him. "She saved all of us. We will always be grateful."

Jake sniffed in misery. "I—I don't know what's wrong with me. I only knew her for a short time, but I feel like part of me has died."

Cylus clicked his tongue. "Stupid human, crying over a dead snake. You didn't see me cry when Panis died."

Astraea turned on him. "Hey, that dead snake just saved your life! You think you and your herd are so strong? Look at you. Vulcan had you down faster than the rest of us. All he had to do was touch you and it was over."

"We would have beaten him," Cylus said.

"Yeah," Darek agreed. "No one defeats a centaur."

Tryn rose up and pointed to the puddle of gray matter. "He just did! He beat all of us. I have never encountered such a creature. With one touch I couldn't move. He drained all my energy. I couldn't fight him—I couldn't do anything!" He looked at the group. "This is worse than I imagined possible. How can we defeat an enemy that we can't even touch?"

"I don't know," Astraea said. "But at least we know how to recognize them now. They won't touch us until they want to hurt us. So we just look for those who avoid physical contact."

"Then what?" Cylus demanded. "How do we defeat them?"

"I—I will help. . . ."

Jake gasped and opened his hands. "Nesso, Nesso, you're alive!"

"I feel terrible. That big monsssster isss bad. Very, very bad. I could tassste the badness in him."

Jake pulled off his gloves and held the snake close as he started to tear up again. "She's alive!"

Astraea exhaled in gratitude. She stroked the small, colorful snake. "Thank you, Nesso. You saved all our lives."

"I am glad I could help," she said. *"And that you will live. But I don't undersssstand. I bit the one that brought me here and nothing happened. Why did thisss one die?"*

When Jake translated, Cylus came closer. "You can talk to it?"

"Her," Jake corrected. "Yes, I can. Those creatures brought her here from another world, but she doesn't know where it is. But I don't understand it either: If Nesso couldn't hurt them before, why could she now?"

"I really don't know," Tryn admitted, rubbing his neck. "But it is important that we find out. Nesso is the only one who could stop Vulcan. Was it just him who was susceptible to her venom, or will it affect all of them now?"

Astraea shrugged. "I hope it's all of them. She's our only hope."

Tryn walked over to the puddle that had once been the Mimic. All that remained was a pile of empty clothes and the wet, gray mess. "Look there are no bones, just this goo."

Astraea gasped. "Wait! He's not the first to die. I heard my father talking to my mom before they were taken. He said they were finding these gray puddles around the prison. He didn't know what they were. But he described the same thing. It's the Mimics. When they die, they turn into this liquid."

"What killed those ones?" Zephyr asked. "We know Nesso killed Vulcan, but what about the others?"

"I don't know," Astraea said. "Until now, we didn't even know it was dead Mimics."

Zephyr was staring into the puddle. "Hey, look, he might have been a bag of goo, but he still wore nice jewelry. He left a ring behind."

Tryn reached for a hay fork and brushed the ring

out of the puddle. Careful not to touch it with his bare hands, he used the gloves to clean it off.

Cylus and his herd backed up. "That is disgusting! I cannot believe you actually did that."

With the gray goo off the ring, Tryn inspected it closer. He started to smile. "I'd do more than that to get my hands on this."

"What is it?" Astraea asked.

Tryn held up the ring. "The key to winning the war."

"What war?" Cylus demanded. "What are you talking about?"

Zephyr snorted. "Haven't you been paying attention? Didn't you hear him saying they were taking Titus from us? Of course it's a war. But not like any that's been fought before. This one is silent, and the only weapon they use is their touch."

"Exactly," Tryn agreed. "But this Mimic has just given us a big weapon to use against them." He handed the ring to Astraea. "It's one of the gems I told you about. This ring will open the Solar Stream."

"The Solar Stream?" Astraea repeated. "How? You said all the gems were on Xanadu."

"All but one," Tryn responded. "There was one lost on Earth. This may be it but I don't know how the Mimics got it."

"Perhaps there are more you don't know about," Zephyr suggested.

"Could be," Tryn said.

Astraea inspected the ring. "This is fantastic." She looked over to the mess that was Vulcan. "I thought we might be able to stop them ourselves, but we can't. We need help from those more powerful than us."

"Who?" Zephyr asked.

Astraea looked at her best friend. "You're not going to like this, but you know who."

"Oh no," Zephyr said quickly. "No, no, no. Don't say it. Don't even think it!"

"We have to. We can't fight these Mimics alone."

"What are you two talking about?" Jake asked.

Astraea looked at everyone. "We have to go to Xanadu to get Emily Jacobs and Pegasus."

29

"OPEN IT NOW," ASTRAEA SAID TO TRYN. "Every moment we delay, they could be taking more Titans away."

"She's right," Cylus agreed. "I want my mother out of Tartarus, and if Pegasus and the others can help, I want to go ask them now."

Tryn looked at the ring and nodded. "You're right. This is bigger than us." He walked up to the stall wall and held up the ring. "Take us to Xanadu!"

Nothing happened.

"Xanadu," Tryn repeated. He looked at the ring and gave it a shake, and then called out Xanadu a final time, but nothing happened.

Cylus snorted. "You said the ring opened the Solar Stream. You lied to us."

"No, I didn't," Tryn said. He studied the ring. "It looks just like the gem from Emily's ring. I could have sworn they were the same."

"Well, it's not," Zephyr said. "We're on our own here."

"No, we're not. We can still get to Xanadu," Tryn said. "There's the arch in Jupiter's palace. We could go there and use it."

"But Jupiter said you couldn't use it," Astraea said.

"Yes, but I believe Jupiter is a Mimic. So I'm not going to listen to anything he—or it—says. I understand if you don't want to come with me. It will be dangerous. But I am going to the palace to try."

"Hey, you're not leaving us behind," Cylus said.

"Yeah," cried the other centaurs.

"Or us," Astraea agreed, standing with Zephyr. "If you're going to the palace, so are we."

"You betcha," Jake agreed. "Let's go."

Astraea turned to him. "Wait. You're not coming."

"What do you mean I'm not coming? Of course I am."

"Jake, it's too dangerous for you," Astraea said. "You could get caught."

"So could you," Jake insisted. "Besides, I'm carrying our special weapon." He held up Nesso. "I'm the only one who can understand her in case we get into trouble."

"*Yesss,*" Nesso said. "*I can help, but only if Jake comesss.*"

"That's blackmail," Tryn said when Jake repeated the snake's message.

"No, it's just smart business," Jake finished. "If Nesso goes, I go."

"Fine!" Cylus shouted. "I don't care who comes. Let's get going!"

They left the stable and started the long walk to Jupiter's palace. This time the centaurs stayed with them. Astraea was sure it had nothing to do with friendship. The centaurs realized that staying close meant there was a small snake that could protect them.

The situation was grim, but it still didn't stop Jake from being awestruck by all the sights of Titus. "This place is unreal," he said to Astraea. "I wish my mom could see it. She'd be blown away."

Astraea frowned. "We don't have strong winds. She couldn't be blown away unless she was very light."

"I meant amazed," Jake corrected.

Each step was a new discovery for Jake, and for Astraea as she tried to see her world through his eyes. They walked past some night dwellers, who smiled at them, showing their sharp teeth.

Jake turned and watched them walk away. "You have vampires here?"

"What's a vampire?" Astraea asked.

"No," Tryn said. "The night dwellers are not vampires. They just look like them—at least that's what my dad told me."

"They really do look like them," Jake agreed. "Did you see those teeth?"

"Enough talking," Cylus complained. "Shut up and just keep walking. You are slowing us down, human."

Jake leaned closer to Astraea. "I don't think he likes me very much."

Astraea looked over at Cylus and the centaurs. "They don't like anyone who isn't a centaur very much. It's just the way they are."

Cylus turned back to Astraea and shot her a dirty look.

"What?" Astraea said. "It's true, isn't it? You don't like anyone else."

"So?"

"All of you, shut up!" Zephyr said, walking beside Astraea. "You two would argue over anything, wouldn't you?"

As they got closer, they saw Brutus the giant standing outside the palace, staring at it.

"Oh wow!" Jake cried. "Everyone, look! There's a giant, I mean a real live giant! He's massive."

Astraea slapped her hand over Jake's mouth. "Be quiet! Giants have really good hearing!"

Jake eyes were huge as he pointed at Brutus and tried talking beneath her hand.

"Yes, Brutus is a giant, we know. He works at our school. But Jake, you have to be quiet, please!"

But it was too late. Jake's voice had caught Brutus's attention, and he took two long strides to reach them. He bent down closer to the ground to ask, "What are you all doing out so late?" He paused and started to sniff the air. "What is that? I have not smelled something like that since . . ." He gasped and his eyes shot to Jake. "You! What are you doing here?"

"Brutus, please," Astraea said. "We can explain!"

"You can explain what you are doing walking around with a human in the middle of the night?"

"Yes, we can," Astraea said. "I promise. But first, I need to touch your hand." She reached out to the giant.

"Astraea, what are you doing?" Zephyr asked.

"Trust me, I have to do it," Astraea said back.

"But if he's one, as a giant, his touch could kill you—or he could squish us with his foot," Cylus said.

Brutus huffed. "How dare you, Cylus. You know I would never hurt anyone. I should tell your mother what you just said."

"Good luck with that!" Cylus shot back.

"Please, Brutus, just touch my hand and we can tell you," Astraea said.

The giant frowned and reached out a massive finger to let Astraea touch it. When nothing happened, she grasped it with both hands and looked back at the others. "He's safe."

"Of course I am safe to be around," Brutus said indignantly.

"I don't mean that," Astraea said apologetically. "I mean you're you and not a Mimic."

"What is a Mimic?"

"We should tell him," Tryn said. "We need all the help we can get, but not here. Let's get away from the palace. We don't want Jupiter to see us."

"See what?" Brutus said. "See that you are hiding a human?"

"That's the least of our worries," Zephyr said. "Come with us and we'll tell you."

They moved away from the palace and entered a large park lined with marble statues. The night dwellers were tending to the grounds but cleared away when Brutus settled down on the grass. He lay down to be closer to them. "All right, I am listening. . . ."

They stood beside the giant's head and told him everything they'd been through, starting with the opening ceremonies, when Astraea had witnessed the capture of the human, up to Vulcan melting in the stable.

"If you go to the stable at my house, you'll see what's left of the Mimic Vulcan," Zephyr said. "But don't touch it without gloves, it's still dangerous."

Cylus remained silent through most of the exchange but came forward and lowered his head. "Brutus, please go to Vulcan's forge and find Panis's body. Take him somewhere safe until this is over. When we free his parents from Tartarus, they will want to see him and honor him properly."

"Yes, do it, please," Render agreed. "He doesn't deserve to be left in the storeroom."

Brutus sat up and looked around.

Astraea expected him to laugh at them or even accuse them of telling stories. Instead he rubbed his chin and nodded. He lay down again and spoke very softly. "I knew something was going on, but I was not sure what. So many strange things are happening." His eyes were shadowed in sadness as he looked down on them. "Jupiter has ordered me to leave my post at Arcadia. I have been assigned to the outer zone of Olympia to keep watch over the nectar orchards. I am to leave here tomorrow."

Astraea gasped and looked at Tryn. "You were right about Jupiter. This proves he's a Mimic. The real Jupiter would never remove Brutus. But they're sending him away so he can't challenge them."

"Do you really think Jupiter is one of those things?" Brutus asked.

"Mimics," Tryn said. "They look like us, but if they touch you, you get weak. If they touch you too long, it's deadly—that's what happened to Panis."

"I have never heard of such things," Brutus said.

"That's why we're here," Astraea said. "We're hoping to use the arch in the palace to get to Xanadu to ask Emily Jacobs and Pegasus for help."

Brutus nodded. "Do not forget Riza. She is powerful. This is a good idea, but it will not work."

"Why not?" Tryn asked.

"Because Jupiter and Pluto have put armed guards all around the palace—you will never get in. That was why I was there. I was trying to figure out what I did wrong and was going to ask Jupiter. Now, with what you have told me, I understand. They don't want me here. Perhaps the other giants and I are too big for them to duplicate."

"It could be," Tryn mused.

"We have to do something to get in," Astraea insisted. "That arch is the only way to get to Xanadu unless you know another way."

Brutus shook his head. "No, it is the only way. Riza saw to that."

"Could you help us?" Zephyr asked. "Maybe you could cause a distraction or something. While the guards are going after you, we could sneak into the palace and use the arch."

Brutus considered and then nodded. "That might work. I have nothing to lose by trying, as I have already been dishonored by being removed from my position at Arcadia."

"There is no dishonor for you," Tryn said. "It is them. You would be a formidable opponent and they know it."

"Well, removing me is not going to work," Brutus said. "If those Mimics are planning to take Titus, they are in for a fight. While you go to Xanadu, I shall reach out to the other giants and the Hundred-handers. We will stop them."

"No, Brutus, you can't fight them now," Astraea said. "They are very powerful, and we're not sure who is a Mimic and who is real. Please wait until we're back from Xanadu with the others."

Brutus rubbed his chin and nodded. "All right, I

see your point. Head back to the palace. I shall be there shortly and will distract everyone. Just be ready to move when I give the signal."

"What signal?" Tryn asked.

Brutus grinned, revealing large white teeth. "You will understand soon enough. Now when this starts, stay to the left side of the palace where the arch is. Do not deviate from that or you may be hurt."

"What are you planning?" Astraea asked.

Brutus chuckled. "You will see. Get moving and good luck."

"You too!" Astraea called. "And thank you!"

They ran out of the park and made their way back to the palace. They ducked behind a row of flowering shrubs not too far from the palace steps. When they peered around, they saw what Brutus was talking about. Guards with swords had been posted all around the building.

"What do they need swords for if they can kill you by grabbing you?" Cylus asked.

"I bet it's for show," Zephyr said. "To make them look like Titans."

The sound of stomping started from behind them.

They all turned and saw Brutus staggering down the street. Astraea started to frown. "Is he . . ."

"He looks like he's drunk as a skunk!" Jake cried.

Soon Brutus started to sing with a thunderous voice that could be heard for miles. He staggered closer and stumbled, nearly falling onto a building.

"This is his distraction," Astraea said.

"But it's not working," Darek said. "Look, the palace guards aren't moving. . . ."

The words were no sooner out of Darek's mouth when Brutus let out a thunderous belch and then stumbled again. He tried to right himself but tripped over his own feet. Tumbling forward, the enormous giant started to fall.

"He's going down!" Tryn cried.

"Go . . . ooo . . . ," Brutus bellowed in a drunken voice.

Moments later the giant crashed down onto the roof of Jupiter's palace and took the entire right side of the building with him. All the guards abandoned their posts and ran toward the immense cloud of dust and rubble.

The doors of the palace burst open as people

poured out and ran away from the crumbling building.

"He did it!" Tryn called. "Come on, now's our chance."

They left their cover and raced up the steps. The whole area was in an uproar as Brutus's loud, drunken laughter and singing continued. The giant tried to rise but belched and fell back down into the palace, causing even more damage. Everyone around them was so focused on fleeing the disaster that they failed to notice the group entering the building.

"It's this way," Tryn called.

Choking dust filled the grand marble entrance, making it difficult to see. Astraea had only been to the palace a few times in her life, but she had never been invited into the council chambers. Following behind Tryn, they all crossed the spacious foyer and ran through the tall double doors to the chamber.

Astraea nearly ran straight into Tryn's back as he stopped abruptly. Ahead of them lay complete destruction. The arch had been knocked down and lay in hundreds of broken pieces on the marble floor.

"That idiot giant broke the arch!" Cylus called furiously as he clopped up to a piece of stone.

"He didn't do it," Tryn said. "The Mimics did. Look around you. Nothing else has been disturbed. This was done days ago. You can see by the way the floor has been cleaned around the pieces."

"What does it mean?" Zephyr asked.

Tryn looked at everyone. "It means we're on our own against the Mimics. No one from Xanadu can help us."

30

THEY FLED THE PALACE BEFORE THE GUARDS could spot them. Outside it was still pandemonium as Brutus sang at the top of his gigantic lungs and flailed his arms around, causing even more damage to the palace.

"Thank you, Brutus," Astraea called softly as they ran away from the area.

After they made it back to the stable, it took them ages to clear up the mess that was Mimic Vulcan. While they worked, they started to draw up their next plan.

"So we know we have to fight them on our own. But how?" Cylus said.

"Yeah, every time they touch us, we collapse," Render said. "It felt terrible; I don't want it to ever happen again."

"We have to find some kind of weapon against them that doesn't require us touching them," Astraea said.

"We have our weapon," Jake said. "We just have to find a way to use it without hurting Nesso." He was holding the snake in his hands and stroking her. He tilted his head to the side. "You know, back home they milk poisonous snakes for their venom to make medicine. I wonder if we could do the same with Nesso. That way we can use her venom, but she wouldn't have to bite the Mimics and get sick."

Cylus approached Jake, slapping him on the back so hard that he nearly knocked him over. "You're pretty smart for a dumb human. Now you're thinking like a warrior."

"And you're pretty strong for a half-naked boy-horse," Jake said.

"Boy-horse?" Cylus raged. "I'm a centaur!"

"No, you're a bully," Astraea said. "All centaurs are."

"We're not bullies," Darek called.

Astraea sighed. Centaurs were known for being strong—and for being natural bullies. They played rough and fought even rougher. Cylus and his herd lived up to the reputation, even if they didn't realize it.

"All right, I'm sorry I called you bullies," Astraea said. "But please, don't hit Jake again. He's human and they're very fragile. You could really hurt him."

Jake stood up. "I'm fine, Astraea. You don't need to fight for me."

Astraea raised her eyebrows. "Against the centaurs? Trust me, I do."

"All right," Cylus said. "We won't hit the stupid human again, even though he deserves it."

"And don't call him stupid, either," Zephyr added. "I told you, that's my job."

Jake looked at Zephyr and then said to Astraea, "What did she just say?"

Astraea grinned. "She told them not to call you stupid."

"Hey, thanks, Zephyr," Jake said.

Zephyr snorted at Astraea. "We really need to work on all those lies you keep telling him."

The long night ended and the sun was up as they continued to refine their plan. It was almost midday before the centaurs prepared to leave.

"All right, so we all know what we are doing?" Astraea said.

Cylus nodded. "Yes. My herd and I are going to talk to the other students to see who has parents acting weird, so we can work out how many Mimics are already here."

"Good," Astraea said. "Zephyr and I are going to start looking at the teachers. We'll try to figure out who we think is real and who might be a Mimic. Then we can decide who we want to tell."

Tryn held up a small container of Mimic goo. "I am going to take this back to my dorm room and work on figuring out what those Mimics really are. My mother was a science officer, and I brought some equipment with me."

"And Nesso and I are going to stay here and collect venom for weapons," Jake said.

"*Yesss . . . ,*" Nesso agreed. "*I can help.*"

"Yes, you can," Jake said. He kissed Nesso softly on the top of her scaled head.

"Oh, that is completely disgusting," Cylus said. "Don't do that again—at least not in front of me. It makes me want to hit you again."

"But you won't," Astraea warned.

"No," Cylus finally said. "I won't."

"So we all have our jobs," Tryn said. "Remember, no one is to talk to anyone about Vulcan, Panis, or what happened at the palace. We don't want a wrong word getting back to the Mimics. So we know nothing."

Cylus huffed. "Do you think we're stupid or something? Of course we won't say anything."

"I'm not calling you stupid," Tryn said. "But after last night, we know just how dangerous these Mimics are. We all have to be careful."

Astraea agreed. "Yes, one mistake and we're all dead."

When the centaurs left, Astraea and the others headed back into the house. Astraea pulled out the ambrosia cake, and Zephyr offered nectar.

While they ate, Tryn remained especially quiet. He was studying the ring. Finally he rose and approached the large kitchen wall. "I really thought this was a

Solar Stream gem. It looks just like Emily's." He put on the ring and pointed it at the wall. "Xanadu!"

Just like before, nothing happened.

Jake stood up. "Maybe you're not saying it right. They didn't speak our language, remember?"

"It shouldn't only work in their language," Tryn said. He frowned and pointed the ring at the wall again. "Earth."

The ring hummed, and then the wall in front of them exploded in a circle of blazing white light. A swirling vortex flashed within the light. Jake jumped back and nearly fell over. "Whoa, that . . . is . . . awesome!"

Tryn grinned. "I was right. This is a Solar Stream gem!" He lowered his hand and it automatically closed the opening. Holding it up again, he said, "Xanadu." Once again, nothing happened. "So Xanadu is blocked somehow," he observed.

"So, like, could that ring send me home?" Jake asked.

"Yes," Tryn said softly. "If you really wish to return to Earth now, we won't stop you." He held up his hand again. "Earth, Los Angeles, California."

The Solar Stream opened again.

Astraea said, "Jake, are you leaving us?"

Jake looked back at her. "Me leaving? No way. I'm staying to find Molly and fight those Mimics. I just wanted to see if it would work."

Tryn's face brightened. "So you're staying?"

"'Course, dude," Jake said, playfully smacking him on the back. "Besides, I can't go anywhere until we figure out how to get Nesso home."

The snake was back in her usual place around his neck. *"But my home isss with you, Jake,"* she hissed softly. *"We are one now."*

"Aw, Nesso." Jake blushed. "I feel the same." He walked away from the blazing light of the Solar Stream and sat down. He handed a small piece of ambrosia to the snake.

Astraea was still standing beside Tryn. "Try Tartarus."

Tryn nodded and lowered his hand to close the Solar Stream. He raised it again and called, "Tartarus." Once again, the Solar Stream opened.

"Yes!" Zephyr cried. "At least we can free the others. I wonder if that ring is limited to just a few places or maybe where the Mimics have been. If it is, it might make it easier for us to find where Nesso

comes from. Then we could bring more of her friends here to help."

Tryn looked at Zephyr in wonder. "I should have thought of that. We can use it to go to Nesso's world."

"So why didn't you?" Zephyr teased. "You're the one with the family from across the universe. You said your mother was a scientist and you love all this science stuff."

Tryn shook his head. "I know. My mother would be horrified if she found out."

Jake mused aloud, "That ring might get us to Nesso's world, but if we don't know what it's called, how can we make it work?"

"Please, one problem at a time!" Astraea cried. "We should get to school. We've missed the morning already." She looked at Jake. "Will you be all right on your own here?"

He nodded. "Go and see how many teachers have been replaced. Nesso and I will start collecting venom."

Astraea was reluctant to leave Jake, but they all had their jobs to do. By the time she, Zephyr, and Tryn made it to school, the lunch break was ending, and they caught up with their classes for the afternoon session.

The first class after lunch was dance, taught by the Muse Terpsichore. Astraea felt awkward and clumsy, but as she watched, she saw Terpsichore touching the students to direct them into a correct movement.

"She's not a Mimic," Astraea whispered to Tryn when they passed each other.

Tryn stopped dancing and considered. "She has no real authority here. So it's true that they are only taking people of power for the first round."

"Until they're all gone," Astraea finished.

The next class they had to attend was the one taught by Vulcan. As Astraea and Tryn met Zephyr there, they wondered what would happen, considering Vulcan was now a puddle of goo.

Cylus and his herd were already in their area when Astraea and her friends entered. They looked at each other briefly, but then looked away.

Astraea leaned into Tryn. "I wonder who they will get to teach the class."

"I don't know," Tryn answered softly. "The big question is, will it be a Mimic?"

They were all settled and waiting when the class door opened.

Astraea couldn't hold in her gasp, while across the room the centaurs shuffled on their hooves. Zephyr whinnied in surprise. Tryn said nothing, but the shock on his face spoke volumes. They were in even deeper trouble than they'd thought.

"All right, who can tell me where we left off?" Vulcan asked.

31

JAKE SAT AT THE KITCHEN TABLE WITH A crystal goblet in front of him. A fine linen cloth was fastened across the top. Nesso was in his hand, waiting to help.

"What do I do?" the snake asked softly.

"I'm not really sure," Jake admitted. "I've only seen this on the Nature Channel on TV. But the guys hold a snake and it bites through the fabric on top of the container and then the venom comes out."

"It doesssn't sssound very pleasssant."

"I know," Jake said. "But it's the only way. Your venom is the only thing that will stop those energy-sapping monsters." He lifted the snake.

"Just give it a try. Bite it like you bit me."

Nesso looked at Jake and tilted her colorful head to the side. *"But you hit me firssst. It hasssn't done anything to me."*

Jake picked up the goblet and lightly tapped Nesso on the nose with it. "There, it just hit you. Bite it back."

Nesso's tongue flicked out of her mouth, and she bit down on the rim until her fangs cut through the linen. Two streams of yellow venom squirted down the inside.

"You did it!" Jake cheered.

When the venom stream stopped, Nesso pulled her fangs back in. *"That wasssn't ssso bad."*

Jake looked at the small pool of venom. "You did so great. How long before you can do it again?"

"I don't know," Nesso said. *"I have never bitten anything twiccce in a day."*

"Don't worry, take a break. I'm going to start working on the arrows."

Jake lifted Nesso back to her position around his neck and then reached for the centaurs' arrows. He began dipping the pointed ends in the venom and putting them aside to dry. "I wonder if this will work."

"*It mussst,*" Nesso said. "*Thossse big, bad thingsss mussst be ssstopped.*"

"Too right," Jake agreed.

When all the arrows were dipped in the venom, Jake made sure the goblet was tightly sealed. There wasn't a lot left in it, but each drop was precious. "Now I guess we just wait to test them."

He walked into the living room and sat down. "This world really needs to get into the mainstream. No games, no TV, no Internet, and no phones. What do these people do for fun?"

"*They danccce,*" Nesso said. "*I have ssseen a lot of dancccing.*"

Jake reached into his backpack, pulled out his cell phone, and tried to turn it on. "This sucks— it's dead." He looked around for somewhere to plug in his charger. "Jeez, they don't even have electricity? These Titans are living in the dark ages. They said they used to visit Earth. Didn't they learn anything?"

With nothing more to do, Jake sat back and started to doze.

✕ ✕ ✕

"Jake, wake up!" Nesso called. *"I jussst heard sssomething."*

Instantly awake, Jake heard the front door open. "Astraea, Zephyr, is that you?"

There was no answer.

"Thisss isss bad," Nesso said. *"Sssomeone isss here. I can hear them."*

Jake got up quietly and dashed back into the kitchen. He hid the arrows on a chair beneath the table but kept them within easy reach. He then put the goblet of venom in a cupboard. Finally he took a seat and waited to see who was coming.

He didn't have long to wait. There was the sound of hooves on the floor and a tall, imposing centaur entered the kitchen. She looked to be in her thirties, with her dark hair piled high on her head. She was dressed in a tunic that covered her torso and draped down her horse legs. She would have been a funny sight were it not for the malevolence revealed on her face.

"Do you wish to tell me what happened here last night?" Her dark eyes seemed to penetrate right through him. But if she recognized him as human, she didn't show it.

"What do you mean? Okay, we did have a bit of a party, but the noise wasn't that bad. I mean, no one complained or called the police."

That comment stunned the centaur for a moment. But then she moved closer. "There was no party. Vulcan was brought here but did not leave. Where is he?"

"Vulcan?" Jake asked. "You mean Spock's planet on *Star Trek*?"

The woman stopped. "I mean Vulcan. He was here. Where is he now?"

Beneath the table, Jake reached for one of the arrows and brought it to his lap. "Look, lady, I don't know who you are or what you're talking about. We had a few friends over last night and then everyone went home. That's it—case closed."

"You are lying to me," she said matter-of-factly. "In fact, you know a lot more than you are saying, and you are going to tell me."

Jake's heart was pounding so loudly, he was sure she could hear it. "Aren't you going to ask me who I am?"

"I know exactly who you are. You are one of the humans we brought here. Somehow you have evaded capture and are masquerading as a Titan. But that doesn't matter now. You are going to tell me what you know, and then you will die."

From the expression on her face, Jake had known she was going to say that. But to hear her *actually* say it shocked him. "Okay, okay," he said. "You want to know what I know. Well, I know that I have to put out the garbage on Tuesdays and recyclables on Friday. And I know how to do a triple jump with my skateboard—but I'm not very good at it yet and fall down a lot." He paused and held up one hand. "Oh wait, I also know why you can't kill me yet. I haven't reached level thirty-six on *The Zombie Dragons of Zar*. I just rescued the Princess of Light out of the Tree of Knowledge and we're trying to get back to her castle, but it's really hard and I don't want to use Internet cheats to win. . . ."

The Mimic took a step back. "What are you talking about? What princess? There are no princesses on Titus."

Jake snorted. "Duh! The Princess of Light comes from the Light Region of Zar. If I don't get her back home, I'll lose the game, and I can't do that because

Ralph Sader bet me my skateboard that I couldn't do it. I can't let him win. I love that skateboard. It was a present from my dad and even signed by Rob Dyrdek. He's my hero in the boarding world and doesn't sign a lot of merchandise. I mean, it's worth a fortune. . . ."

Jake was hoping that Astraea, Tryn, or Zephyr would come back soon. But he could see by the expression on the centaur's face that it wasn't working. He was running out of things to say—and time.

The centaur took a threatening step forward. "I will give you one more chance to tell me what you know. If you do, your death will be swift and painless. If you refuse, your suffering will be unimaginable."

"Jake, tell her," Nesso hissed. *"I will bite her and sssave you."*

Jake gripped the arrow tighter in his fist. "It's funny that you should say that, because I said the exact same thing to Vulcan last night—right before he spilled his guts and told me everything. So I know all about your little plan to invade Titus and then go on to Earth. You are removing Titans and replacing them with your own kind. How's that for knowledge, eh?"

A flash of anger swept across her face and then passed. "Who else knows this?"

"Oh, now that's another question completely. . . ."

"Tell me!" the Mimic centaur demanded.

"Come closer and I'll whisper it to you."

The Mimic tilted her head to the side suspiciously but took several steps closer. "There is nothing you can do to harm me, so do not try anything," she said. "All right, I am closer. Tell me who else knows about us."

For all his life, Jake had avoided violence. The bullies back home had always left him alone, because he was a joker who didn't cause trouble for anyone. But when the Mimic was standing right beside him, he realized he had no choice. He gripped the arrow tightly and swung it up into the side of the centaur's horse body. "I'm so sorry, but you left me no choice."

The Mimic looked at the arrow in her side and frowned. She pulled it out and looked at it curiously. "You think that little stick can hurt me? I feel nothing, but you, on the other hand, will feel everything. . . ."

Her hand flashed out and caught hold of Jake's arm before he could move. He immediately felt the draining of energy. But just as quickly as it started, it stopped. The Mimic staggered back and shook her head. "What is happening? I feel so strange. . . ." Her words trailed off as the skin on her lips and face started to droop.

The illusion of a centaur slipped away as the Mimic reacted the same way Vulcan had. Folds of unsupported gray skin appeared and then simply melted into a puddle of gray goo and empty clothes.

Jake pushed back his chair and jumped away from the spreading mess on the floor. He instinctively reached up to his neck and was reassured to feel Nesso there.

"It worked!" the snake cried. *"I didn't have to bite her!"*

Jake's stomach flipped, and he thought he might throw up. He'd never hurt, let alone killed anything in his life, and even though the Mimic had been threatening him, he still felt guilty for killing it.

"You did the right thing," Nesso said, sensing what Jake was feeling. *"It would have killed usss both."*

"I know, but . . . ," he said.

"I undersssstand. You are a gentle big thing and do not like to hurt anything."

Jake stood unmoving for several minutes, just staring at the mess. But then a thought entered his mind. How had the false centaur known Vulcan had been here? If they'd been followed the previous night, surely the Mimics would have busted in. So did Mimics track by smell? Or worse still, were they linked?

Jake suddenly realized the danger they were in. The Mimics knew about this place, and now two Mimics had died here. Would the others know and come for them?

"Nesso, we're in big trouble. They know about this house. They must be connected somehow."

"Jake, we can't ssstay here. We mussst find the otherss and warn them."

"I know, but I can't go outside in daylight or we'll be caught. We won't be any good to anyone if we're in prison."

"Then we mussst hide and warn them when they return."

Jake agreed. But Zephyr's house wasn't very big, and the stable was open to anyone. Where could they possibly hide and still be able to watch for the others? He looked at the ceiling, hoping for inspiration, and that was exactly what he got.

32

ASTRAEA INSTINCTIVELY REACHED OUT AND caught hold of Tryn's hand. "How can Vulcan be here? We watched him melt!"

"It can't be the same one," Tryn whispered tightly. "Somehow they've already replaced him. But how did they know?" He looked at her and his eyes went wide. "We might have a really big problem. They might be a hive."

"A what?"

"Hive," Tryn said. "With a queen, and the drones are all connected and work together to form a whole. So if one is killed or wounded, another automatically takes over. If that's the case, things just keep getting worse and worse. Stay here. I have an idea."

"What are you going to do?"

"Check on something."

Tryn raised his hand. "Forgive me, Vulcan, but I need to go drink again. Just like yesterday."

Vulcan looked over to Tryn. "Of course, Trynulus. Do what you must."

Tryn whispered to Astraea. "I'm going to the dorm. I'll meet you at Zephyr's house. Tell the others." He glanced over to Cylus and left the room.

Astraea looked over and saw Cylus watching him leave. The centaur had a deep frown on his face. The other members of his herd were pale and whispering to each other.

At the front of the room, Vulcan cleared his throat and reached for a piece of metal. "All right, let's make a bracelet. . . ."

Astraea was moving as though in a dream. She did everything Vulcan instructed and pounded out the metal into the shape of a wide bracelet. All the while her mind was on fire with fear.

After the class, she and Zephyr waited outside the room for Cylus and his herd. But when they appeared, Vulcan also came out. "Cylus, Astraea, Zephyr, please wait. I would like to speak with you and the other centaurs. Come back inside."

Cylus looked fearfully at Astraea, and they all started to walk back into the class.

"This isn't good," Zephyr muttered.

Astraea had only seconds. "Vulcan," she said softly. "I'm so sorry, but Zephyr and I are still on detention. I was told by Themis to bring Cylus and the centaurs with us to her office immediately after class." She looked at Cylus and put her hands on her hips. "You got us detention and now you're causing more trouble? Who did you attack this time?" She widened her eyes and hoped he got the message.

"It—it wasn't our fault. He started it," Cylus cried, going along with the ruse. He looked at Vulcan. "Can I stay here with you instead of going to the office? Themis hates me. She's already making me clean Arcadia Four after school. There is no telling what she'll do to me now."

Vulcan hesitated for a moment, but then his face relaxed. "No, you must speak with Themis first. Then I want you all back here after school."

"Yes, Vulcan, we'll be back," Astraea said. She caught hold of Cylus's arm. "Come on, let's go. Themis said we mustn't delay."

Cylus and his herd looked back at Vulcan and then followed Astraea and Zephyr toward the ramp for four-legged Titans and Olympians. When they reached the main floor, Cylus pulled his arm free of Astraea. "You just saved our lives!" The other centaurs also nodded and offered their thanks.

"For the moment," Astraea said. "Let's forget the last class and get out of here. Tryn said he would meet us at Zephyr's house."

Cylus nodded. "Fine, we'll be there shortly. I don't want to be seen leaving with you, in case Vulcan is watching."

"Good idea," Astraea agreed. "Just get there as soon as you can."

While Cylus and his herd left, Astraea and Zephyr ducked out of the building and hurried back to Zephyr's house.

"Themis will be furious when she hears that we missed the last class as well as our detention," Zephyr said.

"I've been thinking a lot about her." Astraea stopped. "Zeph, she sent us into the orchards and then asked what we'd seen, as though she expected us to see something."

"So?"

"What if she expected us to find Jake? Or maybe even be attacked by that big thing we saw? Also, have you ever seen her touch anyone?"

Zephyr paused. "No, she always keeps her arms behind her back."

"Exactly," Astraea said. "What if she's a Mimic too? She's the head of the school, a position of power. It makes sense that they'd replace her first."

"You think she could be working with Vulcan?"

Astraea nodded. "If she wasn't, he wouldn't have let us leave him and go to her office. He must have known that if we went there, she'd get us. We'd be just as dead."

Zephyr whinnied angrily. "This is getting insane!"

"I know," Astraea agreed. "Zeph, we can't come back to Arcadia—it's too dangerous now. Let's go back to the house and check on Jake. Then we'll wait to see what Tryn was planning. Whatever it is, he'd better tell us soon, because I'm sure the Mimics are onto us."

When Astraea and Zephyr made it back to Zephyr's house, they approached the door and heard a soft *pssst*.

Astraea turned around, looking for the source of the sound.

"Up here," Jake called softly.

Astraea looked up and saw a hand waving at them from the flat roof. "Jake what are you doing up there?"

"Don't speak," he called softly. "We're in terrible danger. Just pretend nothing is wrong and come around to the back of the house."

As Astraea and Zephyr made their way around the house, Zephyr whinnied, "Humans are insane. Most normal people would sleep inside, not on the roof."

"There has to be a reason he's up there," Astraea said.

"Yes, there is," Zephyr insisted. "He's nuts!"

By the time they made it to the back, Jake was peering down from the roof. "Are you really you?"

"Well, who else would we be?" Zephyr nickered.

Astraea nodded. "Of course it's us."

 363

"Prove it," Jake said.

"What?" Zephyr cried. "You tell him if he doesn't come down right now, I'm going to fly up there and kick him off my roof."

Astraea looked up at Jake. "Zephyr says if you don't come down now, she's coming up there to kick you off her roof."

Jake hesitated for a moment and then said, "I guess it's you." He started to climb down and landed on the ground at their feet. "We are *so* toast!" he said. "They know about us!"

"I know!" Astraea cried. "But how do you know?"

"Another Mimic came around today. She looked like one of those horsey people, you know, like Cylus and his gang. She knew Vulcan had been here and wanted to know what happened to him."

Astraea gasped. "What did you tell her?"

"The truth," Jake said.

"What?" Zephyr cried. "Now I'm really going to stomp him!"

When Zephyr took a threatening step forward, Jake backed up and held up his hands. "I don't know what you just said, Zephyr, but please calm down.

Yes, I told her everything, but it was just to test her reaction. When she tried to kill me, I stabbed her with an arrow dipped in Nesso's venom, and she melted just like Vulcan did."

"Really? It worked?" Astraea said.

Jake nodded. "Yep, go see for yourself if you don't believe me. There's a new gray puddle in the kitchen."

Zephyr shook her head. "More dead Mimics? That's it. I'm moving out of my house."

Jake asked Astraea, "What did she just say?"

"That she's moving out."

"Great idea!" Jake said to Zephyr. "They obviously know this is goo central, and I'm sure more will come looking for Vulcan and that other one. I think they might be linked somehow."

The sound of footsteps behind them made everyone jump. "They are connected," Tryn said as he came through the bushes surrounding Zephyr's back garden. "I went to the dorm to check on that Vulcan residue, and from what I can see, the Mimics are single-celled organisms. To function properly, they must be linked at a cellular level. But I'm not sure if they're psychically linked as well."

"I didn't understand a word you just said," Astraea said.

"You mean like bacteria?" Jake asked. He looked to Astraea. "I studied biology at school."

Tryn nodded. He turned to Astraea. "There are billions of cells that work together to make you— you. But the Mimics are different. They have only one cell, which might be why they can copy us. But they aren't like us at all."

"Nope, I still don't understand any of this," Zephyr said to Astraea.

Tryn frowned. "They're kind of like big bubbles. There's only one component to them, so they can change their shape whenever they need to."

"And you think they're all connected?" Astraea asked.

Tryn nodded. "But I can't be completely sure."

"I can," said Jake. "Considering the one that came here today knew that Vulcan had been here. Then she tried to kill me."

"Another one was here?" Tryn cried.

Jake quickly told him what had happened. "At least we know the venom-dipped arrows work."

"That's one good thing," Tryn agreed. "But if they are connected, when we attack one, it's like we attacked all of them. Maybe they can even communicate from great distances."

"Just so I understand," Astraea said, struggling to grasp it all. "If they are single-celled thingies like you said, would it also explain why Vulcan was back at school?"

"What?" Jake cried.

Astraea nodded. "But I don't think he recognized us from last night." She paused and frowned. "But then again, at the end of the class, he did tell us and the centaurs to stay. I panicked, so I told Vulcan that Themis needed to see us. But now they know we're all involved."

Jake nodded. "We need somewhere new to hide. If that Mimic knew Vulcan was here, others must. Now that she's dead too, they'll come looking for her as well."

"We're out of time," Tryn said. "If we are going to do anything to stop them, we have to move now."

"How?" Jake asked. "What can we do?"

Astraea came forward. "We find Cylus and his herd, and then we use that ring to go to Tartarus and free the real Titans!"

33

BEFORE LONG THEY WERE BACK ON THE roof, except for Zephyr, who was in the sky flying in large circles to watch for any signs of attack.

Jake handed out the arrows he had, and while they waited, he asked Nesso to try biting the crystal goblet again. When she did, two streams of yellow venom poured down the side.

"Thank you, Nesso," Astraea said when the snake finished.

"*You are mossst welcome,*" Nesso replied politely.

After Jake translated, he nodded. "Okay, she gave us the first venom this morning, and now it's afternoon. So she can give us venom at least twice a day.

The trouble is, we don't know how many Mimics there are."

"There are more of them than there are us," Tryn said. A wave of sadness swept over his face and he looked away. "I have always prided myself on being just like my mother. She is gentle and strong and has never had to fight for anything. She's always saying there is a peaceful solution to every problem . . . but now . . ."

Jake patted him on the back. "But now it's time for you to become like your dad. He's from Earth, and we humans fight for those we care for."

Tryn nodded, but Astraea could see this would take a heavy toll on her friend. "I don't want to fight either," she said. "But they won't reason with us. They want Titus and don't care who they hurt to get it. They've stolen my parents and so many others. If it means I have to fight and even kill those monsters to get them back, I will."

"Me too," Jake agreed.

Finally Tryn sighed. "You're right. I had hoped we could negotiate with them, but after everything you said about the centaur today, and what Vulcan said to us last night, I know that talking won't work."

"I'm sorry, Tryn. I know you don't like violence, but you are going to have to learn to fight," Astraea said sympathetically.

Tryn turned to her. "When I said my people don't fight, I didn't mean they couldn't. They can—which is why we have avoided it. Once we start, it is difficult to stop."

"Don't worry, Tryn. When this is over, you will stop. We'll help you," Astraea said.

He didn't look convinced and turned away.

They lay on the roof, watching Zephyr circling in the sky.

Jake lay back with his arms crossed behind his head. He sighed. "Who'd have ever dreamed that I'd be here watching a flying hor—I mean Zephyr. She is so beautiful up there, isn't she?"

"Yes, she is," Astraea agreed, feeling proud and grateful that Zephyr was her best friend.

Above them, Zephyr tilted her wings and swept in low. "Here comes Cylus and his herd. Look at what they have with them."

Astraea crawled up to the edge of the roof and peered down. Cylus and his friends had more bows and arrows with them, but they also had swords and daggers strapped to their waists where their torsos became equine. Cylus was carrying a flame-sword.

"They look ready for war," Jake said. He looked at Astraea. "Remind me not to make them mad."

"Cylus!" Astraea called tightly. "Go around to the stable. We'll meet you there."

"What are you doing up there?" Darek called.

"Get to the stable and we'll tell you." Astraea, Tryn, and Jake moved to the back of the roof to climb down.

When they arrived in the stable, Zephyr was already inside, explaining what had happened to Jake and ending with why they were hiding on the roof.

Astraea went up to Cylus. "Where did you get all these weapons—especially that flame-sword?"

Cylus shrugged. "We needed weapons, so we broke into the armory and took them." He held up the flame-sword. "You said there were Shadow Titans, and Minerva told us these were the only things that killed them." He looked at his herd. "These cowards wouldn't take them because they're scared they'll get burned."

Astraea looked over to Render and the others, and they quickly glanced away. Finally she said, "The Mimics will be coming back, looking for the centaur Mimic as well as Vulcan. So whatever we plan to do, we'd better do it soon."

Cylus looked at Jake. "Describe the Mimic centaur. What did she look like?"

Jake shrugged. "Well, she kinda looked like you, if I'm honest. She was tall, had the same color, um, body as you. Her dark hair was piled high on top of her head"—he looked at Astraea—"she must have used a lot of product to get her hair that high!" Then he looked back to Cylus. "Oh, and she had black eyes. . . ."

"That was my mother!" Cylus cried. "You killed her?"

Cylus advanced on Jake and he shied away, holding up his hands. "Hey, hey, dude, dude, I'm sorry, I didn't mean to. But she was going to kill me."

"Cylus, stop," Astraea said. "Leave him alone."

Cylus looked back at her and then reached out for Jake. He patted him forcefully on the shoulder. "Thank you! I've wanted to do that since I found out she wasn't my real mother!"

Jake stood stunned as Cylus congratulated him. The centaur drew a dagger from his hip strap and handed it to him. "Here, this one is my favorite. You've earned it."

Jake looked down on the sharp blade. "No, it's all right. I'm good."

"What?" Cylus said. "You're refusing my gift?"

Astraea leaned in to Jake. "Take the dagger! Centaurs don't give very often, so when they do, it means a lot. It'll offend him if you don't."

Jake looked back at Cylus. "I—I am grateful. I just didn't want to take your favorite away from you. It's so beautiful. But if you mean it . . ." He held out his hand. "Thank you!"

Cylus handed over the dagger and grinned. "You're not bad for a human."

"Um—thanks?" Jake said.

Finally the centaur raised his flame-sword. "All right then, that's another Mimic down. Let's go after the rest. If they want a fight, they'll get one. It is war!"

"No," Astraea insisted. "We can't do this alone, and we don't know who to trust."

"Yes, we do," Cylus insisted. "We have a lot of others from school who are convinced their parents are not their real parents. We have a small army."

"An army of untrained and unarmed fighters," Astraea said. "No, we need real fighters. Those who have been through war before."

"Who's that?" Jake asked.

"Everyone who is locked in Tartarus," Tryn said. He held up his hand to show Vulcan's ring. "This *is* a Solar Stream gem. It won't take us to Xanadu, but it works. It will get us to Tartarus. We can go there and free your families and Jupiter. Then we can return and rise up against the Mimics."

Cylus's eyes were filled with fiery rage. "Fine, then use the ring. I want to go now!"

Despite protests from Cylus and his herd, they took time to smear Nesso's toxic yellow venom on the blade edges of the swords and daggers and dip the new arrowheads.

Nesso tried to offer more, but when she bit into the linen on the goblet, very little came out. *"I am empty,"* she hissed in surprise.

Jake offered her a piece of ambrosia cake after she was settled back around his neck and put an extra-large piece in his backpack for later. "Just rest and build up your strength."

When the venom was dry, Cylus gave daggers to Astraea and Tryn. Tryn received his with a look of despair on his face.

"Cheer up," Cylus said loudly. "We're going into battle."

Tryn looked over to Astraea but said nothing. Finally he nodded.

As they prepared to leave, Zephyr said good-bye to her parents by rubbing her soft muzzle against them.

"I still can't believe those are her parents," Jake whispered to Astraea. "Especially her father. He's so, so wild and dangerous."

"I know," Astraea said. "It shows just how special and precious Zephyr is." She paused and grinned. "Mind you, she gets her temper from her dad. She always wants to stomp people."

"Come on, Zephyr," Cylus called impatiently. "It's time to fight, not blub about leaving your parents."

Zephyr whinnied back angrily, "I am not crying

or blubbing or anything! But there's a chance some of us won't make it back. I want to say good-bye."

That comment stopped everyone. It was true. This wasn't a child's game. Astraea suddenly felt a lump in her throat. Was she ready to do this? Did she have the strength? But imagining her parents in Tartarus hardened her resolve. For those she cared about, she was prepared to do anything.

Jake leaned closer to Astraea while looking at everyone. "What did she just say?"

When Astraea repeated Zephyr's message, Jake nodded. "She's right. . . ."

"She is," Tryn agreed. "So before we go, if anyone doesn't want to come with us, I understand, and there are no bad feelings. We don't know what we are going to face there. My father told me that Tartarus is beyond horrible. So if you want to back out, now is the time."

Cylus shuffled on his hooves. "Just shut up, Tryn, and open the Solar Stream."

"Yes, do it now," Darek said as the other centaurs nodded in agreement.

Jake put his long skateboard in his pack and then

pulled the pack onto his shoulders. "I'm good to go."

Astraea looked at everyone, then turned back to Tryn. "Do it," she said.

Tryn raised the ring to the wall. But before proceeding, he said, "Get your weapons ready. We don't know what we'll encounter." He looked back at the wall. "Take us to the outside of the prison at Tartarus."

The Solar Stream opened immediately with its blazing white swirling light. Tryn started to walk forward with his dagger held high. "This is it, everyone. Let's go."

34

ASTRAEA KNEW VERY LITTLE ABOUT THE Solar Stream. It had been restricted all her life, so as she traveled through the powerful wormhole, she was stunned by the noise and almost unbearable brightness of the colors swirling within it.

But just as quickly as it started, the journey ended, and they emerged out of the light into a place of darkness, blasting wind, and rain. The ground beneath them was sodden, and foul-smelling mud oozed up over their sandals and hooves, while the sky above was alive with scudding black clouds. Lightning flashed on the horizon.

"Is this day or night?" Cylus called above the whipping winds.

"Hey, my hooves are getting stuck," another centaur complained.

Tryn looked around. "My father said it was always the same. Terrible."

"Where to now?" Zephyr called, pulling her hooves free of the mud.

"Over there!" Astraea pointed to a large, carved stone arch with two heavy-looking doors. "That must be it."

Zephyr's feathers were blowing in all directions on her tightly folded wings, and her mane stood on end. Astraea's own long hair whipped painfully across her face, and she wished she'd thought to tie it back. Looking over to Jake, she saw the wind nearly blowing him off his feet, and Tryn had to catch hold of him to keep him upright.

"This place is awful," Cylus called. "How can you fight an enemy in this?"

"Are you sure we want to do this?" Zephyr called.

"No," Astraea said. "But our parents are in there. So are the others." She looked at everyone. "All right, let's go."

They trudged through the thick mud and made

it to the doors. Looking up, Astraea felt very small. This was Tartarus—the prison of all prisons, built to hold prisoners of all shapes and sizes. Her mother had been held here many years ago, and even the Olympians and the Big Three had been imprisoned by Saturn when they were children. This place was nothing but sorrow, pain, and nightmares.

Tryn came forward and grasped one of the large handles. He started to pull, but despite his strength, the door moved only a fraction. "It's the mud around the doors. Cylus, I need your help."

The centaur said nothing but came forward and grasped the handle beside Tryn. Together they heaved and pulled. Slowly the door started to move, and a noxious smell flowed out, making Astraea cough.

By the time the door was wide enough for all of them to enter, Tryn and Cylus were out of breath and the others were gasping for air.

"What is that terrible smell?" Zephyr choked.

"Tartarus," Tryn said. "That is one of the things my father mentioned. It gets worse the deeper you go."

"And you didn't think to warn us?" Cylus said as he pinched his nose shut.

"Would it have made a difference? Your mother is in there. Would you let a bad smell stop you from rescuing her?"

"Of course not," Cylus shot back.

"See, there was no point telling you. We have to be here." Tryn grasped his dagger tighter and entered the prison first.

Astraea and Zephyr were next inside, followed closely by Jake and then the six centaurs.

"The plans in your dad's office showed the cells are on the lower levels," Tryn said. "The stairs should be over somewhere along that wall." He pointed to the roughly cut stone wall.

"Do you think they're really here?" Jake asked softly. "I mean, like, why aren't there any guards or anything?"

"I don't know," Astraea admitted. "But there are burning torches; someone has to maintain them. Besides, we're here now. We have to check."

They found the stairs going down deeper into the foul prison. They were wet and slippery. Astraea had to hold on to the wall to keep from slipping. She looked back and saw Zephyr struggling on her four legs.

"Whose bright idea was it to come here?" Zephyr complained.

"Yeah," a centaur agreed. He was walking slowly on his four hooves and holding on to the wall for support. "These stairs were not built for us."

"They shouldn't be for anyone!" Jake's face was greenish, and he looked like he was about to be sick. "This place should be condemned." His hand was trailing on the wall and touched a patch of thick gray liquid. "Gross! What is that?"

Tryn looked at the liquid and frowned. "It could be from the Mimics. Remember, you said they divided to reproduce. That might be what's left afterward; it's a kind of residue." He leaned closer to touch and then sniff the liquid. "It smells like the Vulcan goo, but it doesn't seem dangerous to touch."

Cylus shook his head. "You are saying that one of those things divided right here on the stairs?"

"Possibly," Tryn said.

"That is *disgusting*. Now I hate them even more," Cylus finished.

When they reached the first level going down, they walked away from the stairs and into a long, dim cor-

ridor. Everyone held up their weapons as they moved silently forward. They approached the first cell on the right and Astraea gasped. A woman was lying on a narrow cot with her back to them.

Astraea looked at the lock on the door. "We need a key."

"You mean like this one?" Darek was standing back, holding a large key.

"Where did you get that?" Tryn asked.

He shrugged. "It was hanging on the wall back there. I thought we might need it." The centaur came forward and inserted the key into the lock. It turned easily and the door swung open.

Astraea was the first in the cell and ran over to the woman. She touched her shoulder and turned her over. "It's Themis!" she cried. "I knew the one at school was a Mimic!"

Themis stirred and opened her eyes. "Stay back!" she cried fearfully.

"Themis, it's me, Astraea. I'm not one of those monsters!"

Themis took a moment to focus and touched Astraea's cheek. "Are you really you?"

"Yes," Astraea said. She looked back at the others. "We've come to get everyone out of here."

Themis sat up and put her arms around Astraea weakly. "I am so sorry I sent you into the orchard. Please forgive me. I never knew those monsters were around. I would never have sent you in there if I had known. I just wanted you to see how hard the night dwellers worked."

"How could you not know?" Zephyr asked. "You are a seer. You should know everything. Especially at Arcadia, considering that those creatures have big areas beneath it where they are storing their food."

"I cannot feel or sense those things that are hurting us—even when they are right in front of me. It is like they are not there, even though they are. Even now, I can't sense them. I feel the Titans and Olympians and you, but not them."

Tryn entered the cell. "Do you know how many are locked in here?"

Themis shook her head. "I lost count—there are too many. I fear I do not even know how long I have been in here. Those terrible things, every time they

touch me I feel so weak. They have not fed us either. We are starving and parched with thirst."

Astraea gasped. "That's unbelievable!"

Zephyr approached her. "Are you strong enough to stand? You can lean on me and I will take you out of here."

"Thank you, child." Themis rose unsteadily to her feet and leaned heavily on Zephyr for support. "We must set the others free before those creatures return."

"We're calling them Mimics," Astraea said. "They can change shape to look like us."

"I have been duplicated twice. I do not think they live very long. But there are so many, they just keep coming back."

Outside the cell, Themis moved away from Zephyr and leaned against the grimy wall. "Leave me here. Go now and free the others. I will be fine."

Astraea hated to leave her behind, but she nodded and went to open the next cell door. Inside they found a Titan. Just like Themis, he was almost too weak to stand and hadn't been given food, nectar, or water either.

"That is why there are no guards," Tryn mused.

"The Mimics are starving everyone to keep them under control." He looked at Jake. "Without ambrosia or nectar, Titans and Olympians become vulnerable. It won't kill them, but it makes them very weak and unable to fight."

"Not to mention the Mimics draining them all the time," Astraea added. She looked down the long corridor of cells and realized just how many there were to check on this level alone. "Zeph, would you keep opening cells and see if you can get everyone outside? I'm going to go look for my parents and Jupiter."

"I'm coming with you," Tryn said.

"Me too," Jake agreed. "I need to find Molly."

They started off at a jog, searching each cell. Though there were many from the ruling council, Astraea's parents and Jupiter were not on this level. They ran back to the growing group. "They're not here. We're going to try the next level down."

Zephyr nodded. "We'll free everyone here. Those stairs are just too slippery for us. Be careful. I still don't like that we haven't seen Mimics here."

"Why would they need guards if their prisoners are too weak to fight?" Tryn asked.

"That, or this is a trap," Cylus suggested. He raised his sword. "But we're ready for them."

Astraea looked at her small group of rescuers and smiled. They were young, inexperienced, and considered worthless by the Mimics. But the Mimics were wrong, and undervaluing the Titan "spawn" would be their undoing. "All right, just keep freeing everyone. We'll be back."

Astraea, Tryn, and Jake ran back to the stairs and went down another level. As they entered the corridor, they saw an open cell door. Jake reached for the key on the wall and they walked quietly down the length of the corridor.

When they approached the open cell, they heard a soft moaning. Astraea's hands flew up to her mouth to keep from screaming when she saw what was inside.

Two Titan-looking Mimics were standing back as an almost formless gray, pulsating Mimic wrapped itself around a female centaur. The centaur's head was lolling weakly to the side and she whimpered in pain as her energy was drained.

Moment by moment, the Mimic holding her was changing shape and slowly taking on the appearance

of the centaur. The more it drew form and energy from the real centaur, the weaker she became. When the transformation was finished, the Mimic released the now unconscious centaur, and she collapsed to the floor.

One of the Titan Mimics turned and looked curiously at Astraea, Tryn, and Jake standing there, watching. "How did you get here?"

The other two Mimics turned with expressions of mild surprise and displeasure on their faces.

"So that's how you're doing it," Tryn said coolly. "When you hold them, you not only drain their energy, you get their genetic imprint to change your shape."

The Mimic centaur remained calm. "We do more than absorb their energy. We gather memories and experiences as well. Our process is efficient and highly successful."

One of the Titan Mimics nodded. "It is how we have defeated every world we have spread to. It is how we will take Titus and continue spreading through-out the universe."

The centaur Mimic noted their weapons and added,

"Who needs foolish weapons like those, when all we require is a touch?"

Jake gasped. "Wait a minute. I know you!" He turned quickly to Astraea and pointed at the centaur. "She's the one who wanted to kill me in Zephyr's kitchen."

The Mimic centaur took a step closer to Jake. "Are you the one who destroyed *our* Lyra? We all felt her fall."

"She was going to kill me," Jake said. "I had no choice."

"There is always a choice, spawn," the Mimic said. "But I will succeed where she failed. You will all die." The Mimic centaur reared on her back legs and charged forward. She caught hold of Jake's arm. "You will not escape this time."

Another Titan Mimic lunged at Tryn, while the third went for Astraea. But Astraea darted away from the reaching hand. She managed to slice the creature's wrist with the tip of her dagger. Then, ducking around her, Astraea went for the Mimics holding Tryn and Jake.

Tryn was helpless in the grip of the Titan Mimic, while Jake gasped and collapsed to the floor. Just like in the barn with Vulcan, it took only a moment to defeat her friends.

Astraea had only seconds. She dragged her dagger's blade along the arm of the creature holding on to Tryn, and then spun around and cut the centaur Mimic holding Jake just as Nesso unfurled from around his neck and bit into the creature's hand.

"Foolish spawn, your little weapons are useless against us. You cannot stop us!" The Mimic who tried to touch her before charged again.

For a terrifying moment, Astraea thought the venom wouldn't work. But then the creature stopped and started to frown. It swayed on its feet as an expression of curiosity crossed its face.

"You're right, I can't stop you," Astraea challenged. "But we know what can!"

Because it had the largest dose of venom from both Astraea's dagger and Nesso, the centaur Mimic was the first to start to dissolve. She released Jake's arm and staggered back. "What—what is happening to me?" Her hand went to her head. "I feel—I feel . . ." Words were soon lost as her face started to lose shape and melt.

The two remaining Mimics were also reacting to the venom. "You—you cannot stop us . . . ," one of them slurred before its mouth dissolved completely.

"It's working," Astraea cried. She lunged forward, caught hold of Jake, Nesso, and Tryn, and hauled them out of the cell as the Mimics melted.

Moments later, all that was left were three gray pools on the filthy cell floor.

Tryn was the first to wake. He shook his head trying to clear it. "He only held my arm for a moment, but I was too weak to fight him, even though I wanted to."

Jake had been held the longest and took him more time to recover. When he awoke, he rubbed his head. "I feel awful. Those Mimics really pack a punch."

"They sure do," Tryn agreed as he climbed unsteadily to his feet. "We can't let them touch us." Astraea handed Nesso back to Jake. "She's unconscious again, but I can see her breathing. She must stop biting them. She's our only hope, and she can't risk her life like that."

"You try stopping her!" Jake said. "I've already told her not to bite them if they go after me, but she won't listen." He cradled the snake in his hands and kept her warm.

"Her loyalty to you is a credit, but it could get her killed," Tryn said.

"Dude, I know. That's what scares me!"

Astraea nodded. "I just wish we had more like her."

The real centaur on the floor moaned and her eyes fluttered open. Astraea stepped around the gray puddles and knelt beside her. "Lyra, you're safe. Cylus is here to rescue you. You just need to rest for a moment."

"Cylus is here?" Lyra moaned. "No, he must get away . . . they will hurt him."

"He's safe, I promise you. He and his herd are helping the others just one level up. He'll be so relieved to know that you're all right."

Lyra nodded and her eyes slowly shut again.

Astraea rose and looked around. "We have to get everyone away from here. Stay with Lyra. I'm going to look for my mom and dad."

She ran out of the cell and down the corridor. Near the end of the long row, she peered inside a cell and saw Jupiter lying on the cot. His hands were bound behind his back and his ankles were in shackles. His wife, Juno, lay on another cot opposite him.

"Jake, Tryn! I've found Jupiter and Juno. Bring the key!"

When the cell was opened, Astraea ran up to Juno while Tryn approached Jupiter. He reached for the chains on the Olympian's wrist and broke them easily. Then he freed Jupiter's ankles.

"Wow!" Jake cried. "You are really strong!"

Tryn nodded and helped Jupiter into a sitting position. He gently patted him on the face. "Jupiter, wake up. You must wake."

Juno opened her eyes, and when she saw Astraea, she embraced her tightly. "Thank you, thank you for finding us." Her eyes went over to Jupiter. "How is he? They have attacked him most."

Jupiter's eyes fluttered open. "I am fine, beloved," he said weakly. He looked at each of them. "Trynulus, Astraea, what are you doing here? How did you find us?"

"It's a long story," Tryn said. "We're here to free you. Please, you must get up. We need your help."

"I am too weak," Jupiter said. "Juno and I were

among the first taken. We have gone without food and been duplicated too many times."

Jake reached into his backpack and pulled out the ambrosia cake he'd been saving. He broke off a small piece to keep for Nesso and split the rest between Jupiter and Juno. "Here, will this help?"

Jupiter's blue eyes landed on Jake. "A human in Tartarus?"

Jake nodded. "Yes, sir. I was brought from Earth, but Astraea, Zephyr, and Tryn have been helping me try to get home."

Jupiter accepted the ambrosia gratefully but handed his share to his wife. "Here, beloved, you need this."

Juno smiled, and her gaunt face lit up. "No, husband, I have my own piece. You eat it. You must regain your strength if we are to fight those monsters."

Jupiter nodded and ate the ambrosia. He rose shakily to his feet. "I am not fully recovered, but I am better. Thank you." He looked around. "Who is with you?"

Astraea answered, "Well, there's me, Tryn, and

Jake. Upstairs there's Zephyr, Cylus, and five other young centaurs."

"That is all?" Jupiter cried. "We have been rescued by children?"

"They are old enough to save us," Juno said gratefully.

"Besides," Astraea added, "the Mimics don't care about us. They call us spawn and don't think of us as a threat. So they leave us alone."

"Which makes us the perfect defenders," Tryn added. "The Mimics won't expect that."

"Mimics?" Jupiter repeated.

"That's what we're calling them," Tryn explained. "They duplicate Titans and Olympians and mimic them. The name just sort of stuck."

Jupiter nodded. "That is exactly what they are." He sank back down on the cot beside Juno. "They have made many duplicates of us. Each time they do, we become weaker. If they did it many more times, I am sure it would kill us."

Tryn nodded. "There have been puddles from dead Mimics found on Titus. I am starting to believe they don't live very long. That's why they've kept you alive, so they can keep making duplicates. But once they've taken Titus, they won't need to anymore."

"How many of our people have been taken?" Jupiter asked. He was leaning over with his head in his hands as he tried to recover. Juno leaned against him and rubbed his back lovingly.

Watching them, Astraea smiled. Jupiter might be the powerful leader of Titus, but it appeared Juno was the stronger. They had been taken together, but she was recovering faster. "We're not sure how many are here," Astraea answered. "But the cells on the first two levels are full. I'm still looking for my mother and father."

Juno nodded. "I have seen them. They are on this level, further down the corridor." She reached for Astraea's hands. "Go to them, child."

"Here." Jake handed the key to Astraea. "Get your parents. We'll stay here and make sure these two are okay."

Astraea ran down the corridor searching for her parents. In the final cell, she saw two cots. Her hands were shaking as she inserted the key in the lock. Throwing open the door, she charged inside. "Mom, Dad!"

Aurora was lying on her side, and her once-lovely

white wings were filthy and askew beneath her. She lifted her head weakly. "Astraea?"

Astraea knelt by her side. "Yes, Mom, it's me. Please, you must get up. We're getting you out of here."

Aurora started to rise, and Astraea moved over to her father. "Dad, wake up."

Astraios opened his eyes. "Wha-what are you doing here?"

"We're rescuing you. Please get up before they come back."

With Astraea's support, her parents made it to their feet and walked slowly from the cell. When they reached Jupiter and Juno, her father looked at her. "Where are the others? Is Hyperion here? What's happening on Titus?"

Astraea, Tryn, and Jake filled them in as quickly as they could, covering everything they had experienced and discovered about the Mimics. "I'm sorry," Astraea finished, looking at Jupiter. "But Brutus sort of destroyed the palace to help us. We were trying to reach the arch to go to Xanadu for help, but the Mimics have destroyed it."

"The palace is the least of our concerns," Jupiter

said. He reached for Astraea's hands. "Thank you for trying to reach Xanadu. You have been brave, and I am grateful. But we are on our own." He shook his head weakly. "I have been such a fool. We knew there was a problem with all the humans and other creatures arriving on Titus. We hid them in the prison for their protection, but we were arrogant to believe we could solve the problem of their arrival without alerting everyone. Our secrecy has allowed the Mimics to slowly take over."

"You must not blame yourself," Juno said to him. "We are all at fault for not being vigilant."

Aurora was shaking her head. "It is so difficult to believe." She looked at her husband. "I am so sorry I ever doubted you, Astraios. There really were humans on Titus."

Astraios nodded. "And now we have been rescued by one." His grateful eyes landed on Jake. "Thank you."

"Nesso is the one to thank." Jake pointed to the snake around his neck. She was awake again and holding on to her tail. "She's way more important than me. We put some of her venom on daggers, and the Mimics melt when we cut them. But she's alone here. If we had more snakes from her world, we could really do a number on those walking bags of goo."

Jupiter peered closely at the snake and frowned. He rubbed his beaded chin. "I am certain I visited her world an age ago and saw snakes just like her. We can go back there and get some more."

"Not without asking first," Jake said defensively. "Nesso and her kind are intelligent. We can't just take them without permission."

"How can they give permission?" Aurora asked.

"It's easy, we just ask," Jake said. "Once Nesso bit me, we could communicate."

Jupiter's eyes opened wide. "Really? One of her kind bit an Olympian and they became gravely ill. But she was never able to communicate with them. How is this possible?"

Tryn came forward. "There must be something in humans or maybe just Jake that makes them compatible."

Nesso released her tail and lifted her head to Jupiter. *"You mussst have hurt one of my kind. We do not bite without provocation."*

When Jake repeated Nesso's message, Jupiter nodded. "Of course. Then we must ensure that we do not provoke your kind again. But we would be grateful for your help."

"We will help," Nesso hissed softly.

Jupiter looked to Jake, and he translated. "She said they would help."

"Thank you," Jupiter said to the snake.

Astraea's parents were holding on to her for support. "What do we do now?" her mother asked. "I am too weak to fight."

"We all are," Jupiter said. "I am still unsure that we can defeat the Mimics. If they catch hold of us, we will be instantly bested."

"I know," Tryn said. "I was holding my dagger, but the moment a Mimic grabbed my arm, I couldn't move."

Astraea held up her own dagger. "But they do work if we can cut them before they touch us. This was dipped in Nesso's venom, and it destroyed three of them easily."

Jupiter nodded. "This may work, but none of us are strong enough to wield a weapon."

"We are," Tryn said. "The Mimics don't consider the youth of Titus a threat. We will be the silent warriors who can defeat them."

Jupiter looked at Tryn and a sad smile rose to his lips. "Tryn, your people are not fighters. They embraced peace long ago. For you to fight now would betray them."

Tryn shook his head. "No, Jupiter. To watch Titus fall to the Mimics when I could have helped would be the true betrayal. My father was human, and they are no strangers to war. That is what this is. It's a war for Titus, and I'm prepared to fight."

Jupiter looked at his wife and then nodded. "And we are grateful." His eyes moved to each of them. "We are grateful to all of you. But right now, we are a liability to you. You must leave us here."

"What? No!" Astraea cried. "You can't stay. They're killing you. You must leave with us now."

"There is nowhere for us to go but back to Titus, and the Mimics are there," Jupiter said. "If we go back in our weakened condition, it could spell disaster—especially as there is only one Nesso to help us."

"Jupiter is correct," Juno said. "We could cause more harm. We must stay here."

"Forgive me for saying this," Tryn started. "But if you think we're going to let you stay here, you're wrong. Look." He held up his ring. "This was on a Mimic Vulcan. It is a Solar Stream gem, and it's how we got here. We can use it to hide all of you somewhere safe until you're strong enough to fight. Unfortunately, it won't open a passage to Xanadu, but there are other places to go."

"Where?" Aurora asked. "If a Mimic had it, they know all the places it opens."

"True," Jake said, stepping forward. "So I think we should send you all to Earth. It is heavily populated, and you could hide there until you recover."

"That is impossible!" Jupiter cried. "Earth has been quarantined. No one is to return there—ever!"

"Um, excuse me, sir," Jake continued. "But I'm from Earth, and I definitely want to go back home."

"I am not talking about you," Jupiter said. "I am speaking of the Olympians and Titans. We are too powerful for your world. Each time we visit, there is a disaster."

"Right now you aren't powerful. You're weak as kittens," Jake said.

"He's right," Tryn agreed. "Earth is perfect. The Mimics duplicate your memories when they duplicate your look. So they must know Earth is quarantined and the last place you would go. It's the perfect place to hide until you regain your strength."

"They are correct," Juno said. "It is the perfect place for us."

Jupiter shook his head. "Beloved, each time we visit Earth, we do more harm than good. We have destroyed cities and ruined lives. I do not want to be responsible for any more hardship."

"What's the alternative?" Astraea asked. "Those Mimics are taking over Titus one person at a time. If you're no longer here for them to make duplicates of, the people of Titus will start to notice that the leadership is missing. The truth will come out. Then all we need is more of Nesso's venom and we can stop them completely. We'll show the Mimics that they can't have Titus."

"Or any other world but their own," Tryn said.

"What are you saying?" Jupiter asked.

Tryn looked at the leader. "I heard that a long time ago when the Nirads were attacking Olympus, you gave a speech. You said everyone had to fight for Olympus and all the worlds that you protect. Isn't that still true? Yes, Olympus is gone, but you are still here. The other worlds the Mimics are taking need your help too."

Juno smiled at her husband. "You did say that. . . ."

Jupiter chuckled softly. "I have never heard my own words used against me so effectively. Yes, as keepers of the Solar Stream, it is our duty to protect other worlds." He started to rise again and looked at everyone gathered there. "Once we are sure that everyone has been freed from their cells, we will go to Earth to regain our strength. Then we will return and take back Titus!"

Astraea, Tryn, and Jake went through all the levels of Tartarus. With each cell they opened, the prisoners were weak but grateful to be free. They made a slow, torturous march to the uppermost level while the search and rescue continued.

Astraea was relieved to discover that out of the

massive prison, only the top three levels contained prisoners. Tryn was especially joyful when they finally found Vulcan on level three. He was as weak as Jupiter, having had multiple duplicates made from him, but he was determined to walk unaided.

When the last cell was opened and everyone had made it to the top level, Astraea was amazed by how many Titans and Olympians had been taken. It was even more disturbing to realize that no one had noticed the change until Jake arrived and set everything in motion.

Another surprise prisoner was Jupiter's brother Pluto. If the Mimics had captured Neptune as well, they would have taken the Big Three without anyone noticing. It was fortunate that Neptune spent a great deal of time in the ocean and so was likely beyond their reach. They all gathered outside the empty cells on the main floor. Jupiter and Pluto were leaning heavily on Zephyr for support, while the weakest prisoners relied on the stronger ones to keep them upright. Gone were the divisions between Olympian and Titan. They were all in this together, and they would need to fight *together* to win.

Astraea stood beside Jake and put her hand on his arm. "I'm so sorry we didn't find Molly here."

Jake turned to her with fear in his eyes. "Where is she? She wasn't in the prison on Titus and she isn't here. What did they do to her?"

Tryn said, "Have you ever considered that she was never taken?"

Jake shook his head. "But that thing, that Shadow Titan, grabbed her first. I saw it before I fell down and hit my head."

"Jake," Astraea said softly, "I promise we'll find her and won't stop searching until we do. Let's just get everyone to Earth and we can keep looking."

Jake nodded, but said nothing.

"Everyone," Jupiter called. "We owe our lives to these brave young people who have freed us. . . ."

Weak cheers rang out, and gratitude was in the air.

"But," Jupiter continued, "none of us are strong enough to take on the Mimics on Titus. Astraea has a team, but they are too few to do it successfully. They have a plan that could work, but it is dangerous. We must leave here and hide until we recover our strength. To do that, we are about to break the quarantine and flee to Earth."

There were gasps and shocked whispers from the gathering.

Jupiter raised his hands. "I know, I know, it is not ideal and not what I would have ever wanted. But we have no choice. We cannot return to Titus. If we did, the Mimics might launch a full attack against us with no one able to stand against them."

"What are we supposed to do on Earth?" Vulcan called. "We cannot just sit around while those monsters take Titus."

"We will not be sitting around," Jupiter said. "We will be drawing up a plan and making weapons. But we must leave before those Mimics return. Each moment we waste puts Titus in greater danger."

Jupiter motioned to Tryn. "Do it."

Tryn looked back at Jake. "You're sure this is the best place?"

Jake nodded. "It's the only place. There are too many strange-looking Titans here to keep them safe anywhere else. Trust me, this will work."

Tryn took off the ring and handed it to Jake. "You

just hold it up and call out your destination. Be as precise as you can."

Jake accepted the ring. He put it on, pointed it at the wall. "Okay, ring, take us to Earth, the United States, Westward Junction in Detroit, Michigan, Reynolds Specialty Steel plant—at night."

The wall exploded with the light of the Solar Stream. Tryn looked back at Jake again. "This is your idea. Lead us in."

Jake turned back to the weak prisoners. "Where we are going is abandoned. You'll all be safe, I promise. Follow me."

Astraea helped support her parents into the blazing, swirling lights of the Solar Stream, leaving Tartarus behind and heading to the uncertainty of Earth.

35

THE JOURNEY THROUGH THE SOLAR STREAM was longer than the one to Tartarus. Once again, it was too loud to talk during the transport. Even if it wasn't, there was little to say. Astraea looked back in despair at the Titans and Olympians. They were leaning on each other for support and looked so vulnerable and weak that it broke her heart to see such powerful beings brought to their knees.

When it ended, they exited the Solar Stream into nighttime. The sky above showed no stars and was filled with dark clouds. There were bright lights in the distance, but around them was completely dark. If it weren't for their Titan vision, they wouldn't have been able to see anything at all.

Astraea felt strange ground beneath her feet and looked down. She saw a track of long steel. Behind her was another track. In the distance she heard a horn blaring and saw a single light driving toward them.

"We're on the tracks!" Jake cried. "Everyone, get off them now. The train is coming!"

Everyone turned and watched the approaching light.

"Go!" Jake cried, pushing the closest Titans away from the tracks. The others finally realized the danger and stumbled away just as the large freight train whooshed past, its horn blaring in protest at them being there.

"What was that?" Cylus cried.

"It's called a freight train," Jake said, panting in relief. "I don't care how powerful you guys are, if a train is coming, you run. They are bigger and heavier than you and will do a number on you if you get hit."

"Why did you bring us here if it's so dangerous?" Astraea asked.

"I didn't, this ring did!" Jake cried. "But my grandfather's company was beside the tracks, so I guess it thought this would be a good place to land." He looked around. "But I can't see anything in this darkness, so I don't know where his building is."

"Really?" Cylus said. "I knew humans were weak, but you are blind, too?"

"I'm not blind, I just don't see in the dark."

Astraea walked up to him. "We do. What are we looking for?"

"The building was made of red bricks and stood three stories tall. There was an old rusty sign in front that said, 'Reynolds Specialty Steel.'"

Astraea looked around and saw many old broken-down buildings. Several had signs, but she couldn't read human language.

"There it is." Tryn pointed directly ahead.

"Really?" Jake said. "I can't see anything but Zephyr, because she's glowing."

Zephyr walked up to Jake, shaking her head. "I can't believe I'm going to do this, but would you like to ride on my back? But," she quickly added, "it's only to stop you from falling over and breaking your neck before we get to safety. So don't get any dumb ideas that I like you or anything like that. . . ."

Jake looked at Astraea. "What did she say?"

"She's offering you a ride on her back so you don't trip and fall."

"Really? Cool! Thanks, Zephyr!" Jake reached out and patted her glowing neck. "You're the best."

Zephyr gave Astraea a withering look. "Astraea, will you *ever* tell him what I actually say?"

Astraea chuckled and shook her head. She leaned closer and whispered, "Not until you say something nice."

"Yeah, like that's ever going to happen!" Zephyr whinnied.

Astraea was still laughing as she showed Jake how to climb up on Zephyr's back. She settled his legs beneath Zephyr's folded wings.

"You're all set," she said to Jake. "Just hold on to her mane."

"This is so awesome," Jake said. "I've never been on a horse before."

"What did he say?" Zephyr cried. "Get him off! Get him off right now, before I throw him off!"

Juno approached Zephyr and laid a hand on her rear flank. "He did not mean to offend you. But humans do not understand the difference between us. I am asking you to remain calm and let him stay where he is."

Zephyr looked back at Juno and bowed her head. "Of course, anything you say. Would you like to ride too?"

Her face wrinkled in a smile. "Thank you, child. I am well enough to walk—as long as it is not far. I have not been back to Earth in a very long time, and none of this looks familiar."

"We don't have far to go," Tryn said. "I see what Jake is talking about. It is just ahead."

They crossed a second set of tracks and made their way over a cracked asphalt road. Up ahead was a tall fence with barbed wire at the top. Farther along was a gate with a chain locking it shut.

Astraea saw weeds and other plants pushing through the asphalt, while the building itself had broken windows on the upper floors and wooden slats covering the downstairs ones. There were painted messages on the building that made no sense. "This area looks deserted."

"It is," Jake responded. "That's why I thought of it. My dad said this whole area used to make cars and parts for cars, but most of the industry left, leaving all this behind."

Jupiter nodded. "Your choice is very wise—thank you."

"What is a car?" Astraea asked.

Jupiter pointed to a large road in the distance. "Look way ahead, down there on that road. Those moving things with the white lights in front and red at the rear are cars. Humans use them to get around. We have had some experience with them in the past."

"Really?" Cylus said. "Wait, Chiron told me that when he last visited Earth, he and the others with him were captured and taken away. Did they use cars?"

Jupiter nodded. "And trucks, I believe." He looked at the gathering of Titans and Olympians. "Remember, we are visitors here. Everyone must be on their guard. We must not expose ourselves to humans or do any damage. Let us get inside and then we can rest and start to recover."

They fell silent and walked like a zombie army across the deserted road to the fence entrance. Tryn jogged up to the gate and caught hold of the lock on its thick chain. He pulled out his lockpick kit and opened it in seconds, then pushed the gate open. "Once everyone is inside, I'll lock it again."

One by one the Titans and Olympians filed through the gate and were standing in a parking area that was overgrown with grass and weeds. Very little of the original pavement remained.

Once the gate was relocked, Tryn joined the others walking up to the freight doors.

Cylus and Render caught hold of the door handles and started to pull. The doors creaked and moaned, but finally surrendered to the centaurs' strength.

"Very good," Jupiter said. "Everyone inside. Then we can rest."

The moment they entered, they were struck by the smells of damp, decay, and rust, and the sound of dripping water. After they'd moved farther inside, the doors were shut and sealed behind them, casting them into total darkness.

"All right," Jupiter said. "First we need light. Those of you who are strong enough to move, look around you, and see if there is anything we can use to construct torches."

Astraea tapped Jake on the leg. "Stay here with Zephyr. I'll go see if I can find something."

"Be careful," Jake said. "This place has been closed for a long time. There still might be some old machinery in here and things you can hurt yourself on."

Astraea settled her parents on the floor before going to search for something to use to make torches. Most of the prisoners were too weak to join the search, so it was mainly her, Tryn, and the centaurs moving around.

Going deeper into the abandoned metal plant, Astraea saw immense machines rising like monsters from the darkness. She could see well enough, but at night the world became black and white to her Titan eyes.

All around her she saw piles of scrap and rusty metal as well as the huge machines. When she rounded a corner and was looking up at a machine that made no sense to her, she tripped over a pile of old oily rags and fell down into the middle of them.

"I think I found something!" she called out.

Tryn came running first, followed by Render and two other centaurs. Astraea held up a rag. "This will burn, won't it?"

Tryn sniffed the rag. "That's machine oil. It sure will. I found a barrel on the other side. If we can find some wood, we can start a fire and then work on the torches."

By dawn they had a fire blazing in the barrel, and torches were being made from pipes with oily rags wrapped at the end. They wouldn't last long, but it was a start.

With the arrival of day, light poured in through the cracks of the boards on the windows, and they could see exactly where they were and started to explore.

"What did you say this place was?" Vulcan asked Jake. He was gazing around at all the immense abandoned equipment.

"My grandfather used to make specialty steel for the car industry. But the plant closed a long time ago. After my grandfather died, my dad brought me here when they were holding an auction to sell off everything that was valuable. This is all that's left. Dad says no one wants these big old machines and forges anymore. I think he's planning to sell everything off for scrap."

Vulcan eyes went wide. "Did you say forges?"

Jake nodded. "They're here somewhere. I don't remember what they look like. But they used them to make molds and important parts."

Vulcan started to shake his head. "With all of Earth available to us, you brought us to a forge?"

Jake shrugged. "I'm sorry. It was the only place I could think of."

Vulcan reached out and pulled Jake into a bear hug. "There is no need to apologize, boy. I thank you for bringing me here. I am feeling better already."

"You can use these forges?"

Vulcan laughed heartily. "With your forges and all these steel machines, we can melt them down and make all the weapons we need to defeat the Mimics trying to take our world!"

36

DESPITE VULCAN'S EARLY EXCITEMENT OVER the forges, he was too weak to do much more than sit down and look longingly at the equipment. All the Tartarus prisoners were weak and ran out of energy too quickly to do anything in the building.

Astraea was standing back with Zephyr, Tryn, and Jake. "They need ambrosia or nectar soon. They won't be able to recover without it."

"Is there anything like it here on Earth?" Jake asked.

"Not really," Tryn said.

Astraea looked at Tryn. "We could always go back to Titus to get some."

Jupiter was sitting down against the wall and over-heard their conversation. He called them over. "Take that thought from your mind. It would be too dangerous for you to return. If the Mimics have discovered our escape, it will lead back to you. They will be hunting you."

"But you can't go without food. None of us can," Astraea called.

"We will have to find something else," Jupiter said.

"Wait!" Tryn snapped his fingers. "Sugar! I remember talking to Pegasus a long time ago. He said when he came to Earth, he ate sugar. It kept him going. Paelen, too. They did lose their strength, but it kept them alive. One of Pegasus's favorite foods was chocolate ice cream. Emily still makes it for him."

"Yes, of course," Jupiter said. "But how do we get some?"

"We'd have to buy it," Jake offered. "I've still got some cash with me in my backpack, but we'll need more if we plan to stay here long."

Jupiter looked down at his hand, pulled off one of his gold rings, and held it out to Jake. "I seem to recall gold being valuable here. Is this worth anything?"

Jake looked at the large gold ring. "Whoa, is that real?"

Jupiter nodded. "Yes."

"I bet this would bring in enough to buy a truck-load of sugar!" He handed the ring back to Jupiter. "If we have to stay long, I'm sure we could sell it or find a pawnshop or something." He looked at the large gathering of Titans and Olympians. "Guess we should get you guys some clothes, too. You can't go walking around dressed like that."

His eyes landed on the centaurs, satyrs, and Aurora with her large wings. "And some of you can't be seen walking around at all."

Juno turned to Aurora. "Or flying. I am sorry, but I believe while we are here, you must stay grounded."

"I am too weak to go anywhere, walking or flying," Aurora said.

Jupiter looked over to Vulcan. "Take today and rest." His eyes trailed to everyone in the area. "All of us can take the day. But tomorrow, regardless of how weak or sick we are, we must find a way to turn these machines on and make the weapons we need to defend Titus."

With everyone else lying down on the filthy floor, Astraea and her friends explored the main part of the building. The damp smell of decay was everywhere, and there were puddles of water from old ruptured pipes. Finally Astraea stopped. "They're all so weak. I've never seen my mother looking so pale, and my dad can barely stand. They need ambrosia."

"I know," Tryn agreed. "But after what we've done, the Mimics must know it was us. Going back for ambrosia now, before we're ready, would be madness."

"Yes, it would," Zephyr said. "But it wouldn't be to go for nectar."

"What?" Astraea said. "They'll catch us."

Jake looked at Zephyr and back to Astraea. "What? What did she say? Who will catch us?"

Astraea translated, "Zephyr said we should go back to Titus for nectar, not ambrosia. But it's crazy. They'll catch us."

"Yes, they will!" Jake cried.

Zephyr snorted. "No, they won't. Not if we only go into the nectar orchards. The night dwellers are there. If we tell them what's happening, they would give us jugs of it. We could bring it right back and help everyone."

"It'll be dangerous," Astraea said.

"What will?" Jake cried. "You're still not talking about going back, are you?" He looked at Zephyr. "Astraea's right. It's too dangerous to go back right now."

Zephyr snorted, "What's dangerous is leaving our people weak with no nutrition. I may not like Pegasus, but I know what he went through here. Human food is just no good for us. We're all right now, but in a few days, we will be as weak as the others. Then what good will we be to Titus?"

Astraea looked at Tryn. "She's right. We have to go back."

"Wait," Jake said. "What could Zephyr have possibly said to make you change your mind? Going back there is insane."

"Jake, we have to," Astraea insisted. "But we're only going into the nectar orchards. We won't go anywhere near the palace or our homes—just the orchards."

"But Jupiter said not to," Jake insisted. "Won't he

go ballistic when he finds out what we've done?"

"Not 'we,'" Tryn said. "Us. You have to stay here."

Jake started to shake his head. "No way! If you're going back, so am I."

"Not this time, Jake," Tryn said. "Right now, you are the most important person here. We can't risk you getting caught by the Mimics."

"What's so special about me?" Jake asked.

Tryn pointed to the snake around his neck. "You and Nesso. You're the only one who can talk to Nesso, and she's the only one with venom that can stop the Mimics. Plus, you're human, and this is your world. If we're caught on Titus, Jupiter and the others will need your help to live here until they are strong enough to open the Solar Stream on their own and get to Nesso's home to gather more snakes."

"He'sss right," Nesso said. *"We mussst ssstay here to take care of the weak big thingsss."*

"Please stay and help them," Astraea said. "We won't be long. We'll just go, grab some nectar, and come right back. You won't even miss us."

Jake looked at each of them skeptically and then back to the resting Titans and Olympians. "All right,

I'll stay—but only if you promise to take Cylus and his herd with you. They may be permanently angry, but they're really strong."

"All right, fine. If you stay, we'll take the centaurs," Astraea agreed.

They moved quietly though the resting Titans and Olympians and gathered their daggers. Jupiter was on the floor snoring softly beside Juno, while Pluto snoozed not far away. Cylus was near his mother. She was lying down fully, but Cylus's head and torso were up, keeping watch over her.

Tryn motioned to Cylus and pointed to his flame-sword. Then he pointed to the other young centaurs and silently motioned for them to follow.

Cylus nodded and clambered carefully to his hooves. He quietly gathered his group and told them to grab their weapons. They all followed Tryn to the back area of the plant.

Cylus clopped up to them. "What do you want?"

"We're going back to Titus," Astraea said.

"You are going back for ambrosia. I was thinking of doing the same thing. My mother is so weak, she needs it," he said.

"We can't go for ambrosia," Astraea said. "We would have to go to our homes for that, and it's too dangerous. But we are thinking the Mimics won't be looking for us in the nectar orchards. It's just as good as ambrosia. We are hoping the night dwellers will help."

"Even if they don't," Darek said, "we're taking it anyway. My parents can barely stand."

Cylus nodded. "Fine. When do we go?"

"Right now," Tryn said. He looked back at Jake. "If we're not back by tonight, tell Jupiter what we've done. Jake, you have to help them—you're the only one who can."

Jake nodded. "You just be careful."

"We will," Astraea said.

Tryn walked up to a wall and raised his ring. "Take us back to Titus, the biggest nectar orchard, nighttime."

Immediately the Solar Stream opened on the wall. Tryn looked back at the others. "Are you ready?"

"Enough talk," Cylus said as he and his herd barged forward and entered the Solar Stream.

Astraea looked back at Jake, smiled, shrugged, and followed the centaurs.

37

THE JOURNEY SEEMED SOMEHOW SHORTER as Astraea stayed close to Zephyr. When they emerged from the blazing light, they found themselves in the sweet-smelling nectar orchard.

It took a moment for their eyes to adjust to the nectar orchard at night after the blazing brightness of the Solar Stream. When they could see again, they saw a group of night dwellers looking at them curiously.

The centaurs charged forward. "Give us your nectar, now!"

"Cylus, stop doing that," Astraea called. "We need their help—we don't have to threaten them!" She approached a middle-aged night dweller. "I'm sorry about him. Please, can you call the night dwellers together? We need your help. Jupiter and all of Titus are in big trouble."

"My mother is too!" Cylus put in. He raised his flame-sword. "So give me your nectar now or else."

Astraea reached over to Cylus and forced his flame-sword down. "If you don't stop threatening the night dwellers right now, I swear you'll regret it!"

"What are you attacking me for?" Cylus cried. "You know we need it. They have it. So we'll just take it."

"No, we won't," Tryn said. "We ask. If they say no, we'll gather our own."

The night dwellers seemed overwhelmed at their sudden arrival. "What are you talking about?" an older night dweller said softly. "We just saw Jupiter a while ago." He started to back away fearfully. "He told us you are in big trouble and we should tell him if we see you. What have you done?"

Astraea felt her stomach drop. She looked around. "They knew we'd be coming back for supplies! This could be a trap."

"You must listen to us," Tryn implored. "The Jupiter you saw is an imposter. He comes from a species that is trying to take Titus from us. The real Jupiter is hurt and needs help. We need the nectar to save him."

The man backed away farther. "Jupiter said you would say that."

"Please, listen to us," Astraea begged. "Titus *is* being invaded. We are all in terrible danger." Her eyes landed on the two young night dwellers who had helped her and Zephyr. "You remember us, don't you? You helped us a few days ago by filling our urns with nectar for our detention. Won't you help us again?"

The night dwellers were muttering among themselves when a larger group of other night dwellers arrived.

"What is happening here?" asked one of the newcomers. This dweller looked older than everyone. But like the others with him, he was carrying a jug.

Astraea walked up to the new night dweller. "We were just explaining how we need your help. Titus is being invaded by creatures that are making duplicates of everyone. Jupiter and the others need this nectar. Please, let me have your jug."

The night dweller handed over his jug. But when Astraea received it, she discovered it was empty.

"If you expect us to believe you," he said softly, "you should tell us where you have hidden Jupiter and the others."

The hair on the back of Astraea's neck rose instantly. "Um, what?" She reached out to touch the night dweller, but he pulled back his hand.

Astraea looked back at Zephyr and shouted, "He's a Mimic!"

The words were barely out of her mouth when the Mimic's hand wrapped around her wrist. "What have you done with Jupiter? Tell me!"

Astraea had never felt anything like it. It was like she had been instantly frozen and was unable to move, scream, or fight. She could feel her strength ebbing away as the Mimic stole her energy. She was helpless in his lethal grip.

Astraea couldn't breathe as stars flashed before her eyes. The sound of rushing water filled her ears as the stars faded and were replaced by darkness.

38

"ASTRAEA, WAKE UP!" THE VOICE WAS FILLED with fear. "Please, wake up."

"Mom?"

"I'm not your mother, silly," Zephyr said. "Get up. We don't have a lot of time."

Tryn was kneeling beside her and helped her rise. "That Mimic got you good. You hit the ground fast."

Astraea climbed unsteadily to her feet and rubbed a sore wing. "He got me bad. I feel awful, and I landed on my wing."

One of the young night dwellers who had helped her before brought forth a small cup and offered it to Astraea. "I hope this helps."

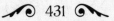

Astraea thanked her and drank the sweet nectar. Almost immediately her strength started to return, but it did nothing to dull the memory of the experience. She had never felt more sick or helpless before in her life. She realized now why Tryn hadn't been able to fight in the cell at Tartarus. No one could fight against the Mimics.

Astraea looked around and saw the night dwellers running from tree to tree, gathering as much nectar as they could. Three of the centaurs were posted around the area with their bows held high and at the ready. Two centaurs were missing.

"What happened after that thing got me?" Astraea asked.

"It was insane," Zephyr said. "After you went down, the other Mimics charged and started grabbing night dwellers and then coming after us." She looked around at the centaurs with renewed admiration. "I have to say, those centaurs can move fast. They shot all the Mimics with their poisoned arrows." She nodded toward the grass. "You can see them there."

"I'd rather not, thanks. I've seen more than enough Mimic puddles."

"After that, Cylus sent two on patrol, while the others are guarding the night dwellers as they gather more nectar for us. Look how much we've got."

Beside Astraea was a collection of jugs filled to overflowing with sweet nectar. Across from her, Cylus was wrapping a cloth around a night dweller's arm. The night dweller was sitting against a tree and looking green. "What happened to him?"

"At one point it was impossible to tell the real night dwellers from the Mimics, so he was shot with an arrow by mistake. It was only a graze, but Nesso's venom made him really sick."

"That's terrible," Astraea said.

"He doesn't mind," Zephyr said. "After what he saw, he said he was grateful we were here." She paused and then finished, "The night dwellers have to come with us. They aren't safe here after they witnessed the Mimics."

Zephyr was right. Mimics seemed to know when Titans discovered their secret or who was around when one of them died. But would the night dwellers be any safer on Earth? "I agree," Astraea said. "We'd better get going."

The centaur Darek barged through the trees. His eyes were huge with fear. "Shadow Titans are coming! Grab the nectar! We have to go, now!"

Tryn called over to the working night dwellers. "Everyone, gather your jugs, we have to leave!"

Astraea and Tryn picked up two jugs each, while the night dwellers gathered what they had and ran up to them. The centaurs also came closer but kept their bows high and ready to fight. Nerves on their flanks twitched as they readied themselves for the fight.

"Open the Solar Stream!" Cylus cried as he raised his flame-sword.

"Hurry!" Darek cried. "They were right behind me!"

Tryn held up his ring and called softly, "Earth, Detroit, Michigan, Westward Junction and into the Reynolds Specialty Steel plant. Now!"

The Solar Stream opened and Tryn shouted, "Everyone, go!"

They all ran forward into the blazing light. Astraea looked around and saw that all the night dwellers, centaurs, Zephyr, and Tryn had made it in. But then her eyes beheld a terrible sight. Three huge Shadow Titans had also followed them into the Solar Stream.

"Look!" Astraea cried fruitlessly as the Solar Stream stole her voice. But calling was unnecessary. The centaurs were looking around within the light and when their eyes landed on the Shadow Titans, they instantly raised their bows. But the arrows they loosed were stolen away by the swirling vortex and vanished. No matter how many they shot, not one hit their target.

Cylus swung his flame-sword but was unable to strike the Shadow Titans.

Tryn handed his jugs to a night dweller and pulled out his dagger. He shouted to Astraea, "Your dagger, use your dagger!" He was trying to walk within the Solar Stream, but like Cylus, he found that moving was next to impossible. Finally he surrendered and stopped trying. But he kept his dagger high and eyes locked on the Shadows.

Astraea also handed over her jugs and pulled her dagger free. She turned and faced the Shadow Titans. Fighting within the confines of the Solar Stream might be impossible, but Astraea was going to be ready for them the moment they emerged on Earth.

With each passing moment, Astraea's heart beat

faster. She was facing the Shadow Titans and realized just how horrible the war in the past must have been. Three of the creatures were terrifying. What if she had to face a battalion of them?

When they arrived back on Earth, because she and Tryn were facing backward, they tumbled out of the end of the Solar Stream and onto the filthy floor of the plant.

The three Shadow Titans appeared right after them with their weapons raised high. Tryn was on his feet first and charging at the monstrosities, with Astraea right behind him. But even before they reached their targets, arrows whizzed past them and struck the black armor of the Shadows.

Most of the arrows bounced off the protective armor. But when one struck a shoulder joint in the armor, it cut through to the creature inside. The creature howled, staggered backward, and started to melt.

"They're Mimics!" Tryn shouted. "Go for the joints in the armor!" But the Mimics were moving targets, and hitting the small joints with the arrows was difficult.

Seeing this, Tryn ran forward and threw himself

down on the greasy floor. He slid the rest of the way right into the legs of one of the remaining creatures. He stabbed his dagger into the ankle joint.

Astraea did the same thing. But her dagger struck the Mimic in the knee joint. In the same flowing move, she rolled away from the creature. But even though it had been poisoned, it didn't stop charging at her.

As the Shadow Titan raised its sword to strike Astraea, Cylus dashed forward and blocked the blow with his flame-sword. He followed through with a swing that struck the Shadow Titan's armored head, and it was cut from the body. When the helmet rolled away, they all gasped to find that it was empty.

After a few more hits with the flame-sword, Cylus cut the Shadow Titan down into pieces of empty armor.

"Whoa, that was awesome!" Jake shouted as he raced forward and helped Astraea to her feet. "Are you okay? You guys are proper ninjas!"

"Thanks . . . I think," Astraea said. She looked at Cylus. "Thank you for saving my life."

Cylus shuffled on his hooves. "Now we're even after you saved me at school."

"What is going on here?" Jupiter demanded.

He, Pluto, Juno, and several other weakened Titans arrived and stared in confusion at the gathering of night dwellers. Then their eyes went wide at the sight of the fallen attackers.

Astraea's father approached one of the sets of armor and gazed at the spreading pools on the floor. "Shadow Titans? How is this possible?"

"No, Dad," Astraea said. "They're Mimics wearing Shadow Titan armor—except for that empty one. I don't know what that is." She looked back at Tryn. "They've learned that we have a weapon against them and are wearing the armor to protect themselves."

Pluto lifted the empty Shadow Titan helmet. "This is no Mimic. It is a genuine Shadow Titan," he uttered with an ashen face. "They have resurrected the Shadow Titans and have discovered how to control them."

"That is impossible!" Jupiter cried. "We ended them!"

"Apparently not," Pluto said. "Look for yourself."

Jupiter received the dark green armor head, and his jaw dropped. "This is real—I would know it anywhere. But how?"

"Wait," Cylus cried. "Are you saying that I fought a real Shadow Titan?"

Jupiter looked at everyone and slowly nodded. "Yes, that is exactly what I am saying."

"I think I'm going to pass out." Cylus leaned into his mother.

"Shadow Titans and Mimics working together?" Tryn said. "We're going to have to adapt how we fight."

"Astraea!" Aurora cried. "Where have you been?"

Astraea looked guiltily at her mother. "Please don't be angry. We had to do it."

"Do what?" Jupiter said. He was still holding the helmet. "Child, what have you done? How did these things get here?"

Astraea walked over to a night dweller and asked for a jug. She carried it back to her mother. "We went back to Titus to get nectar for you."

"I forbade you to go!" Jupiter cried.

Tryn faced Jupiter. "Technically speaking, you said we couldn't go back for ambrosia. You never said anything about nectar."

39

EVERYONE GATHERED TOGETHER IN THE center of the large, dead manufacturing plant and listened to the away team as they explained what had happened.

"They know you're no longer in Tartarus," Tryn said, "and they're looking for you."

Astraea nodded. "They're probably looking for us too. It was a trap in the orchard, like they were waiting for us. They wanted to know where we've moved you."

Jupiter shook his head. "It was reckless and dangerous for you to go back there. It could have been a disaster, especially if they are using Shadow Titans to

fight for them." His eyes landed on Tryn. "That ring you wear is the only way off this world for us in our weakened condition. You might have lost it, and we would have been trapped here."

Tryn dropped his head. "I'm sorry, Jupiter, but it was a risk we had to take. You are all so weak. Without nectar, you will grow even weaker. We had no choice."

"Do not think that we are ungrateful," Jupiter said, "but the risk was still too great. I forbid you to go back there for any reason until we are ready to take on the Mimics and their fighters."

Aurora had her arm around Astraea. "After everything those things did to us, I cannot bear the thought of them hurting you."

"I understand, but it turned out all right," Astraea said. "And you have the nectar you need to get strong again."

"For now," Jupiter said. "But it will not last indefinitely."

"Then we had better think of some way to take our world back soon," Vulcan said. He was holding on to the helmet of one of the Shadow Titans.

"Especially now, if they have an army of Shadow Titans and are wearing the armor themselves."

Jake raised his hand. "Excuse me, but I think you should know. It was one of those things that took me from my home in LA. And it's what took Nesso from her world."

Jupiter paused and rubbed his bearded chin. "How is this possible? The Shadow Titans were from our past, and most recently from underground here on Earth. But we destroyed them all. A Mimic could not have known about them."

"Perhaps they have seen them in our memories," Juno suggested.

"Yes," Cylus's mother agreed. "I was in the first war. My memories—and nightmares—are filled with them."

"All right, they might have seen them in our memories. But how did they re-create them?"

Tryn was standing beside Astraea, listening intently. When the conversation slowed, he started to speak. "I am sorry, but I think I know another reason they knew about the Shadow Titans and maybe even where to get the armor."

Aurora turned to him. "How?"

Tryn looked over at Jake. "Jake and I were under Arcadia Two when we saw them take you and Astraios through the Solar Stream. The Mimics were speaking their own language, but then there was one among them who was different. I am sure he was a Titan."

Gasps filled the air.

"What?" Astraios said. "I don't remember that."

Astraea looked at her parents. "Dad, do you or Mom remember anything of your capture?"

Aurora and Astraios looked at each other and shrugged. "Actually, now that you mention it, no," Aurora said. She looked at the other prisoners. "Does anyone remember their capture?"

"I just remember waking up in Tartarus," Pluto said softly.

"As do I," Jupiter agreed.

"I recall nothing," Themis said. "The last thing I do remember is being in my office at Arcadia."

Every other prisoner nodded.

"They somehow blocked your memories," Tryn said. "But there was a Titan beneath Arcadia talking to the Mimics, and he sounded really bitter."

Jupiter turned sharply to him. "Do you realize what you are saying?"

Tryn nodded. "Yes. I am saying that Titus has a traitor."

A heavy silence filled the plant as the Titans and Olympians quietly consumed a cup of nectar each. The remaining nectar was stored safely away and would be rationed to ensure that it lasted as long as possible.

As their energy slowly returned, everyone set to work clearing away refuse and rubble from the area. Then scrap metal was brought in and piled in a single area for Vulcan to go through. He was working with Astraea's father and Render's mother, figuring out what each machine was and its function.

When Astraea, Zephyr, Tryn, and Jake offered to help, Jupiter took them aside. "I know you are anxious to contribute," he said. "And you have, more than you know. But for now, I must ask you to take it easy and rest. I am working on a plan for you, and you will need every ounce of strength you possess." Jupiter then instructed the centaurs to keep practicing their bow and sword work.

"And . . . ," Zephyr said as Jupiter walked away. She looked at Astraea. "Why didn't he tell us the plan? What are we supposed to do now?"

"I guess we just wait."

Zephyr whinnied in frustration. "You know I hate waiting!"

"Me too, but what choice have we got?"

Jake reached into his backpack and pulled out his skateboard. After putting it down on the smooth concrete floor, he started to ride it through the area.

Tryn jogged beside him, and when Jake finished, he handed the board to Tryn. "Give it a try. The floor here is great."

They took turns going through the mostly empty main floor of the building, skirting around the big machines, under the broken-down conveyer belt, and around the forge where Vulcan was working. Several times they nearly struck working Titans and dodged out of the way of Olympians with the sound of angry shouts following behind them.

While Tryn was taking another turn, Jake approached Astraea. His face was glowing with excitement. "You really should let me teach you.

Boarding always makes me feel better." His smile broadened, and he petted the snake around his neck. "Nesso loves it too!"

"It'sss very exccciting," Nesso agreed. *"I love boarding."*

Astraea shook her head. "Thanks, but I don't think anything could make me feel better right now."

"Hey, your mom and dad are safe and getting stronger. What's all this about?"

Astraea was leaning against Zephyr. "What are we supposed to do now? The Mimics are using Shadow Titans, and now they know that we know about them. If they don't have Jupiter to make duplicates of, what are they going to do? Are they going to start attacking everyone?"

"And what about the traitor?" Zephyr added. "If someone has betrayed us, who is it?"

"Yes, that too," Astraea agreed.

Jake looked at Zephyr. "What did she say?"

Zephyr snorted, "Don't tell him this time, and let's see if he can figure it out."

Astraea shook her head. "She was wondering about the traitor."

"You really aren't any fun anymore, Astraea," Zephyr complained.

Jake shook his head also. "Yeah, I mean, what kind of person would betray his own people?"

"A very angry one," Vulcan said. He approached, holding on to Jake's skateboard. Tryn was standing behind him and shrugged apologetically, as if to say that Vulcan had taken it from him without permission.

"This is yours?" Vulcan said, peering closely at the polished skateboard.

"Yes, sir," Jake said. "My dad gave it to me. It's my favorite thing in the world." He leaned over his board and pointed to a signature. "Look, it's signed by my boarding hero. My dad had it enameled after that to protect the autograph."

Vulcan nodded but looked like he hadn't understood a word Jake had said. "Do you mind if I borrow it for a while?"

Jake looked from Astraea to Tryn. Finally he said, "Um, sure, I guess."

Vulcan mumbled a few words and walked up to Jake. He caught hold of a couple of strands of his blond hair and plucked them out.

"Ouch!" Jake cried. "What did you do that for?"

"Need them . . . ," Vulcan muttered as he walked away with the skateboard.

Tryn shrugged. "He did the same thing to me but wouldn't tell me why."

Jake rubbed his scalp. "He's not gonna keep it, is he? I love that board."

Astraea didn't know what to tell him. Vulcan had a way of borrowing things and forgetting to return them. Worse still, her mother once said that Vulcan had borrowed a piece of jewelry from her, then took it all apart because he needed the jewel inside it. "I'm—I'm sure he'll return it."

"Yeah," Zephyr laughed. "But not in your lifetime!"

Jake looked at Zephyr and shrugged.

"She says he will give it back," Astraea lied.

"I did not!" Zephyr snorted angrily. "Astraea, you are impossible!"

Astraea laughed and hugged Zephyr's white neck. "And you are the best!" She looked at Jake and Tryn. "Since they don't need us to help, why don't we finish looking around? I haven't been upstairs yet."

"Me neither," Tryn agreed.

"Stairs, how wonderful," Zephyr complained as she followed behind them.

The stairs were deeper than they expected, and Zephyr was able to follow them up. Walking onto the second level, they noticed that this floor did have glass windows—most were cracked or broken, but at least they weren't boarded up like on the main floor. They let in the light and revealed that it was approaching sunset.

Like downstairs, there was more abandoned equipment. Several Titans were working with Olympians, looking at the strange machines. They gave Astraea and her friends only a passing glance.

They walked up to a broken window and peered outside. The weather was gray and moody as a soft drizzly rain wet the pavement. Directly across from them was another derelict building. It, too, had all its windows broken and the main floor boarded up. The two buildings shared a common driveway that was overgrown with grass and weeds, but also had a load of old tires dumped in the middle of it. There were burned patches on the ground, showing signs of a possible bonfire.

Astraea stared in wonder at the abandoned area. "I have never seen anything like this before."

"Yeah, it's pretty depressing," Jake said. "But in my grandfather's time, this place was one of the busiest areas in the country." He reached into his backpack and pulled out his cell phone. He tried to turn it on, but it was still dead. "I wish the power was on. I could charge this and call home."

Beyond the abandoned buildings, they saw other buildings. "What are those?" Astraea asked.

Jake looked out the window and then back at her quizzically. "They're houses. That's where people live. From what I can see, that area doesn't look abandoned. If you look farther ahead there, you can see they're actually building more homes."

Tryn's eyes were wide with excitement. "So this is Earth."

"I wouldn't judge all of Earth by what you see here," Jake said. "This is an industrial area that died when the industry left. . . ." He paused and looked around. "But by the looks of things, they're getting better. Look, we're not too far from downtown, and it looks busy. Hey, maybe I can find a phone there and call my mom. I need to let her know I'm okay and to find out if Molly is home."

"What's a phone?" Zephyr asked. When Astraea repeated the question, Jake held up his cell phone.

"This is a cell phone. When it's charged, I can use this to call anyone I want, or send texts or do almost anything. So if you were on the other side of the city or even the world, I could use it to call you and speak with you. But it needs electricity to be charged, and there isn't any here."

Astraea took the phone from Jake and looked at it curiously. "You can do all that with this little thing?"

"Sure. There's a camera, too, so I can take pictures."

"It's wonderful," Astraea said. "I wish we had these on Titus."

"I'm surprised you don't. We've had phones forever." Jake leaned out of the broken window. "I think I can see a bar down the road. I'm sure they must have a phone in there that I could use."

"Oh, great. I'm coming too," Astraea said.

Jake looked horrified. "You can't! Astraea, you have wings. If anyone saw them, they'd take you away."

"Stupid wings," Astraea moped. "I can't fly with them, and I can't go out, either. What good are they?"

"Besides," Jake continued, "you're not dressed like a human. I still have my clothes in my bag from when I was taken." He looked down at his tunic. "There is no way I'm going out in this dress."

Tryn looked at Jake. "You're not wearing a dress— it's a tunic." Then to Astraea he said, "At least you can hide your wings with a coat or something. I have this silver skin that's going to be a nightmare to hide."

Zephyr whinnied to Astraea, "I don't know what you're making such a fuss about. This is Earth, and it's filled with idiot humans who can't tell what I am. To them, I'm just a flying horse. Why would you want to see more of it or them?"

"What did she say?" Jake asked.

"She doesn't understand why I'm making a fuss," Astraea said. "She said Earth is filled with humans who would only call her a flying horse."

"*Idiot* humans!" Zephyr whinnied. "Why won't you ever tell him what I actually say?"

Jake blushed and smiled at Zephyr. "You won't

ever let me forget that I called you a horse, will you?"

Zephyr snorted, "Not if I can help it!"

Astraea smiled. "She says not to worry about it."

"Astraea!" Zephyr cried.

40

JAKE PICKED UP HIS BACKPACK AND SLUNG it over his shoulder. He was wearing the clothes he had worn when the others first found him in the orchard. "I won't be long. I'll just call my mom and come right back. I'll save the sightseeing for another time."

"Just be careful," Astraea said. She reached out and stroked Nesso. "You're carrying precious cargo." She leaned closer and spoke to the snake. "Are you sure you don't want to stay here with us?"

"Thank you, but I belong with Jake," Nesso hissed.

Jake smiled. "She says thank you, but she wants to stay with me."

Astraea nodded. "Then don't you let anything happen to her. She bit the Mimics for you. If anyone goes for her, you bite them."

"Me bite someone?" Jake laughed. "Yeah, right, like that's gonna happen! But don't worry, I'll keep her safe."

Jake felt strange leaving the others behind as he exited the building and closed the doors behind him. He hadn't known them very long at all, but already he felt they were the closest friends he'd ever had.

Tryn had lent him his lockpick set to get out of the gate, but no matter how much Jake worked on the old lock, it wouldn't open. Giving up, he found he was thin enough to slip through the opening between the two gates.

Jake stood on the street and gazed around. Suddenly the area looked strange and uninviting compared to what he'd seen on Titus. The sky was gray and moody and the streets were wet, dirty, and filled with potholes and weeds growing through the asphalt. Around him the derelict buildings looked eerie and threatening, with their broken windows and graffiti tagging on the boards sealing them closed.

Granted, he'd spent the last few years in LA, but they had come back to Detroit for visits. He couldn't remember it ever looking so desolate before. Had his time on Titus changed him so much?

Jake set his shoulders and started to move with determination. He walked along the empty street until he left Westward Junction behind and was moving into a more populated area. Each time he passed someone, he instinctively reached up to his neck to make sure Nesso was still there.

"I'm fine, Jake, don't worry about me. Jussst call your mother."

"I will. When we go into the bar, don't move or let anyone know that you're alive, okay?"

"I won't," Nesso promised.

Before long they reached the street with the bar that he'd seen from the window. As evening set in, it was becoming more and more busy. Jake pushed open the door and entered the dark bar, and he was immediately struck by the smell of stale beer.

Men of all ages were seated on high stools before the long oak bar, while a few couples sat at the small round tables and booths.

"Hey, kid, you're too young to come in here," called a man from behind the bar.

Jake looked over and saw hundreds of glasses hanging from a rack above the bar and tall beer taps poking up from beneath it. He nodded and walked over to the bartender. "I'm sorry, but my cell died and I really need to find a phone to call my mom."

The bartender was pulling one of the taps and filling a pint glass with beer. He looked at Jake. "You lost?"

"Sort of," Jake said. "I really need to reach her, but there aren't any phones on the street." He looked around and saw a public phone on the wall at the back near a sign leading to the toilets. "Can I use that one? I promise to leave when I'm done."

The bartender shook his head. "Sorry, that one hasn't worked in ages. With everyone using a cell these days, there's no point. Let me see your phone."

Jake reached into his bag, pulled out his cell phone, and handed it over. When the bartender checked and found it had no charge, he nodded and handed it back. "Sorry, kid. I can't be too careful around here." He called over to another man taking glasses out of

the dishwasher. "Hey, Jimmy, take over for a minute. I'm taking this lost lamb to the office to use the phone. I'll be right back."

"Sure, boss," Jimmy said as he closed the dishwasher and moved to take a drink order.

"Follow me," the boss said. He looked at Jake and frowned. "You're not from around here, are you?"

"I was born in Detroit, but my mom moved us out to LA a few years ago."

The man looked like he was barely listening as he led Jake to the back of the bar. He pushed open a door that had the sign PRIVATE posted on it. "Forget the mess. The phone is on my desk. Try not to move things, I got a system."

Jake stood staring at the disaster of an office. There were stacks of papers on the desk that looked ready to topple over. He couldn't see a phone at first and had to follow the telephone cable to find it.

When Jake picked up the receiver, he looked at the man. "I won't be long. But to be honest, my mom is going to go nuclear when she hears me. Can I have a bit of privacy?"

The bartender studied Jake for a moment. "Sure.

But I'll be right out here and will hear if you start going through my stuff."

"I won't, I promise," Jake said. "And I can pay for the call."

"Forget it, kid. Just help an old lady across the street or something to pay me back."

"How about I help save Titus from a bunch of Mimics?"

"Sure, whatever," the bartender said as he closed the door.

Jake dialed the number, not sure what he was going to tell his mom. What could he say? That he'd been kidnapped by a monster and taken to another planet? That would go down really well. He had no idea what to say and had to hope something would come to him.

By the third ring, he heard the receiver being picked up. "Hello?"

Jake gasped and could barely speak. "M-Moles, is that you?"

"Jake!" Molly cried. "Where are you?"

Jake could hardly believe that she was safe. "What happened to you? How did you get away from the Shadow Titan?"

"The what?" Molly said. "Jake, are you crazy? Have you hit your head again?"

"Yeah, I did hit my head," he said quickly. "When I saw that thing grab you. Don't you remember? I fell off my skateboard and hit the curb. We were on our way to the pier to see Dad."

"Yes, we were, and you just left me there. Mom went nuts when you didn't come home! She called the police and everything. They said you probably ran away."

Jake suddenly realized that like everyone else who encountered the Mimics, Molly couldn't remember a thing. He barely could, but he had no idea how Molly had gotten away from them. Had she fought? Screamed? Run away? He didn't know and wondered if he ever would.

"Where is Mom? I need to speak with her."

"She's not here. She and Richard are taking Billy to the doctor for his checkup."

"Who's Billy?"

"He's our baby brother."

"Brother? Mom's had the baby already?"

"Yeah, like two months ago. He's so cute. When are you coming home to see him?"

His mother had the baby? She still had two weeks to go before he was due. Now his baby brother was two months old? "Moles, answer me: How long have I been gone? What's the date?"

"That's a stupid question."

"Tell me!" Jake shouted.

"Jeez, Jake, you don't need to bite my ear off. You ran away on July thirteenth, and now it's September twenty-ninth and school has started again."

"What?" Jake cried. "That can't be right. I've only been gone a few days." He looked around the small office and saw a newspaper lying on a mountain of files. He pulled it closer and read the date on the top. SEPTEMBER 29 . . .

"Jake, where are you?" Molly demanded. "What happened to you?"

"I—I'm safe," he promised. "I was taken, but now I'm safe."

"When are you coming home?"

When was he coming home? Speaking to Molly, he felt such a huge sense of relief that she was safe. But the Titans weren't. It would be so easy to tell Molly where he was. Then his father would come to

get him. But then what? What about Astraea, Tryn, and Zephyr, and all the others? What would happen to them if he and Nesso stayed?

Jake knew he couldn't stay. His sister was safe, that was the main thing. But there were others who needed him. "Molly," he finally said. "Listen to me very carefully. I have to go somewhere far away. But I'm not running away, I promise. Do you hear me? Tell Mom I'm not running away. I will be back. I just need to help some very special people."

"What are you talking about?" Molly demanded. "Jake, come home. Mom has been crying ever since you left."

"I know, and I'm so sorry. But I'm needed here. I hope you can understand. I am helping some very special people. Please tell Mom and Dad that I love them and I'll be back. Just not for a while. Would you do that for me, please?"

"Jake, I don't understand. Where are you?"

"I wish I could explain, but I can't, at least not now. There isn't time. Just tell Mom and Dad and even Richard that I *will* be back."

He could hear Molly's voice catch. "But—I miss you."

"I miss you, too," Jake said softly. "Moles, listen, when I come back, I promise to tell you everything. I might even be able to show you some amazing things. But you have to trust me. I'm doing this to help others."

The bartender opened the door and nodded to Jake. "Almost finished?"

"Yes, sir," Jake said. He focused on the call again. "Molly, I have to go. Whatever happens, please remember that I love you—you big slob."

"Jake, no, please tell me where you are."

"I can't. But I promise to be back as soon as possible. Give a big kiss to Billy for me and tell him his big brother loves him."

"But you haven't even met him," Molly said in a whisper.

"I will, soon." Jake felt his throat tightening. "Molly, please tell Mom I'm sorry I've hurt her. But I will be back."

He pulled the phone from his ear and heard his sister's voice calling his name as he hung it up.

"You okay, kid?" the bartender asked.

Jake sniffed. "Yeah, I'm fine."

"Look, I heard part of what you said. Are you in some kind of trouble? Can I help?"

Jake smiled. "No, it's all right. My family thinks I ran away, but I didn't. Now I have to do something before I go home—but I don't think they'll understand."

"You sure you're not in trouble?"

"Me? No, but some good friends are, so I'm staying to help."

The bartender looked doubtful but nodded. "Okay, but if things get bad, you come back here. I got a boy a bit older than you, and I'd like to think someone else would help him if he got into trouble."

Jake smiled again and walked toward the office door. "Thanks, that's real nice of you."

"Anytime," the bartender said as he stood back and Jake walked out.

41

TRYN WAS STANDING AT THE WINDOW, gazing out. "I hope he comes back."

Astraea nodded. "He will."

Zephyr nodded. "Only because Vulcan has his board thing."

Astraea laughed and patted Zephyr on the neck. "You're not very trusting, are you?"

Zephyr snorted and shook her head. "Not when it comes to humans."

Around them everyone seemed to be busy, but nothing appeared to be getting done. The piles of scrap metal had been moved to one area and the aisles were now clear.

They left the windows and returned to the main floor, where a crowd was gathering at the forge. Vulcan and Juno were standing with Jupiter and Pluto. Pluto put his hand on his brother's shoulder while Jupiter raised his arms and a large flash of forked lightning shot from his hands and into the old forge.

The long-dead furnace creaked and moaned in protest but finally burst to life as flames shot out of it. Almost immediately the plant seemed to radiate with heat and light.

Vulcan roared with joy upon seeing the flashing flames. He looked at the others. "Do not just stand there—bring me some steel so I can start making the weapons we need to free Titus!"

Everyone cheered. But then Astraea looked at Jupiter and Pluto and saw the toll that sharing their powers and lighting the forge had taken on them. They were both standing back and leaning heavily against the wall.

"Stay here. I'll be right back," Astraea said to Zephyr. She dashed away and ran to their supply of nectar. She picked up an old cup, poured it full of the thick, sweet liquid, and brought it back to Jupiter and Pluto.

"Here, I think you both need this."

Jupiter's tired eyes sparkled with gratitude. "I have had my ration for the day. I will be fine."

Pluto waved the cup away. "Save it for the others."

"But you both used a lot of power to light the forge. Please, take my ration. I don't really need it yet."

"You will," Jupiter said weakly. "We just need to rest a bit and we will be fine."

The sound of running made Astraea turn. Jake was tearing through the plant at top speed. He had grocery bags in both hands. When he stopped and saw the flames burning in the forge, he couldn't hide his surprise. "You lit the forge and I missed it. Nuts!"

"Jupiter and Pluto did it," Astraea said. "But they drained their energy and won't drink any nectar."

Jake put down the bags he was carrying. "Didn't you say that when you guys came to Earth, you ate sugar?"

Tryn nodded and Jake grinned. "Well then, be prepared for a sugar overdose!" He bent down, reached into the first bag, and took out a box. As he opened it, he explained, "These are sugar-glazed doughnuts. Try one."

Tryn was the first to reach into the box. "My dad told me about doughnuts. . . ." When he took his first bite, he smiled. "This is wonderful."

Astraea also took a doughnut and tried it. A wide smile crossed her face. "It's almost as good as ambrosia."

Jake picked up a doughnut and offered it to Zephyr. "Here, try this."

"I refuse to be *fed* by a human!" Zephyr turned away, but then her nostrils started to twitch and she nickered. She turned back and finally took the doughnut. "Don't think this changes anything," she said with her mouth full.

"She says thank you," Astraea said.

Zephyr nearly choked and spit crumbs everywhere. "What?" She gave Astraea a dirty look and then stole a second doughnut from the box.

Astraea led Jake over to Jupiter and Pluto and gave him a nudge. "Give them some. They just used a lot of power to light the forge and need the sugar."

Jake looked into the flames. "I wish I'd seen it." He shuffled his feet and held out the box of doughnuts. "Um, Jupiter, Pluto, sirs, would you like a doughnut?"

Jupiter raised his head. "Where did these come from?"

"I had some money with me, and since I went out to call my mother, I bought them on the way back. There's a grocery store not too far from here. It has a lot of junk food that should be good for you."

"You went out?" Jupiter asked.

Jake nodded. "Yes, sir. I really needed to call my mother and tell her I was safe."

Pluto stood upright. His face was calm, but his eyes flashed. "Did you tell anyone about us being here?"

Jake looked fearfully at Pluto. "No, sir, I didn't say anything, I swear! I didn't even reach my mother." His eyes went back to Astraea. "I spoke to Molly. She's home. She wasn't taken by the Mimics!"

"Explain yourself," Jupiter said. "Who is Molly?"

Astraea took over for Jake. "His sister was attacked at the same time as Jake. It was a Mimic in armor or a Shadow Titan that got them. We found Jake in the nectar orchard by Arcadia but couldn't find his sister. Now it seems that they didn't take her, just Jake."

"I'm so relieved," Jake said. "But Moles is just like

everyone else—she can't remember what happened. They think I've run away. And guess what, my mom has already had the baby. I've been gone over two months! How is that possible? I was only in Titus a few days."

Jupiter nodded. "Time moves differently between our two worlds. A day on Titus is weeks here. Did you tell your sister about us?"

"No, sir. I just said I've been helping friends and will be home once you're safe."

Jupiter came forward and put his arm around him. "You have been a great help and I am grateful." He looked at everyone around him. "So let us get to work so we can reclaim our world and get this boy home to his family as soon as possible."

42

THE FOOD WAS DISTRIBUTED AMONG THE Titans and Olympians, giving them renewed energy and a determination to get to work.

Jupiter and Pluto called Astraea, Zephyr, Tryn, and Jake over. They also asked Astraea's parents to join them. When they were all together, Jupiter said to Astraea and her team, "You have done so much for us, and we will be eternally grateful. But now I must ask you for more. We realize that you will be integral in freeing Titus from the Mimics. So I must ask you to leave us while you still have the strength to do it."

"You want us to go back to Titus?" Astraea asked.

Jupiter shook his head. "No, you must go to Nesso's

world and find more snakes like her." He looked over at Jake. "Implore them to help us. They will be our only salvation against the Mimics." He paused. "Though I remain uncertain what to do about the Shadow Titans with only one flame-sword here. We can only hope that Vulcan comes up with something."

Astraea felt her mother's arm tense around her. She looked up at her and saw the fear in Aurora's eyes. Astraea knew her mother didn't want her to go, but said nothing. Finally she smiled weakly and nodded.

"We'll go," Astraea said. "And we won't come back until we have convinced them to join us."

Jupiter nodded tiredly. "Thank you."

"Clear the way—let me though," Vulcan said gruffly.

The Titans and Olympians parted to allow Vulcan to approach. He walked up to Jake and held out his skateboard. "This one is yours and will serve only you." Then he handed another to Tryn. "And this one is yours. Try them out and see how they work for you."

Jake looked at his board and cried, "What have you done to it?"

Vulcan smiled. "I improved it."

Jake's eyes were huge. "But—but you cut it in half!" He held it up to Astraea. "Look what he did to my skateboard! He cut right through my Rob Dyrdek autograph and glued a piece of metal to it."

"Yes," Vulcan said. "So you have half of the original and Tryn has the other half. The back part now has wings and the power to fly. You simply tell it where you want to go and it will take you there."

"F-fly?" Jake cried.

Vulcan smiled a big, toothy grin. "Yes, fly. I made Mercury's sandals fly; this is the same principle. Now your boards fly."

Astraea could see the pain in Jake's face. He had loved that strange board, and now it was changed. "Try it," she suggested.

Tryn put his down on the concrete floor and climbed on. He pushed off and the new skateboard rolled easily down the aisle. "Fly me to the end of the building." Instantly tiny metal wings appeared out of the back wheels, lifted the board off the ground, and flew down the length of the big plant.

"Jake," Tryn called, "this is wonderful. Try it!"

Jake was still looking at his damaged board, and his chin started to quiver.

Zephyr nudged Astraea. "Look, look, he's going to cry!"

"Be nice," Astraea said to her as she walked over to Jake. "I'm so sorry. I know how much that meant to you."

"It was the last really big gift my dad gave me before he and my mom got divorced. Now it's ruined."

"But it's for a good cause, and now it flies. Why don't you try it?"

Jake looked at her miserably. "It already flew down the road."

"Please try it." She pointed up at Tryn. "Look how much fun Tryn is having, and you know he doesn't like to show his emotions."

Jake looked up as Tryn whooshed by with a huge grin on his face. "Come on up, Jake, it's great!"

Jake walked away from the group and put down the board. He climbed on and pushed off. It seemed to move as well as it had before.

"Just tell it to fly!" Tryn called as he passed overhead again.

Jake looked down at the board and repeated Tryn's command. "Fly me to the end of the building."

Tiny wings appeared out of Jake's rear wheels. They flapped just like the hummingbirds on Titus did, moving so quickly they could no longer be seen.

Jake cried out as the board lifted him off the ground. He lost his balance and started to fall, but the board seemed to know it and readjusted itself beneath his feet.

"It will not let you fall," Vulcan called. "Be confident and it will work with you."

"Jake," Tryn called as he flew up beside him and hovered. "It works the same way as it did on the ground, but this time it's in the air. The balancing is the same."

After a couple of uncertain moments, Jake's posture changed and he rebalanced himself on the flying board. It rose high above the heads of everyone and carried him smoothly down the length of the building.

"See!" Tryn called.

From her position on the floor, Astraea smiled as

Jake's confidence grew. Soon he and Tryn were flying together all around the building. She saw them duck into the stairwell and disappear upstairs.

Several minutes later they returned. They touched down on the ground and pulled up in front of Astraea. Jake's disappointment had vanished and been replaced by excitement.

"This is awesome!" Jake beamed as he stepped off the skateboard and the wings vanished into the rear wheels. "It's just like the hoverboard from *Back to the Future*! You just lean into where you want to go and the board takes you there!" He looked at Vulcan. "Thanks so much!"

"No, thank you for getting me out of Tartarus."

"Hey, I helped," Zephyr cried. "What do I get?"

Vulcan laughed. "Would you like a flying board too?"

Zephyr snorted. "I've got my own wings, thank you very much."

Astraea smiled at Jake. "I thought you were upset about your board being cut in half."

"I was," Jake admitted. "But this is so much better. Maybe I can get this one autographed too!"

"After we free Titus," Tryn said.

Jake's smile vanished. "Yes, after we free Titus."

Vulcan nodded. "So they work for you?"

"Yes, thank you, Vulcan," Tryn said. "You are right, they will serve us well."

Vulcan mumbled a few words and then walked back toward the forge. Jupiter came forward. "I hate to say this, but it is time for you to go. Each moment we delay, you will be growing weaker, and disaster could be befalling Titus."

"You're right," Tryn said. "I'll gather my things."

"Me too," Jake said.

Astraea and Zephyr stood with her parents. She hugged her mother tightly and then her father.

"I wish we could come with you," her father said.

"We'll be fine," Astraea promised. "Nesso is so sweet, I'm sure the others will be too. You just stay here and get stronger."

"Be careful," her mother said as tears filled her eyes. "Don't take any unnecessary risks." She kissed Astraea and then Zephyr. "I love you both very much."

"We love you, too," Zephyr answered.

Astraea hugged her mother again. "Don't let any-one see you."

Her mother nodded.

Tryn and Jake returned. Jake had his board in his backpack. "All set."

Cylus, Darek, and Render clopped up to them, holding their bows and quivers full of arrows. "We're ready," Cylus said. "Let's go!"

"But we're only going to get some snakes. We won't be long," Astraea said.

"And who's going to protect you if you get into trouble?" Cylus challenged. "You? Tryn or that weak human? You saw what I did with that Shadow Titan. I can fight, you can't. We are coming."

"Hey, I can fight just as well as anyone," Astraea said.

"Me too!" Zephyr added.

The three centaurs started to laugh, stopping only when Jupiter approached. "Thank you, Cylus, Darek, and Render. I am sure you will be a great help to them." He turned to Astraea. "They are excellent fighters, and this is too important to all of us." He started to walk forward. "Come, it is time."

Jupiter's word was law, and Astraea didn't argue.

She looked at Zephyr, sighed heavily, and followed him to one of the building's big walls.

"Where are we going?" Tryn said. "What is the world called?"

Jupiter answered, "I am certain that we saw snakes like Nesso on Zomos. But it is an unknown world. When one of us was bitten and nearly died, we left it immediately and did not return. I remember it was a world much like Xanadu—wild with a lot of life, both plant and animal. I am sorry that I cannot tell you more because we did not linger."

Tryn nodded. "We'll just have to find out for ourselves." He looked at Astraea. "Are you ready?"

Astraea nodded and held on to Zephyr. "Are you?"

Zephyr snorted. "If I say no, can I stay?"

"No," Astraea said.

Zephyr sighed. "Then yes, I'm as ready as I'll ever be."

Tryn looked back at the Titans and Olympians and nodded. "We will be back soon." He held the ring up to the wall and called, "Zomos!" Instantly the Solar Stream opened as the wall was covered in blazing white light.

"Stay safe!" Aurora called.

Astraea nodded at her parents. "We will. You stay safe too!"

Jake looked down at Nesso. "You're going home, Nesso!"

Astraea watched the snake lift her head and hiss something back to him. Jake smiled and blushed, but what Nesso said remained a mystery as they walked confidently into the Solar Stream.

ACKNOWLEDGMENTS

There are always so many people deserving thanks in the creation of any book. But in this case, I want to say an extra special and massive thanks to my darling editor, Fiona Simpson at Aladdin, who cares as much about the world of Olympus and Titus as I do. It was Fiona who invited me to follow the Pegasus series with Titans. You're the absolute best, Fiona. I know I owe you big time for this—would T. H. be enough?

As always I'd also like to thank my agent, Veronique Baxter, for her continued support.

I would also like to add my heartfelt thanks to Jennifer Ollinger from the Detroit Visitors Bureau, for taking me on a long-distance tour of Detroit (she was there; I was still in England) so that I had somewhere for my Olympians and Titans to land. I would also like to thank Kim Rusinow from Destination Detroit and Police Lieutenant Mark Deluca for their assistance in finding places for my characters and finding what they might encounter there. You guys are the best!

And, of course, I would like to thank my family for putting up with me pulling out all my mythology textbooks again and for wandering around the house muttering to myself about Jupiter. . . . You guys are awesome!

Finally, I'd like to thank you, the reader, for taking these books into your heart. I write for you. . . . Just remember to be nice to each other and to care for the animals of the world. They are counting on you. . . .

NOW GET A SNEAK PEEK
OF THE NEXT BOOK!

TITANS BOOK 2:
THE MISSING

WITH A WEAKENED JUPITER, AND TARTARUS prisoners hidden on Earth, Astraea, Zephyr, and their team head to Nesso's jungle world to seek the help of the snakes in the struggle against the Mimics.

But nothing goes to plan. The moment they arrive, they encounter a world filled with dangers they never imagined possible—from massive hungry dinosaurs to a blisteringly hot sun. Soon Zephyr is critically wounded by a giant poisonous serpent, and Astraea suffers a broken leg. Without ambrosia or nectar to heal them, the group soon realize they are in serious trouble. But where can they go for help?

With Zephyr's life slipping away, Jake and Tryn use their new flying skateboards to try to make it to Xanadu, where they hope to find ambrosia for Zephyr and to enlist the help of the Xan, Riza, and Emily Jacobs to join the fight against the Mimics.

When the teams split up, Astraea and the three centaurs Cylus, Darek, and Render must use all their cunning to keep Zephyr safe and alive. But danger comes in many forms, including the unexpected arrival of Mimics and Shadow Titans intent on destroying the snakes before they can be used against them.

Things aren't any easier for Jake and Tryn as they make it to Xanadu only to find that the Mimics have attacked first and taken everyone away. Everyone, that is, except for one lone Olympian that they left for dead—Pegasus.

The hope Jake and Tryn desperately needed from Xanadu is no longer there; they soon discover that what they thought was a new enemy of Titus is in fact a very old enemy of the Xan—the Mimics, uncaring and unstoppable, with ambitious plans for conquering the universe.

The young heroes are on their own. Somehow they must find a way to not only save Zephyr and Pegasus but also stop the Mimics before it's too late.

JOIN US ON THE NEXT
EXCITING ADVENTURE.

ABOUT THE AUTHOR

KATE O'HEARN was born in Canada, was raised in New York City, and has traveled all over the United States. She currently resides in England. Kate is the author of the Pegasus series, the Shadow of the Dragon series, and the Valkyrie series. Visit her at KateOHearn.com.

ABOUT THE AUTHOR

KATE O'HEARN was born in Canada, was raised in New York City, and has traveled all over the United States. She currently resides in England. Kate is the author of the Pegasus series, the Shadow of the Dragon series, and the Valkyrie series. Visit her at KateOHearn.com.